THE FACILITATOR

C.A. SOLE

Helifish Books

Published in 2025 by Helifish Books

Copyright © 2025 CA Sole

ISBN: 978-1-0682067-0-2 (Paperback)
ISBN: 978-1-0682067-1-9 (ebook-ePub)
ISBN: 978-1-0682067-2-6 (PDF)

British Library Cataloguing in Publication Data
A CIP catalogue record for this book is available from the British Library

I am sincerely grateful to my wife and others who have provided invaluable input to make this a better book.

THE FACILITATOR

PART ONE

CHAPTER ONE

The Summer Solstice

ON A clear morning during the summer solstice, anyone standing in the centre of the ancient stone circle of Stonehenge can look through the entrance and watch the sun rising behind and eventually topping the Heel Stone to the north-east. It's a much photographed event and thousands of people, some of them Druids, Pagans – old religion followers – and tourists spend the night drinking mead and smoking weed as they wait to celebrate the sunrise.

The Heel Stone is almost five metres high, leans towards the main circle and is rough-hewn, with an angled cleft on one side. For an agile person, it is not difficult to climb.

Dressed in a white robe with a brown belt and a leather, broad-brimmed hat sporting four feathers was a self-proclaimed druid who called himself Hengist Bluestone. His companion was a middle-aged woman wearing a feather headdress and a purple robe. Her head and drowsy, slow-blinking eyes slid from one scene to the next as she took in the action without comment. She cupped a joint in her left hand, which occasionally rose in slow motion to her lips.

An hour after midnight the moon had not yet risen but, it being midsummer, astronomical twilight gave sufficient illumination for outlines to be seen. Hengist, whose real name was Fred, stroked his long grey beard as he watched a lithe individual dressed in tight black clothing approach the Heel Stone. Using the cleft and multiple handholds above it, he (or was it a she? Hengist couldn't tell) scaled the stone carrying a bag about the size of a football. A few others looked on with little interest. They were too involved being at one with nature and Gaia and their sun god to consider human things.

But soon enough a murmur of disapproval ran through the crowd, and Hengist, his beard wagging as he spoke, went so far as to call out, 'Hey, you can't be doing that. You can't climb the stones. It's sacrilegious. Come down.'

The figure stopped what it was doing. It stood upright on the peak of the stone, appearing tall, when seen from below, and dominant. Its face turned and looked directly at Hengist. All that was visible was a black balaclava beneath the wearer's hood, the features hidden. Hengist felt rather than saw the eyes singling him out, boring into him. He opened his mouth to say something else, but it went dry and he couldn't continue. He swallowed and looked away.

'Wha?' said his companion, drawing on her joint. She released a cloud of pungent smoke. 'Wha's going on? Why's he up there? Here, you want a drag?' She offered her joint with a wavy hand, but Hengist was too unnerved. He ignored her.

The figure tipped the bag upside down on top of the Heel Stone and gently eased it off the contents. It required a slight adjustment to stay in place, but it did. Satisfied that the object was stable, the figure descended the stone with precise, delicate moves to about halfway down, then jumped the last six feet.

No one could say where he went.

'I saw death, Melody,' Hengist said, clearly shaken. 'Death looked me in the eye.'

'Ooh. Have a drag, my darling druid.'

He took the joint. 'I will. I need it.'

More people were drawn to the Heel Stone as rumours spread, but in the dark no one could see what the object on top of it was.

0452 hours, sunrise. The orange glow behind the stone grew, throwing it and its new crown into silhouette. Cheers rang out from the inner circle and around. The religious prayed, others raised their arms to heaven and gave thanks for this new gift. All were happy.

Until a piercing scream rang out.

The sky brightened, and the crowd could make out detail at last. Their euphoria, which had grown as the sun rose, petered out, giving way to more wails rending the morning air.

Hengist peered up with his imperfect eyes. 'What is it?'

Melody emerged from her clouded semi-conscious state. She clutched his hand. 'It's… it's a devil's head. It's staring at us, Hengist, *at us*. Let's go. *Now.*'

The flesh was bloodless, the eyes sunken and dark. A piece of paper was stuck to the forehead. The hair was lank and shoulder length, with strands of grey. A week's stubble did not hide sunken cheeks and a pointed chin.

The police reported later that the note said: HE HAD IT COMING – RATEL.

CHAPTER TWO

Sunday 28th August

LUKE HARTFIELD was planning something horrific, something so alien to him that he would never in a million years have imagined he would do such a thing.

The pub table he was sitting at was about five yards from the river's edge. The wood, untreated, grey and with circular water stains, was hot to his bare arms. Half an hour ago his beer had been cold. Now the last dribble had warmed and he longed to replenish it, but if he left the table for the bar someone would sneak in and take his place.

The midday sun bore through his shirt. He wiped beads of sweat from his head, thinking he should have brought a hat or used sun cream. The trouble was, he was too focused on the dominant issue in his life to even consider the mundane.

The garden tables were all occupied, mostly by families. Dogs tied to table legs, water bowls nearby; kids playing tag amongst the tables; waiters armed with giant burgers swerving to avoid them. He appeared to be the exception as the lone man at a bench built for six. He felt a little ashamed and prayed no newcomers would ask to share, because he'd be duty-bound to agree. To his left was an elderly couple nursing gins and tonic, at a guess. To his right was a family with some noisy, poorly behaved and screaming children. Glaring at them, he caught the eye of their father and saw the challenge there: *Don't you dare complain, they're only kids having fun.* But he wasn't alone: the old couple were also showing signs of irritation at the noise.

Thoughts popped into his head, sometimes two at once. He would scribble one down in his notebook and in doing so forget the other. Was it the distraction of those noisy brats, or just his overloaded brain? No. The gravity of his plan was making him so nervous that he was losing concentration.

Luke studied his notes. He could barely read them, his writing was so squiggly. He put his pencil down and stared at his hands; they trembled. He clenched his fists for a minute, driving his nails into his palms, then released, holding the fingers out straight. They still quivered. They didn't normally, but then what he was plotting was not a normal activity of his.

His table looked out over a broad pool in the river. Just upstream from him was a lock which enabled canal boats bound eastwards towards the Thames to drop down to the lower level. Conversely, West bound canal traffic would gain height as they passed through the lock.

The river and the canal joined at a point between Luke and the lock chamber's heavy oak lower doors, creating a strong cross-current in the pool which affected boats coming out of the lock. People would gather on the pub lawn to gawk, as it was entertaining to see how different skippers frantically twirled their wheels to deal with the swing.

Luke drew his notebook towards him and readied his pencil above the page, but the thought that had been worth noting had vanished into the ether along with a mass of other things he wanted to remember. He ground his teeth. There was one chance to get this right, and to that end he had decided to plan and record every move he had to make. Sound advice, but ever since he had committed himself to the project, his behaviour had become erratic (and was becoming more so as the moment neared) – like that of an octogenarian: where was his phone, his car keys? Had he cleaned his teeth that morning? Stopping mid-sentence and unable to remember what he was saying, or why he had left the room.

If this current inability to concentrate persisted, he was going to fluff it. He had to pull himself together – his future depended on it.

'Hello. Sorry, but are these seats taken? Every other table is in use.' The speaker was a young woman. Behind her were a grey-haired couple, one of whom was using a crutch. The old man looked exhausted.

'Please, help yourselves,' Luke said. 'I was about to leave anyway.' He downed the last of his beer and stood.

Damn. He would never be able to think with someone else at the table. He ambled round the pub lawn and noted the two CCTV cameras covering it from the building. They were unlikely be a problem. Next was to look for any form of surveillance covering the lock itself.

Luke had known very little about canals and the vital role they played in the Industrial Revolution. They were history, part of the landscape, and frequented nowadays by people with strange tastes as far as he was concerned. Yet he had spent an hour the previous day, Saturday, sitting on a log in a natural recess in the vegetation above the lock and watching as long, narrow canal boats were manoeuvred into the chamber, crew members rushed about closing the gates, opening and closing the sluices and paying out the mooring ropes as the water drained from the chamber and their boats descended gracefully to the lower level.

With the aid of his shaky drawings of the different parts and mechanisms of the lock, he identified what he would have to do to fill the chamber if it was empty when he returned to undertake his task. One thing he noticed was that the windlasses the crews used to open and close the sluices all came from the boats themselves. None was available for public use. Since he didn't have a boat, he'd have to buy his own windlass – which he would do that afternoon.

His thoughts strayed from how he was going to execute his plan to why he, a successful, middle-aged accountant, was taking such extreme measures. His relationship with Mary had deteriorated to such an extent that it was hard to imagine it getting any lower. They barely spoke and no longer shared a bed. In the evenings, she would cook a single hamburger or heat a lone pot of instant noodles. After that she would go to bed, or maybe go out, leaving him to his own devices.

Luke was at a loss as to why things had come to this, and since discussing even the blandest of subjects usually resulted in a senseless row, he seldom opened a conversation. Mary had no such reservations. In fact, she seemed to gain strength from a good shouting match.

'You haven't forgotten we're going to a quiz at the cricket club tonight?' she had once said, putting her breakfast bowl in the dishwasher.

'No,' he lied. 'Who's going?'

'Who d'you think? Usual crowd, of course.'

Which meant her friends, not his. Never mind: if Luke kept a low profile and said little, he would avoid confrontation with the mob, most of whom he regarded as thick. A quiz night with them was trying. Luke preferred to let them argue and make mistakes rather than show them up with his usually superior knowledge.

The question that set things off that night was: What is the name of the Icelandic volcano that erupted in 2010 and caused havoc to air traffic throughout Europe? Only the correct spelling will qualify.

The team huddled together, keeping their voices low so the competition couldn't hear.

'Come on, Luke. You know these things.'

'Eyjafjallajökull.' Luke spelt it out.

'Nah. There's only one 'l' in the first pair.' Neil, a successful businessman with a taste for glossy suits, colourful waistcoats and shocking ties, said.

Luke shrugged. 'If you say so.' Bloody ignoramus. You want my advice then argue when I tell you the truth.

Of course, the revised spelling was incorrect, and Mary's team only came second. She rounded on her husband as the results were read out. 'You timid little wimp. Why don't you stand up for yourself? You were right, you should have insisted. It's the same in bed—' She stood glaring down at him.

Luke felt the heat spreading up his cheeks. He balled his fists, but forced his arms to his sides. He stared back at her. She was going to pay for this embarrassment, but he wasn't going to turn the issue into a public spectacle.

'—When you manage to get it up there's no will in you, no balls to back it up, no vigour. Pathetic.'

Luke waited until she was about to launch into finer detail, then said, 'Necrophilia has never been my thing, so it's a bit difficult to raise enthusiasm when I'm faced with an inert body.'

The sneer on Mary's lips vanished, a flush hit her cheeks. She opened her mouth but words failed her. Neil stood behind her and gently pushed her down into her seat from behind. He began to massage her neck, soothing the anger out of her.

Luke had nodded to himself. So that's the fat slob she's fucking. What on earth does she see in him – unless it's money or just someone to flaunt at me? It couldn't be his body. The man was not just fat, he wasn't firm, he was pudgy with soft white squidgy flesh. He made huge commissions from selling high-value properties, but the word was that he was into drugs – using and dealing. Whatever, it was immaterial.

A timid little wimp was what she'd called him. If she had done that at home in private, that would have been one thing. But for her to say it in public and to follow the insult with an explicit description of his failings in bed – which was a gross exaggeration – was both extremely embarrassing, disloyal, and, to his mind, unforgivable. Even some of her friends had initially shrunk from her vitriol. Unfortunately, Luke had retaliated with his necrophilia line. This, of course, lent some truth to her words, and the mood had turned against him.

If she could see him now, sitting here, plotting a murder, she would have to retract the 'timid' accusation at least. Maybe the thought that her husband was about to kill would scare her silly. He had an insane desire to disclose everything just to see her reaction.

She was having an affair, of course. Luke had known for some time, but once he'd pushed out the dent in his pride he realised he no longer cared. In fact, it was good, because he now had a licence to play the field himself.

His latest passion was becoming serious, so Mary was now a major obstacle in his life. The trouble was that she would fight him at every level if he mentioned divorce.

Everything was going in her favour at the moment. She organised her own entertainment with her female friends (or so she claimed), had a good sex life (which she couldn't be bothered to hide), and took great pleasure in humiliating her husband and spending his money. Whereas Luke had to keep his affair secret so as not to give her any ammunition in the event of a divorce.

She would try to take him for at least half his wealth and publicise his failings in a vindictive tirade guaranteed to make its way onto the front pages.

There had to be a simpler way. And this was it.

Luke felt he held the moral high ground: he had never done anything unforgivable to her in public. She, on the other hand, was going to pay for her disloyalty – and so was her lover.

So yes, there would be justice, and the first step in that process was going to happen the very next morning.

2

Luke arrived home a little drunk. What had started as a calming pint while he plotted his crime became another, as one more element that could not be ignored tore at his nerves. Then there was another, and more. The sun had had its effect as well. The skin on his head was red, tight and tender.

He should refrain from drinking any more. Tomorrow morning was going to test his nerves, courage and determination. Failure could spell absolute disaster... To hell with it, one more beer isn't going to make a difference. He levered the top off the bottle as Mary came in.

She used to be a very attractive woman, but the years had added a few pounds to her figure. She was still alluring, though, and was still followed by looks from admiring men and critical women to which she might respond with a superior and teasing smile. For Luke, she reserved a sour expression.

She was wearing a little red dress, a style more suited to someone half her age. It revealed well-shaped legs and a deep cleavage. What a waste of a good body, Luke thought.

'I'll be out tonight,' she said and picked up the bottle top, turning it over and over in her fingers. 'I feel like getting smashed, so I'll crash at Janet's place.'

Long ago, suspicion would have risen in Luke at such a statement. She was his wife, after all. But now, if she wanted to go and get stuffed by Neil, or another bloke or maybe a whole gang of them, she should go. She was the least important person in his life. Another had taken over, and she was worth killing for.

He looked up at Mary with a knowing smirk on his face. 'Go and enjoy the night.' He stopped short of adding, 'While you can.'

That she wasn't used to her cuckold grinning at her was obvious. Her eyes narrowed. 'What are you going to do? Get more pissed, watch porn and have a wank?' She flicked the bottle top in his direction to emphasise her contempt.

Luke's grin widened. 'Hardly. I shall be away from tomorrow, back on Friday night. There's a business workshop in Newcastle I'm attending, so you won't have to lie about your movements.'

Mary glared, but said nothing. She slammed the door on the way out.

3

Sunrise was at 06.08 on Monday the 29th of August, or thirty-eight minutes after his target was due to reach the lock. Luke was naturally a cautious planner, but on this day, with such an important event at its start, he was overly so and was there before five. Everything had to be ready, in particular that the lock chamber was set up for a boat going downstream, meaning that it was full.

Even though it was standard practice for boaters to leave the lock full, the water level was low when he arrived, so there was work to be done.

A clear sky had dropped the previous day's heat, and it felt chilly. The brighter stars were still visible in the face of the approaching dawn when Luke, armed with a windlass and a second-hand boat hook that he'd purchased, checked that the lower gates were shut and that its sluices were fully closed before running up to the top gate and opening its paddles. Water flooded in. He watched it rise, mesmerised. The moment was drawing closer. He glanced up the towpath, checking to see if his victim was in sight. Not yet. Why did anyone want to run before dawn, anyway? Idiotic.

The chamber was almost full. Once it was, with the water at the same height on both sides of the upper gates, the heavy structures could be moved to full open; but Luke left them closed.

Time was marching on – 05.24. He retreated to his lair, as he thought of it, amongst the bushes, and sat on the log. He pulled out a torch and a crumpled page of typing given to him by the secretive organiser. He'd read it twice before, but he had to ensure he got the plan right the first time. A second attempt was out of the question.

The writer, whoever he or she was, had been thorough:

§

Your target runs every single morning without fail, barring ill health. He always takes the same route unless he's away on business or holiday. He's very set in his ways, very boring, doesn't even run the route in reverse. From his house on the edge of the park, he takes suburban streets to run onto a large area of waste ground. A rough track across this space leads to the towpath beside the canal. A mile and a half along there and he reaches the lock at five-thirty every morning. This is recorded daily on his Apple Watch, and varies by no more than two minutes either side of his target.

He wears an orange T-shirt (he's got several), pale blue shorts and Nike Zoom Fly pink and orange running shoes (these seem to be his sole daring challenge to the world of conformity).

It is suggested that the optimum method of disposal is by drowning. In case you are not aware, the canals themselves are quite shallow – some were only designed for boats with a draft of three and a half feet. This is not deep enough for your purpose. However, the lock chamber on this run is much deeper as the canal drops in height by almost ten feet.

If you don't know, you will need to learn how to work the lock to ensure its chamber is full, i.e. the water is at the upper level. Your job will be to get him into the full lock chamber and keep him there for a short while. He's a big man and quite strong, but he can't swim. If he's in the water long enough, he'll drown. Be careful, because there is a fixed ladder for climbing out of the lock. You must keep the target away from that. If he escapes you will be in trouble.

§

Luke shivered. It wasn't that cold, his breath did not become steam, but the tremor began at the nape of his neck and crept down his spine. His jacket was inadequate. No, it wasn't the jacket, it was fear. A brief attempt at a precise slotting of the instructions into his breast pocket failed in favour of his trembling fingers crumpling the paper in.

05.26: four minutes to go, but no sign of the runner.

There was still time to pull out. And then what? More of Mary's shit, that's what. Courage now and a better future awaited. Give up now and life would always be miserable.

05.28: still no sign. Suddenly Luke hoped his victim would never appear. Hoped that the decision to give up would be taken from him. In time he'd be able to believe he would never consider murdering a stranger – anyone.

05.30: he's late. Maybe today is a sick day and he's not coming.

05.32: feet pounded the dirt. In the growing light, Luke made out a runner with a heavy step, a man lacking the spring and flexibility of a young athlete. His orange T-shirt and the flash of pink and orange running shoes were hideous, and a futile attempt to portray youth in an older man – but who cares?

Luke left his lair in the bushes and ran to the side of the lock chamber. He stared down into the murk before fishing around with the boat hook and acting as if a life depended on it. Prod, hook. *Damn* – lost it… Probe… Where's it gone?

The runner was a few yards away. Luke looked up, surprised. 'Thank God. Help me. There's a man in here, I can't get him out. I think he's alive. We have to get him out.'

The runner slowed, ran on the spot. 'What's the matter?'

'There's a man in the water. Help me, I think he's alive.'

The runner muttered some swear word, but came up to the edge of the chamber. He was a big man, taller and heavier than Luke as he stood beside him. 'I don't see anything.'

'He's gone down… Hang on, I've hooked something.' Luke pretended to pull on the boat hook.

The runner leaned over the edge, peering into the water.

Luke stepped back and pushed.

The man teetered. Off balance, he flung a hand backwards. Too late – he'd gone over the tipping point. Already falling, he scrabbled behind for support and caught a fistful of Luke's jacket. He toppled forward.

Luke went with him.

An involuntary gasp – Luke's head was in the clear air. The runner couldn't swim – did he take in water with that gasp?

The lock was a maelstrom of flailing arms. A big, strong man – a non-swimmer in a panic – fought to stay afloat. Wild, thrashing hands bashed at Luke's head. Luke dodged the blows, reaching between them to push the man down, and so keep himself up. He ducked below the surface to pop up and punch the runner in the face to make him fight for breath.

Loud, hoarse gulps for air came from the frantic man. He had a longer reach and got a hand on Luke's shoulder, pushing him under.

But Luke kept his head. Now that he'd started, he had to win this. He had to. To give up now was unthinkable. His attempt to kill would be exposed. He was smaller and lighter, with shorter arms than his victim. His weight had to be used to force the man under.

The runner was weakening. But their fight was taking them towards the ladder. The runner must have seen that it was almost within reach, because a sudden surge of energy boosted his efforts. He stretched an arm for the rungs.

Luke kicked against the wall and pushed their locked bodies away. He dived, robbing the runner of his support. In the filthy murk, in the dark, he imagined his way around behind the man, surfaced and got his hands on those broad shoulders.

As quickly as it had begun, so it ended. The runner floated face down. Luke gave the body a shove towards the middle.

He clung to the ladder until the heat of the fight evaporated. With effort, he dragged one foot after the other to clamber out of the lock chamber and stand on the edge, his back to the water; he couldn't look at his victim. Immobility had a grip on him, until his shivering in dawn's breeze became too much to control. He ran the few steps to the bushes and allowed his stomach to hurl its contents over the leaves.

He had killed a man he didn't know for a reason he didn't know.

Retching over and over again, he panted, gathered his things, the boat hook, the windlass and a bag. All he could think of was the heated seat of his car waiting for him.

But first there was a phone call to make.

4

Later, after Luke had showered and packed a small case for his trip up North, he put on a suit and left. Mary had not put in an appearance. Presumably she was still hungover, or more likely being treated to breakfast in Neil's bed. With a bit of luck she'd choke on the toast.

A bullish sentiment, but he definitely didn't feel on the front foot. At his company, he gave Jane, the receptionist, a forced smile and continued to his office. Jane followed him in and put a small package down on his desk. 'Courier came. I signed for it. Hope you don't mind.'

'Of course not. Thanks.'

'Are you all right, Luke? You're looking very pale today. Not coming down with anything, are you?' She was short, with a round, pretty face and hair down to her waist. Her thick glasses had heavy, tortoise-shell frames, which magnified her eyes and gave her an owlish look. She always wore, what Luke imagined was, an expensive perfume. It was delicate and enticing, and he wondered who gave it to her, because her salary was unlikely to stretch to such a luxury. The HR Manager claimed that Jane fancied Luke, at which he had scoffed in embarrassment.

'No, I'm fine. You remember I'm going to Newcastle after lunch, only back on Friday.' He breathed in her scent, but its magic didn't work today.

'Yes.' Concern was written across her face. Her eyes never left him, as if she expected him to drop dead right there in front of her.

Luke had expected this package on Friday and was fretting it was going to be late. In the process of ordering it, he'd had to answer a set of questions regarding his identity and why he wanted such a noxious substance. Lying his way through that, he'd requested delivery to his company address. It was far too dangerous to have it delivered to his home. Mary had the nosey habit of opening everything, even mail not addressed to her.

When the other staff were taking their lunch break, Luke took a pair of latex gloves and a plastic film canister from his desk drawer. The canister, used for holding a roll of 35mm photographic film, was black with a grey pop-on/off cap.

With the gloves on, he unwrapped the parcel to disclose a manufacturer's box containing a bottle with a child-proof lid. His unsteady fingers tipped two capsules out of the canister onto his desk. He split each one by pulling the blue top off the white bottom part of the casing. He tipped the powder into his rubbish bin, and then, with great care, filled the casing with granules from the bottle and replaced the blue top. With both capsules in the canister, he snapped the grey lid on and gave the thing a wipe to erase his fingerprints.

Now to get the film container to the shady character who was organising everything. Luke slipped out of the office and headed for the nearby park, putting on his leather gloves.

As instructed, he sat on an unoccupied bench facing the pond, took the film canister from his pocket and wiped it yet again, even though he hadn't touched it without gloves on. He settled back to wait. Ten minutes went by. Come on. I've a train to catch.

His mind seemed to be attached to the murder with a rubber band. Every moment he wasn't occupied, his thoughts sprang back to his crime. He had killed a man, a man he didn't know. Had the poor fellow a family? Were his wife and children grieving: in tears, not eating, not sleeping, worried sick about where the future would take them without their breadwinner? How could he make it better for them?

He would find out who the runner was; how could he atone without knowing? It should be simple enough: watch the press for identification of the body and take it from there. Decide on compensation depending on the number and financial status of his family. Had to be a very tight and limited investigation, though, because there were other people who had to be protected. He had contracted to do that, and, for Luke, his word was sacred.

Images flashed through his mind: water streaming down the runner's head as he surfaced, plastering strands of hair to his forehead and cascading over his wild, angry, confused and questioning eyes, flooding over his gaping mouth, which sucked it in and tried to cough it out. Luke knew this image would never leave him. Throughout the years ahead, he would think of it in the middle of the night. He would think of it during moments of peace. It was never going to leave him alone.

Another image. Standing on the side of the lock, water dripping off him onto the grass, and beginning to shiver more from shock than cold. Two metres away, the body lay face down on the surface. As he watched, first the legs vanished into the murk, and then the bright orange T-shirt, which blended well with the colour of the canal, faded from view. In time it would surface as the internal build-up of gasses gave it floatation. Where would that be? Would it stay in the lock or would it be driven downstream by the rush of water when the lock emptied?

What evidence had he left behind? He had scouted for CCTV cameras, but was there a hidden one? Were the police already following a lead towards him? How could he make amends? Should he go to the police now and confess and take his punishment? At least in jail he would be free of Mary for decades. But then he would have to tell them about the man who set this up, and that would lead to other people being arrested.

His own conscience would be eased by confessing, but the fallout for others? What to do?

Luke glanced at his watch. Time was passing, he would have to go to the station soon. Then he remembered he was supposed to hold the film canister in his hand but slightly away from his body so that it could be seen by someone nearby but not from a distance.

A figure in a grey hoodie sauntered past, his head down to his phone. He walked on some twenty yards, then turned as if he'd forgotten something and came back. That was the signal. Luke stood, left the canister on the bench and walked away.

All he had to do now was go up to Newcastle until the end of the week and make sure everyone knew about it. He would use his credit card up there and be seen in the hotel and on CCTV cameras. By the end of those few days, but for his nagging remorse, he would be able to rebuild his life in a more pleasant form.

CHAPTER THREE

Monday 29th August

TWO COMMUNICATIONS interrupted Millie York's ten day break in the Dolomites. The first was on Monday morning at about eight o'clock, a simple text: *Task completed. Deal must close Friday midday.* She deleted the message and slid the phone back into her pocket. How long would it take for the second call to come through? There was going to be a second call, and maybe more. They could start this afternoon, they could be days away. She needed that call to give her legitimacy. In the meantime, as long as she was home before Friday, she would continue her climbing holiday, or that second call was made.

A feeling of satisfaction, elation almost, filtered through her. A massive portal to a fulfilling life was opening, and a tingle of self-satisfaction caused a smile. She had planned a difficult solo climb for herself in an hour, but suddenly and uncharacteristically, she decided to do nothing. After that brief text, today had become the perfect day to do nothing but lounge around and indulge in the excellent local food, and drink a good deal more Prosecco than normal. Today was a day for thought in an alpine meadow under a cloudless sky.

To have a decent coffee was her first priority. That urge satisfied, she bought some supplies, stuffed them in her tiny climbing pack and set off for the long grassy slopes below the towering Tofane range that dominates the town of Cortina d'Ampezzo.

She passed chalets and houses with wide overhanging eaves and balconies, some with flower boxes dripping with colour. Small trees in pots at street level, and yet more flower boxes. Leaving the outskirts of the town behind, she stopped on what, in winter, was a ski slope. To her right, as she took in the magnificent view of the massif ahead, was a ski lift. Idle now, its masts stood in line like giant telephone poles queuing for the snow.

Millie took off her pack and arranged it on the ground as a pillow. She lay down and closed her eyes. The sun's heat was fierce and she pulled her hat down over her face. With the smell of grass in her nostrils and her mind on her pleasures, she soon fell asleep.

She got her kicks in two ways: on a rock face and through martial arts. She didn't dedicate herself to the latter, she wasn't a follower of any one discipline. Rather what she practised was advanced self-defence or hand-to-hand combat techniques. She liked the sport because she took great pleasure in defeating a rival. From each win she felt increasingly self-assured and powerful. And the skills might come in useful out of the ring some day.

It was climbing she really loved. The exposure, the risk, the test of her strength and agility sent thrills up and down her spine. She excelled at it, and she knew it. Other club members would halt their own activity to watch her speed and grace with a mixture of envy and admiration. Naturally, there was always a jealous peer or two looking for an opportunity to criticise, but she ignored them.

Of course, she had started her career being second on the rope following a leader, but her ability had progressed at a rapid pace, and now she led climbs. With a ruthless disregard for the feelings of her less-able companion, she would push herself, tackling more difficult pitches at every opportunity, never hiding her impatience as she waited for her partner to catch up. She had recently begun solo climbing, dispensing with the safety (and drag) of a slower partner. She had set herself the goal of free solo, climbing without the safeguards of equipment – one of her dream achievements would be to complete a free solo ascent of El Capitan in Yosemite.

This drive of hers, this conquer-all, spare-nothing, selfish attitude drove her at work, too. It affected both her employees and Mike, and she had lost any shred of popularity and respect she might have had in the early days.

Such reactions were of no concern to her.

On her back in the mountain meadow, she soaked up the sun and dreamed. At some time in her fantasies, her thoughts switched to the current situation and, after half an hour, she woke.

She co-owned her company with Mike Spencer, a man who, at fifty-four, was prematurely slowing down. Set in his ways, he followed a strict daily routine. From the time he woke (04.45) until he went to bed (21.45), every activity began at a certain time: breakfast at 07.45 after a run and a shower, lunch at 1300, dinner at 2000. 'Look,' he boasted to anyone who would listen, 'My Apple watch keeps me on schedule. It checks my fitness, counts my steps and measures my heart rate. Technology, that's what it's about. You've got to embrace the tech.'

With this close monitoring of his personal life, his own business took second place. If he couldn't measure activity on his watch or connected gadgets, he stuck with the status quo and rejected fresh ideas.

A few weeks previously, they'd had a stinking row, fortunately out of earshot of the staff. Mike was sitting at his desk, looking out over three trays, each with it own pile of documents. His computer sat to one side, the monitor sleeping with a digital depiction of the time bouncing round the screen on a random route.

Millie paced the limited space in front of Mike's desk, clutching a sheet of paper which crackled. As it often was at work, her long blonde hair was stretched back into a bun. The resulting tension in her face gave her a severe uncompromising look, which she thought was entirely appropriate for her position in the company. Now, impatience radiated from her.

'Mike, I think we should be expanding this business.'

'Let's not have this argument again, Millie. I explained last time that we don't have the capital to open another branch.'

'I'm not talking about another branch this time. I mean we buy out a struggling rival for a low price. Squires, for instance. They're not doing well and the owners are old and about to retire. They'll be selling up soon for what they can get and by approaching them now, we'll get ahead of any competition.'

Mike gave an impatient sigh. 'For the last time, Millie, we don't have the capital.'

'Then borrow it. No one's got a million under the mattress waiting to be used. They borrow from investors so they can grow. Why won't you do that?'

'Because you have to repay that loan and that costs money. We're doing very comfortably as we are.'

'*God.* Have you no ambition, no desire to grow at all? I want to build an empire. We have the skills, we have knowhow, we have the people to get started. The timing couldn't be better. Another couple of small companies under our umbrella and you could retire rich and happy.'

'I'm comfortable as I am, and happy without losing sleep not knowing how we're going to repay a massive debt.'

Millie had stopped pacing and was staring out of the window. '*For heaven's sake.* You're a dinosaur, Mike. Have you no desire to be successful, to outdo the competition, to be rich? Your trouble is, you don't have the courage to take a chance. You're a stick-in-the-mud who's too afraid of the extra work involved.'

'Millie – *Millie*, turn round and look at me. I may be a dinosaur, but you're young and reckless and you'll fail. If we do what you want, we'll be in deep water, and I for one can't swim—'

'So you keep telling everyone.'

'It's a metaphor, Millie. It means we'll be in debt over our heads and I'm not prepared to deal with that—'

'I'm not stupid. I know what you mean.' She crumpled the paper into a tiny ball in one hand and threw it across the room. It flew past Mike to hit the wall behind him and bounce into the waste basket.

If Mike was angry at her rudeness in his office, he gave no sign. 'The point is moot, however. I'm the senior partner by quite a margin. I control the purse strings, and I say we're not doing it.'

Millie had clenched her jaw so hard it hurt. Mike was holding her back, but that was going to change.

The ways to get what she wanted were limited, and however much she studied her options she kept coming back to one definite solution. It was extreme, and initially she didn't want to consider it, but as time passed and other options died a weak death, Millie accepted it was the only way to go – but how?

She searched the regular internet and got nowhere. She downloaded the Tor browser, which gave her access to the dark net, and after hours of scrolling through unhelpful sites found what she thought she was looking for – a killer for hire. But it wasn't quite like that. It was more complicated and involved personal input. But it was less expensive and less risky. It was run by a shadowy character who called himself (or was it herself?), The Facilitator.

Millie had to wait about two weeks while this curious individual concocted a plan. It took this long, he or she explained, because two parties were involved. The tasks of the two protagonists had to be coordinated, and both had to ensure they stuck to their side of the bargain.

Having completed her application to join the scheme, she was told to take a holiday, so she organised a week's climbing in the Dolomites to get out of the way. When she came back, any obstacles to her future success would have been removed. All she had left to do was fulfil her side of the contract.

That morning's text was confirmation that things were moving in the direction she'd chosen. For them to continue, she had to go home and take control.

But when exactly? She had a company to run. With Mike gone, there was no one competent enough to do that for more than a couple of days. But, if she went back too early – as in leave before she had been advised officially that Mike was missing – questions could be asked as to why she had felt it necessary to cut her holiday short: had she known something would happen? On the other hand, she now had an obligation to fulfil – her part of the deal had to be done before Friday.

The Prosecco was still cold. She drank straight from the bottle. The bread and bresaola were delicious, and the cheese demanded more wine. Hey-ho, I could spend my life like this… That was rubbish of course. She was a person of action, a leader, aggressive and not to be taken for granted. She had to have a battle to fight, and to win, to be satisfied. Even ladies of action need to relax, Millie mused as she gazed out over the meadows and the little town below her. She turned to admire the great rock mountains behind, then lay back in the grass in a wine-assisted sleep.

She was woken by her phone. A panicked young man from her office told her that Mike had been missing all day, and that his body had been found in the canal. 'Please come back as soon as you can, Ms York. It's chaos here. It's so sad.'

Sadder still for you, was Millie's reaction. As one of Mike's weak-willed acolytes, young Brian would be among the first she was going to fire in her shake-up of the company.

It would be best to leave tomorrow, Tuesday, on the first train. Three hours to Marco Polo Airport, Venice, wait around, then another two and a half hours to Gatwick. She'd be back home before dark. That gave her two full days and nights to get her final brief and do the deed.

She took another swig of Prosecco. It was going to be very interesting to see how she would handle this new and significant challenge. Facing challenges was the essence of her life, but this one was extreme. Most people would shy away altogether, some would attempt it with trepidation, but a very few, like Millie, would look forward to it. The reason she was eager to face the challenge was not the killing of a stranger in itself, but to study her own reactions to the act. Shame, revulsion, remorse and concern for the bereaved? Or power and enjoyment? The former were entirely human; the latter would indicate at least some measure of psychopathy.

2

On Wednesday, the last day of August, Millie adjusted the scarf covering her mouth and nose – it itched and had to be tucked well into the wetsuit hood. She stared out from the dark protection of a weeping willow, through the screen of its pendulous branchlets, across the garden in front of her, to the house on the far side of the lawn.

On a warm summer night, her outfit felt clammy and restrictive. But Millie classed that as a mild irritation. What was more important was to ensure no trace of herself was left behind, and the suit should do that.

Occasional wisps of grey cloud drifted across a crescent moon, dimming the light and robbing the scene of detail as they passed. Across the expanse of lawn, under a tall hedge, was a bench, and nearby, an elaborate birdbath. Paths of crunchy pebbles, like spokes to a wheel hub, converged on a central pond. A statue of the huntress Diana, her hand to a leaping deer, searched for distant quarry.

Millie wondered, not for the first time, how Diana reconciled petting a gentle animal like a deer to hunting its family to death. Much like me, she thought, priding herself on an honest self-examination. The human race was there to be exploited by the progressive few. The strong would always tread on the weak. And Millie had no intention of ever being trodden on. She considered herself one of the rulers, and therefore had every right to brush aside anything or any person in her way.

From where she stood in deep shadow, she had a clear view of the house. It was exactly as it had been described to her. An orangery had been built on the outside below the first floor. Its flat roof, surmounted along its centre by a glass lantern for light, would serve as the ideal platform for entry through the bedroom window.

The clouds were dissipating, the arrows in Diana's quiver became more distinct, and the young deer at her side revealed a broken antler, Millie noted without interest. A fox trotted across the lawn and disappeared through the hedge. The church clock struck three, the gongs ringing heavily from nearby. A light gust of air cooled her forehead, her only exposed skin.

Millie retreated into the security of the greater darkness, her mind running over the detailed instructions she'd been given. A key item was that a ladder always lay against the wall on the side of the house; she could use that to gain access to the flat roof.

A final strand of cloud dimmed the scene. Millie ran across the lawn, leapt clear of the crunchy paths and gained the shelter of the house. The ladder was there. She looked at it and hesitated a moment, because although it would make entry easier, it might make a noise.

In one smooth movement, Millie leapt and gripped the edge of the flat roof. She pulled herself up to chest height and swung a leg up and on to the surface, just as if she was coming out of a swimming pool.

Next, the window. The instructions had been clear and precise. The target always slept with the main window closed and the fanlight open. There being no children, the child safety catch had been removed, the notes said. The curtains were always open. The bed was close to the window, so care would be needed not to fall on it when climbing in. More positive was the assurance that no one could be seen on the roof or at the window as the house was isolated and surrounded by tall trees … Unless the observer was in the garden.

Millie took two steps across the roof to reach the window. It was precisely as described. So far everything was going exactly to plan, but she had yet to get inside and the possibility of the subject waking was always present. Millie studied the woman through the glass. It would have been nice to know her name. She was lying on her side facing the window. Long brown hair had flopped across her face, which was squished. She was snuffling, possibly drunk? The brief said it was likely.

The fanlight opened easily and without a sound. Millie reached up as high as she could and then down to the catch of the main window. *Damn.* She could touch the handle, but even at full stretch she couldn't press the button to release it. The only way was to get closer, which meant crouching on the windowsill – only a few inches wide. That was nothing to a free solo climber, but it did spell out to her that the unexpected could still ruin her plans.

With the window open, she stretched one leg over the sill and down to the carpet inside. She had to cling to the frame to get her other leg in without falling on top of the sleeping woman. Millie took another close look at the sleeper – no change. A faint whiff of alcohol hung in the air.

§

Her routine never varies, the information sheet said. *She gets up at five in the morning no matter the weather or the light. Much of the year it's dark at five, as it is now. Because it's dark and she doesn't want to disturb me, at night she prepares her medication for the morning, putting the blood pressure pills in an old film canister. She just opens the canister and pops the medication in her mouth, washing them down with her night's water. You will be given an identical canister with the same number of pills inside. All you have to do is swap the canister I've provided for the original. According to her routine, she will swallow the substitute pills and it will all be over. You should be long gone when she gets up. Warning: handle the canister with care and do not open it yourself in case the pills have split. They contain potassium cyanide.*

§

To the left, in the corner, was a chest of drawers, its top a shambles of miscellaneous make-up jars and creams. Millie switched on her head torch. She had stuck black insulating tape over the lens, leaving a tiny hole. The result was a pencil beam with no stray light to wake the sleeping body.

Next to the chest was a chair with clothes strewn over it. Shoes, a bra, T-shirt and knickers lay on the carpet: a tripping hazard. A full length mirror flashed her torch beam back at her, and she quickly looked away.

Returning to the chest top, the beam picked out the film canister immediately. The pills clicked against the inside as Millie picked it up. She took a similar one from the belt pouch she wore over the wetsuit and put that in its place. The original she put in her pouch. The new pills also gave a satisfactory couple of clicks as she put them down in exactly the same spot.

She switched off her torch and looked back to the bed. The woman was still snuffling. A sound of bedclothes, a faint squeak from the mattress. Yet she was still.

Christ. Millie froze. Someone else was in the bed. She shrank into the corner, deeper into the darkness.

'Mmmmh.' Pure pleasure.

A faint chuckle.

'Mmmmh. What a way to wake a girl. Don't stop.'

'Would you like something bigger?'

A giggle. Heavier movement from the bed.

Millie bit her lip to stop a snort of laughter. She had to get out of there before they put a light on or got up. Or, on the other hand she could strip and join them for a surprise three-some. She bit her lip again. Nah: revolting, and probably inadequate.

Exit through the window was out of the question, it was too close to the bed. It would have to be the door and an unknown route out of the house.

The woman was giving off little squeaking sounds. The man grunted occasionally. Was he the reason Millie was there with her little pills?

The copulating couple were fully occupied under heaving bedclothes. Millie left her corner, stepped over the clothing and crept to the door.

The handle gave a loud squeak.

'What?' The mound in the bed stilled. The blanket was thrown back, and a naked white figure struggled to free itself from the sheets. The man was almost on his feet. Millie threw the door open and ran. Where the hell were the stairs? She touched a banister, turned a corner and nearly fell off the top step. A hand brushed against her, searching for a grip on her arm.

'Stop, you bastard. I'll fucking kill you.'

Down the stairs at breakneck speed. Where the hell was a door to the outside? There, across the wide hall. How was it locked?

The bare white figure, a portly spectre, was slower than her but almost at the bottom step. Millie turned the handle. The door gave a slight click but wouldn't budge. Higher up was another latch. She opened that and gripped the lower knob again. She was almost out of the door, halfway to the freedom of the outside.

But the pale, flabby ghost caught her,. his fingers digging into the arm of her neoprene wetsuit. 'You little bastard. What the fuck were you doing? Spying? Looking for diamonds, eh? You're going to get the shit knocked out of you before I call the cops.'

He yanked her into the house. She didn't resist, instead going with him. Expecting her to pull back, he went off balance. Millie reached down, grabbed his naked balls and squeezed. As a climber, she could hold the weight of her body on the fingers of one hand.

'*Aah.*' The man dropped Millie's arm to fight her grip on his tackle. But he wasn't going to win that battle. He punched at her. She dodged and deflected another blow.

From the top of the stairs, the woman called, 'Neil what's happening? Are you all right?'

'*Aaah. Christ. Help.*'

Millie looked at the unsightly lump of squirming flesh in her grip. His eyes were tight shut, his lips parted and his teeth clenched.

He was funny.

The last time she'd done this – to her stepfather – she'd crushed his testicles like this, but harder; then she had rolled across the bed while holding on. He'd screamed and screamed – worse than this fat slob. It had taken a couple of years, until she was sixteen, to grow big enough and train hard enough to be able to do it. 'You're never going to hurt me or any other girl again, because you're not going to have the balls to do it, you bastard. For years you've used me. Never again, not with me, nor anyone.'

And she had yanked – hard.

And, just like the woman on the stairs above them, her mother had made weak attempts to stop her from a distance. Her mother – too pathetic to challenge her partner about his abuse, too pathetic to save her daughter. It didn't take Millie long to realise that no one was going to help her, that she was going to have to do it herself. She challenged her neutered stepfather to go to the police, packed a bag, called her mother a few choice names, and left.

She'd learned: dominate them, or they will dominate you.

Now, with this slob Neil, she saw the funny side and laughed as she tightened her grip one last time.

Then she was through the door and running. She ran and giggled the half mile to her van, expunging her doubts and easing the tension that had been building without her noticing.

She'd effectively killed someone. The thought hit her halfway along. What did it mean? Did she feel terrible, remorseful? No – if anything she felt uplifted and powerful. Another human's life lay in her hands. And in any case there was still time for her to run back to the house and stop what's-her-name from taking her pills. But no – there was a contract to uphold.

So honouring a contract was of greater value than a life? Yes, because the contract enabled her to take control of the company and to better her own life, whereas this other woman's existence was of no consequence to Millie at all.

Perhaps, though, it was too soon for all this reflection. A couple of hours could pass before the capsules of potassium cyanide slid down the cheating woman's throat.

Millie reached her car. She needed to make a call to say the job was done, the future cast in her favour. But, panting, her forearms on the bonnet and her head in her hands, she got the giggles. '*Forget Dead Man Walking*,' she said out loud, 'this was *One Corpse Copulating*.' And she laughed out loud again.

PART TWO

CHAPTER FOUR

Monday 12th September

FERDY FELLOWES surveyed the waste and debris that littered his lounge from the past week: Indian takeaway punnets from Sunday night; two, no three, dirty plates (and there were more in the kitchen); a pile of beer cans (Guinness, Old Speckled Hen, Fosters); and two brands of IPA bottles by the single armchair. A used fork glinted from its lair under the couch.

It was Monday, and every Monday Ferdy cleaned and tidied his house. He flattened a thin-crust pizza box (thick crusts added bulk, not taste), balanced empty packets of nuts and cheese and onion crisps on it in his left hand and collected two beer bottles in his right. Kicking a can ahead of him as he walked to the kitchen, he dumped the dirty stuff in the rubbish and put the bottles to one side for recycling – he considered himself diligent for that.

'I am ze Archduke Ferdinand. Dum-di-dum.' He liked to sing that as he tidied, although couldn't explain why. Maybe it made him feel more important than he was which, he admitted, wasn't very important at all.

Running hot water into the sink, he dumped the dirty plates in it to soak and turned his attention to the rest of the ground floor, which consisted of a hall, a cupboard and a sitting room. The kitchen was surprisingly spacious. This was because a previous occupant had broken down an interior wall to open it up to include another room. A door at the end led to a long narrow garden hidden from the neighbours by a six-foot wooden fence.

The garden would be better described as a weed patch. There was so much sense in the slogan of *No Mow May* that Ferdy followed *No Mow From May to May*. His front entrance was similar, with two pot plants that were only watered just before they died.

The top floor comprised two bedrooms and a shared bathroom in which a big man could touch all four walls from the centre. Ferdy couldn't, he was too small.

His prize for living in this cramped semidetached house was the fact that it had a basement. And it was in this subterranean den that this inconspicuous five-foot-seven-inch man conducted much of his life and made his living. In contrast to the rest of the property, Ferdy kept it neat and clean. A long table against one wall held two computers. Their monitors were large and displayed exceptionally sharp images, read-able from the stairs. Further along was a bank of phone char-gers and a neat rack of adaptors. There was no filing cabinet, only a cupboard with IT accessories, a headset and cables in it. Ferdy did not keep paperwork.

The doorbell chimed its annoying 'ding-dong bell'.

'One day, when I get around to it, I'm going to dong its bloody ding,' he muttered as he scuttled down the stairs to answer it. The door camera showed a wide-brimmed hat covering a head held down.

It was raining. On the step, pressed close to the door and taking shelter under its ridiculously short canopy stood the most beautiful young woman Ferdy had ever set eyes on. She stood below him on the step, but her head was almost level with his. Strands of dark-red, almost auburn, hair that had escaped being gathered in a ponytail clung to her damp cheeks beneath a green fedora.

Ferdy mouthed a 'Hello', but no sound came out. He opened his mouth to try again, but she forestalled him with a brilliant smile. Teeth whiter than white with the slightest gap in the front. Tiny smile lines bracketed her mouth.

'Hi,' she said, edging forward away from the rain and putting one foot on the door-sill. 'A friend told me you fix computers. I hope you don't mind me popping round unan-nounced, but I didn't know how to contact you. I think my screen's died. Either that or the lead to it is broken.'

Ferdy hesitated. He glanced behind him at the mess. He'd cleared most of it, but a few beer cans still cluttered the floor.

The couch, whose wide seat had collapsed on one side, looked as if someone had slept there with a discarded blanket and all the cushions piled up at one end. A truly terrible print of a bowl of fruit on the wall behind had a lean to the right. Why had he only noticed that now, when it was too late to correct it? The fork was still under the couch.

Shame hit him. The poor woman was getting wet and he was embarrassed at being the slob he was. His mouth was dry, but he managed, 'You'd better come in. It's wet.' He waved a hand at the state of the lounge. 'Sorry…'

He stood back out of her way and moved partly behind the open door. She stepped inside and, closing the door behind her, looked down at him. She must be at least five-ten in her socks, he thought, but in those country boots – close on six foot.

'My name's Sally Kemp.' She thrust out a cold, damp hand. Her grip was firm.

'Ferdy,' he croaked.

She unslung a satchel from her shoulder while looking for a clear space to put it.

Ferdy leapt into action. With one sweep of his arm and no thought to damage, he cleared the end of the table, dumping noisy detritus on the floor. 'S… sorry… th-th-there's some space for you.'

She smiled her disarming smile. 'Don't fret, Ferdy. You should see my place, it's just as bad. I'm only respectable when I go out. At home I'm a real slob.'

Ferdy had serious doubts about that. 'So, what's wrong with your machine?'

'Well, the screen's got little bright spots evenly spaced across the bottom and sometimes it stays black when it should be alive.'

Ferdy was standing beside her, their shoulders brushing against each other occasionally. He imagined a heart attack coming on, and why was all the moisture in his mouth escaping as sweat from his head? 'D-does the camera work?'

'No. Silly me, I forgot that – no, it doesn't. What does that tell you?'

'I think you're right, the screen is on its way out. Let me take the serial number and I'll order the right one. It'll take about two or three days if they have stock.'

'Um… er, will it be expensive?'

'I'm not sure what they're charging these days, but it might be up to four hundred pounds.'

Sally took a step back, her eyes wide. 'Oh, I didn't realise it would be so much. I think I'd better carry on with it the way it is and come back when it really fails and I have more money.' Her eyes were a deep, deep green, the green of unfathomable depths. The creamy skin of her face was dusted with a sprinkle of freckles so fine he hadn't noticed them to begin with.

Ferdy forced himself to concentrate; his voice gained some confidence. 'That's just off the top of my head. Let me get you a firm quote and we'll talk again. How much are you prepared to spend?'

Sally laughed nervously. 'You don't expect me to answer that, do you?'

'It's worth a try. I'll be back in a minute or two.' He took the laptop and went into the hall to access the basement. Down there, he copied the machine's model and serial number and opened his own computer.

'What are you doing? Can I watch and learn something?' Sally was standing on the stairs behind him.

Ferdy jumped. She'd been so quiet. 'Please don't come down here.'

'Oh, sorry.' She dropped her eyes, her bubbly spirit evaporated, and she turned to go. He could so easily take her in his arms and hug her better. 'It's all right, not to worry. I'll see you upstairs.'

Back in the lounge, Sally had a nervous look. 'I'm really sorry. I wasn't prying, I was just curious.'

'It's all right.' Her beauty, those eyes, her redder-than-auburn hair and her very sweetness had reduced him to a love-struck idiot. But Sally had been in the wrong, and in his gut reaction of snapping at her, he was back as head of his own domain instead of being a captivated idiot. 'I tell you what. I'll only charge you at cost.'

'That's so good of you. Thanks so much, you're a real sweetie.'

2

Ferdy watched as Sally walked away. Ignoring the rain, she adopted a brisk, confident pace with long strides. The street, lined on both sides with plane trees and small semidetached houses like Ferdy's, curved round to the left. Sally was visible for a short distance until she vanished behind the trees. Before doing so, she looked back and waved. How did she know he was watching? Ferdy covered his embarrassment at being caught staring after her with a quick retreat.

As he closed the door, he noticed the old witch across the road standing under her own porch with a broom in her hand. She appeared as a stereotypical house-proud woman from the sixties, perhaps imitating her mother, as she was probably around sixty-five: flowery apron, hair under a scarf, stockings and furry slippers. She was either a spinster or a widow; whatever, Ferdy had never seen a man around her house in five years.

She spent much of her time watching her neighbours, frequently cleaning outside so as to get a better view. Ferdy was convinced, even though they had never spoken, that she disliked him personally and spied on him more than any of her other targets. At that particular moment, the crone was showing undue interest in Sally walking away. Then she turned her head and shot a disapproving look directly at him.

He shut her out, the miserable cow. What wouldn't she give to look like Sally again. Not that she ever could have done.

He slumped back against the wall. Bloody hell, what just happened? How come someone like Sally even touched the fringes of my life? He asked himself. She's stunning, and she's sweet too. Lovely.

At school, Ferdy had been teased and bullied as the runt of the litter. This drove him to keep his own company until a classmate stood up for him. She defended him and forced the bullies to back off. He responded to her with adoration and a willingness to do anything for her. So much so that they called him her 'puppy'.

Then the scene changed. Once she had him feeding from her hand, she began to control him herself, using little tactics like eating half his lunch and getting him to clean the mud off her shoes. Had she plotted this mastery from the very beginning? Was it all for her own ends, her defence of him? He didn't know, but he reckoned it was highly likely. And once again he lost faith in others.

But now, he determined: with Sally, I must have courage. I can't go on living in solitude with no friends and being too scared to talk to a woman. I have to try and make something of this – but I'm not going to let her dominate me. I know the signs now, and I'll back out if I see a life of subservience coming.

Ferdy was successful in his business. Hiding behind a shadowy persona, this meek little man used threats and a take-it-or-leave-it attitude to compel his clients to adhere to their side of an agreement. He kept it impersonal, maintaining a distance from his customers.

A personal relationship with any of them would be the height of stupidity. It would require closeness, trust and respect. and needs. Feelings would be involved. And feelings were irrelevant in his business – in fact they were dangerous.

Ferdy's heart was thumping in his chest at the very thought of asking Sally out. He had to conquer his nerves, overcome his innate reserve and at least suggest they meet for a drink or something. She could only say no.

With his house now tidy, if not really clean for the first time that week, Ferdy retired to his basement – his den of wickedness, as he thought of it. The room served as his refuge from the world. Whenever the weather was foul, or the stress of his business weighed on him, he would retreat to his computers rather than watch TV. Down there he could keep tabs on his clients, reply to their messages, alleviate their concerns and spend hours researching them to ensure they were genuine and not investigators.

He switched on his computers and, as he did first thing every day, brought up the Tor browser and Onion Mail on the dark web. The secure and anonymous email client was essential to his business and he took pride in answering every mail and message as soon as he saw them.

Ferdy knew his customers were generally nervous in their dealings with him. They were dipping their toes into dark waters uncertain of what lurked beneath the surface. His prompt and reliable responses helped them settle. Edgy clients were a risk: calm and confident ones were more likely to dot their Is and cross their Ts and thus reduce their risk.

A message popped up on his screen as he opened the mail.

I want Cecil dead. He mistreats me, he abuses me and beats me. My body is covered in so many bruises. I'm sore and cannot carry on like this. Please help me. I understand what's required and am willing to do my part. I can't afford to hire a professional, and your concept seems secure and effective. Tell me what I must do. I can't take this any longer. I hate him. Ivan.

There are two sides to every story. Not that not hearing Cecil's side worried Ferdy: a client was a client, and provided he or she paid the fees and kept their part of the deal, they deserved to get satisfaction. Ivan had foolishly added his address and mobile number to the message.

Ferdy answered:

Ivan, I feel for you. Yours must be a terrible situation and I'd love to offer you a speedy solution. I assume you understand the concept of this business – it requires two parties to make it work. Unfortunately, I have no one who can reciprocate at the moment. Do not worry about this, because possible customers contact me almost daily and I'm sure a suitable person will be available very soon.

In the meantime, I suggest we get started on your induction. This is important as you must fully understand how the process works and what your commitments are before signing the contract.

I like to conduct personal interviews. No written record is held, no email, and there is value in one-to-one communication. I see we live fairly close to each other. Meet me in the cemetery at St Mary's church at 0100 hrs tonight – i.e. tomorrow morning.

You will not see me, but I will be there. Enter the cemetery via the wooden wicket gate and take the path to the right. Stop at the fourth headstone, face the church, put your hand on the top of the stone and wait. Do not turn around. I will speak to you.

   Confirm you will attend tonight with an immediate reply.

3

Ferdy passed through the wicket gate half an hour before Ivan was due. The gate gave a high-pitched squeal on closing. Several parishioners had complained about that to the vicar. They said it set them on edge; it upset their mood and ruined their contemplation of the sermon after the service. The vicar had said he was going to oil the hinges, but he seemed to have fallen by the wayside on that one.

Having closed the gate, Ferdy stopped where he was for a minute. He always felt at peace in the graveyard – as if at one with the permanent residents. Ask anyone to imagine a cemetery at midnight, and they will scour their memories for a, probably stereotypical, image not unlike the one confronting Ferdy. Yew trees, some almost as old as the medieval church itself, were spaced evenly amongst the graves. In summer they provided deep, cool shade; in winter they offered protection from the rain or snow.

Facing Ferdy that night, a low quarter moon sent thin shafts of light between the yews to bless the odd lucky gravestone before creeping round to bestow its favours on the next. He took the path and turned right at the fourth tombstone. A single dead posy lay at its foot. He stared at it for a moment –

dead flowers on a grave are particularly sad, somehow – then he vanished into the dark recess beneath a yew.

Someone had broken the tip off a branch. Ferdy swept it from the bench and sat down. With twenty-five minutes before Ivan was due to appear, he relaxed. He enjoyed these interviews. Face to face in a normal situation, Ferdy would take a back seat and never try to dominate a relationship. But here, as the professional, the organiser, the expert, he had absolute control, always hidden in the darkness, confident and able to observe the would-be murderer. The killer who might be going to experience a feeling of power over his victim was, during those minutes, under Ferdy's thumb.

He stretched out his legs and glanced around. That someone else would be here was highly unlikely, but it was wise to be cautious. But there was nothing to be seen and nothing to hear except the whisper of a breeze through the branches.

Ferdy slouched and let his mind drift to the pleasures of Sally Kemp. She was stunningly pretty, and lithe as a gymnast. Not that he'd seen her exercising, of course, but he could tell from the way she moved. She had shown that she was kind, and she was incredibly seductive – all terms that could be summed up in one word: 'wonderful'. There really was no other way to describe her.

Letting his imagination get far ahead of him, he worried how she would react when she became aware of his feet. Would she laugh? He'd been teased enough over them throughout his life, from primary school onwards. It would be devastating if *she* mocked him.

And what about when she found out what he did? Would she remain as wonderful when she learned what his professional name was and what it meant? How on earth could he keep the secret from her when she had the run of his house? He couldn't shut her out of the basement forever. Would he lose her? Or worse, maybe, would she report him to the police?

Hold on a minute, you're entering Cloud Cuckoo Land. Just how likely is it that she'll even consider going out with you, let alone have the relationship you're assuming? She saw the mess the house was in when she was there. What is the likelihood any woman is going to go out with a man that lives like that?

The wicket gate screeched. Ferdy jerked out of his reverie and withdrew deep into the tree's shadow.

The crunch of hesitant steps came closer. A slight figure passed through a moonbeam into shadow then reached the fourth grave. He turned to face the church and put his hand on the headstone as Ferdy had ordered.

No one else approached and silence prevailed. The figure, Ivan, could not keep still, shifting his weight from one foot to the other, putting his free hand to his face. Ferdy gave him five minutes.

'Hello?' Ivan called softly.

On the telephone, Ferdy used a voice changer to avoid recognition. In person he could not do that, so he adopted a variety of accents: South African, Australian, New Zealand, Canadian – he was a good mimic. He could do an excellent French accent too, but the trouble with using a foreign one was that the client might speak that language better than Ferdy could.

'Hello. Is anyone there?'

Ferdy knew that the dark, ominous atmosphere of the cemetery at night would make Ivan even more nervous than he already was. '*Ja*. Don't turn round.'

'I won't. I won't. Promise.'

'All right, man. Just relax, Ivan. Nobody's gonna kill you – not yet, anyway.' Ferdy laughed.

'Heh,' was all Ivan could manage.

'For everyone's sake we want to be sure you are a safe person, okay? I'm gonna ask you some questions again, 'cause if you are a danger, then all of us are in danger. You understand?'

'Y-yes.'

'All right. Have you ever been arrested on suspicion of committing a crime, or suspected of a crime?'

'No.'

'Have your fingerprints ever been taken?'

'No.'

'Have you ever had a sample of DNA taken, even if you were totally innocent of a crime?'

'No. Why are you asking me these things? I'm not a criminal.'

'Because, Ivan, if the cops find DNA or fingerprints at the crime scene and it matches your sample that's already on their data base, it'll be curtains, even if you never did nothing wrong. Once they've got you, they'll be after the person who wanted your victim dead. Then they'll ask questions about how you were connected to that person, which means they'll come after me. So you see, man, everyone will be affected.'

'I see.'

'All right. The full terms of the agreement are on my website. I will give you a password to get to it; you must read and agree to those terms. Now, I need to emphasise a couple of things. They're in the agreement, but you need to agree in person, right here and now or there's no point in going further.'

'O-okay.'

'If you don't complete your side of the agreement – in other words, if you don't carry out the act you agreed to, you will lose your life. And I personally will see to that. Is that clear, Ivan my friend?'

Ivan's gulp was audible. His voice was weak. 'Yes, sir.'

'You will provide all the personal information about yourself that I ask for. That info will only be used to facilitate the contract. It will not be used against you in any way. You won't get any personal info about me, nor any about your opposite number. He or she will not know anything about you either. You will never meet that person. It's essential you remain unknown to each other, so all communication is through me. You need to know that I will keep an accurate record of all the info you and your oppo' give me until both sides of the contract are complete. Then I will destroy it. There will be no record of our deal, so you will be quite safe in that respect.'

'Okay.'

'You will give me all the info that your contracted partner will need to complete the task. That info must be accurate and complete. You can suggest the best way for your task to be carried out, and an alternative way if you want. That will be good, in fact. In turn, you will be given all the information you will need for your side of the deal. Okay?'

'Yes.'

'If the info you provide to assist the other party to carry out your wishes is incorrect or incomplete and puts that party in danger or at risk of arrest, then you will lose your life. Is that clear?'

'Yes.' Ivan's voice had become hoarse.

'To be sure you understand, man, this is deadly serious. And by deadly, I mean *deadly*. Several lives will depend on the actions and decisions made by you and your oppo' number. This is why it's essential for you to acknowledge that you will join that guy whose head you're leaning on if you put the plan and therefore people's future in jeopardy. I will make sure of this – personally. Got it?'

Ivan's hand shot off the gravestone as if it were red hot. 'Oh, sorry.' Then, to Ferdy, 'Yes, I understand.'

'Are you sure you can go through with this, Ivan?'

Silence.

'Ivan? …Look, man, I don't give a shit whether you're up for this or not. What matters to me and to the other party is that you stick to your word. If you want to give this up now, no problem – but if you continue …Ivan, your life and everyone else's depends on you sticking to your obligations.'

'I understand. I do want to do this.'

'All right, man. I talk tough, but I'm also here to support you. You and me is finished for now. I still have to find another person to join in this deal. It won't take long: you'd be surprised by the number of people who want other people dead.

'Now, comms: I will keep a phone specially for you. No one else will know the number. For routine stuff, leave a message on my website. For emergency stuff, use the phone. To do this, you must buy a cheap phone – a burner, they call it, a pay-as-you-go thing – and give me the number. You will not call me using any other number. Okay?'

'Yes.'

'Your oppo will get exactly the same brief. One more thing: you must not leave any trace of yourself at the crime scene. By this I mean dropping stuff that belongs to you, and especially DNA. The best way to protect against that is to wear a wet suit or a gimp suit – something that will prevent you losing hair or skin samples that could identify you later, maybe years later. Buy one, and when you finished your task, you burn that suit. You don't throw it in the tip, you burn it, every last piece of ash. Now, go and study my website.'

CHAPTER FIVE

Wednesday 14th September

FERDY WAS cleaning for the third time that week. 'I am ze Archduke Ferdinand. In ze morgen I vill be shot.' Why this stupid ear worm would not leave him during his housework, he didn't know, but it had become a fixture. He tried to think of following lines, but they only made it worse.

He was so acutely embarrassed at Sally seeing the pigsty of his lounge, that he swore he'd clean up first thing every morning from now on. The trouble was, he admitted, such resolutions only lasted for a few days. He was so besotted with her, though, that he might just stick to this one.

Ding-dong bell. 'Pussy's in the effing well,' he grumbled, as he put three beer bottles in the kitchen and padded to the front door.

Ever since he was first teased about his feet at school (and the problem became more pronounced as he grew), he had tried to hide them. When opening a door, he would pull it back towards him and step behind it so his feet stayed out of sight. It was an awkward manoeuvre, as he tended to be off balance and used the door as support while he peered around it at the visitor.

'Hi,' Sally said with a bright smile. Ferdy had initially been captivated by her overall beauty. On seeing her again, though, the details that contributed to her attractiveness became apparent. Fine laugh lines bracketed her lips when she smiled, he noticed, and a sparse sprinkling of minute freckles dotted her porcelain skin.

She was dressed casually on this occasion in ripped jeans, boots and a green top which set off her auburn hair. 'I was passing and thought I'd save you a call if my computer's ready.'

'Oh, sorry, it should have been, but they don't have a spare screen. It should be ready tomorrow, though… Um, would you like to come in anyway? I've tidied the place.'

'Love to.'

Ferdy looked beyond her before he closed the door. The net curtains in the crone's front window were closed, but held to one side by an invisible spying hand.

'Sorry, very presumptuous of me, but do you have coffee?'

'Of course. No problem. It'll be a few minutes, though. I don't have instant, and this will be the first time with new beans. I'll have to set up the machine from scratch; set the weight and the timing, select the grind size... You'll have to be patient, I'm afraid.'

Sally touched his arm. 'Take your time. I was thinking of getting a machine for myself, actually, but not a complicated one like yours. I'll watch, if that's okay.'

Ferdy knew he was ridiculous in being so fastidious about his coffee, but he savoured it, enjoyed experimenting with it and had invested in one of the most expensive machines on the market – close to a thousand pounds. He was single, he argued, with no one else to spend his money on, so why not?

'I'll be as quick as I can,' he said. 'I enjoy getting the details right; somehow it makes the coffee more enjoyable – worthwhile.'

'Don't worry, Ferdy. I'm fascinated.' She put her fingers up to her lips, adding a coquettish smile. 'I appreciate your attention to detail. I'm like that myself, actually.'

In the other room, his private phone rang.

Ferdy was in a comfortable little bubble with Sally here. He was enjoying it and was fully occupied in looking for ways to extend it. He wandered over to the phone, annoyed that it had disturbed his moment; he hoped it would stop before he reached it.

Clients did not call on this phone; they didn't know the number. Initial contact was made via untraceable messages on the dark web. Later contact, when necessary, was made via phone, but Ferdy always gave them a different number and discarded the instrument when the matter was concluded. He had given no one the number of this phone. He jerked out of his bubble of pleasure, shot a quick glance in Sally's direction and retreated to the garden.

Although the rain had cleared in the night, the grass was still wet and, due to its length, Ferdy's trousers were soon soaked below the knee. He didn't notice, the call had his full attention.

The voice on the other end of the line was female, soft and pleasant with a faint Scottish accent. 'Felix Fellowes?'

'It's Ferdy, actually. How did you get this number?'

'Yes, Ferdy to your customers, but I know your real name is Felix. I know a lot about you, actually.'

What the hell? 'How did you know how to contact me directly?'

The woman gave a short laugh. 'That is not for now. I have a job for your spare client, or even for you, if you'd prefer, although I doubt it.'

Ferdy shivered. How the hell did she know what his real name was and that Ivan was in the wings, waiting for his turn to participate? – with dread, probably.

Although sweet and warm on first impressions, the woman's voice was devoid of emotion. It would have been equally at home discussing various methods of torture and going soppy over a litter of puppies. 'There is an old woman, her name is Simone. It is necessary that she dies before the end of this month. She is going to change her will, and her appointment with the solicitor has been made for Thursday the 29th. If she is able to make the change, I will lose a very large sum of money. I will take care of any outstanding jobs you have, in return for this.'

'*Stop*. Hang on a minute. Are you talking about murder? I don't murder people. You've got the wrong person, wrong number.'

'I know you don't murder people, Ferdy/Felix, but you help others do it, don't you?'

'You're talking rubbish. This is a dangerous conversation. Goodbye.'

'*Don't hang up*.' Sharp words cut his bravado. 'Ferdy/Felix, have you heard of Ratel?'

Of course he'd heard of Ratel. Half the country knew of Ratel, the killer for hire who had evaded identification and capture for nine years. Now, the name, and a growing suspicion of what was in store, caused Ferdy's neck to crawl. He glanced at the house. Sally was looking out of the kitchen window. She waved at him. He raised an unenthusiastic paw.

'Yes, of course,' he said.

'My name is Alison – Ali. In a different life, I am Ratel. I research every aspect of my work to the finest detail. Your parents were David and Helen. You had a friend, Phil, who murdered his wife and confessed to you. This set you on your current path of helping others carve a better future for themselves.'

Ferdy gasped. How the hell…? Phil had been so mentally abused by his wife that he had contemplated suicide. Then he thought, why should he die when she was the evil one? Somehow, thanks to a catalogue of errors in the investigation, he got away with it, but was almost overcome with remorse and frightened silly about being discovered. In mental turmoil, he opened up to Ferdy hoping for some sort of release from his guilt. Ferdy had been appalled that his good, mild mannered and generous friend had been driven to take such drastic action. By the time he learned of Phil's trouble, it was too late to help him fight his case, but he saw an opportunity to make a living by helping others have their partners or opponents removed with virtually no risk to themselves.

'Well, Ferdy?'

Ali's knowledge was incredible. Either she was genuine, or this was an elaborate sting by the police. But surely the police would simply arrest and question him? She had to be genuine. 'You've been very thorough,' he said.

'I always am. Are you going to do what I want, or…?'

'Prove you're Ratel, and I'll see to it. It's simply too dangerous for me to accept clients at face value. If you are Ratel, surely you understand that?'

'You will get your proof when Ivan's problem is solved. You should send him on holiday immediately.'

'If you are Ratel, why don't you deal with Simone yourself?'

'Ferdy, – I'll call you Ferdy now that we're in business – maybe I've misjudged your intelligence. As a beneficiary of Simone's will, I will be high on the list of suspects for her murder. I cannot afford to have the police that close to me. It has to be done by someone else.'

'How do you want me to send the instructions for killing Ivan's Cecil – that's his name, by the way.'

'It is not necessary. I already have my plan for Cecil.'

Ferdy shivered again. This was a disaster. How did this woman get all this information? How did she know of Ivan and that he had no reciprocating client? How did she get into his data when the dark web was so secure? What did she know of past clients? Were all his contacts now compromised?

Sally was still at the kitchen window. She raised both her hands in a *what's-going-on?* gesture. Ferdy waved back and tapped his watch.

Suppressing his rising panic, he said, 'All right. I will get Ivan out of the way tomorrow, then you can deal with Cecil and give me proof that you're Ratel. In turn, I'll get Ivan on the job as soon as you tell me you're out of the way in Spain, say, or wherever – and ready. No payment from you will be necessary until Simone is dealt with. Is that okay?'

'That's good. When will I see results on my side?'

'I'll be honest with you, Ali – what do I call you, Ali or Ratel? – I'm having difficulty with Ivan, so to commit to a schedule I may not be able to meet would be dishonest.'

It might have been Ferdy's imagination, but it seemed that although her tone remained calm and soothing, a menace had crept in. 'As I already told you, my name is Ali. I will neither tolerate weakness nor imprecise results. Nor do I accept excuses. If this Ivan is not up to it, then you will have to complete the deal. I will have removed Cecil from his life. I expect Simone to be removed from mine. Either he does it, or you do. It makes no difference to me.'

'It will be done. How do you wish to communicate? You can phone me on this number, but how do I contact you?'

'It will not be necessary.' She cut the call.

Sally opened the door for Ferdy to go inside. 'That was a long call. Everything all right?'

'Yes, fine thanks. Just business.' He brushed a hand over his face. It was damp with sweat.

2

After Sally had gone, Ferdy slumped onto his couch, his mind a jumble of conflicting emotions. She was fantastic. Something had to be done about her. She seemed to like him and was comfortable in his company. Ask her out – but, what if she says no?

Ask her out, ask her out, ask her out.

I will, but…

Do it.

Okay, okay, I'll do it.

When?

Um…

On another tack – Ratel. Why had Ali chosen that creature as her icon? He looked it up.

§

It is a shy and retiring badger-like animal, a little over two to three feet long and a bit less than one foot high. It has a thick, tough and elastic skin. This enables it to withstand bites and manoeuvre within its skin to fight its adversary with little harm to itself. The honey badger is generally peaceful. However, if it is attacked or threatened in some way it will not hesitate to fight against seemingly impossible odds. Once in a fight, nothing short of death will defeat it. It has been recorded as killing much larger creatures such as wildebeest and waterbuck. One technique – Ferdy noted with horror – was the ratel's habit of climbing the legs of a male adversary and attacking the testicles, ripping them and causing the animal to die from blood loss. People have made pets of honey badgers and report that they can be tamed to some extent. They are intelligent and may be affectionate.

§

How much of the honey badger's character had Ali adopted?

Ferdy selected the phone he was using for Ivan and punched in his number. 'Ivan, my friend. Okay, man, things are moving. I've got a partner for your, er, venture and he's ready to act. So, I need to confirm your commitment. Are you sure you want to go through with this?'

There was silence at first. 'Ivan, you there?'

Ivan answered with a brief cry and a sniff. 'I'm so sore, Facilitator. He did terrible things to me last night. All his friends were watching, and some … I've got bruises everywhere, and my bum—'

'I don't want to know, Ivan. Does this mean you want to go ahead as we discussed?'

'I didn't want to, but now I do. I want him to feel pain.'

'Good man. Okay, Ivan, listen carefully. Go away. Go away tonight or latest tomorrow morning, okay?'

'All right. Oh, I … I don't know. This is a big step, Facilitator. I mean we're talking about killing Cecil. Isn't that going too far? What do you think, Facilitator? Do you think I should do it?'

'Look at it another way, Ivan, my friend. If you don't do something, when is this treatment of you going to stop? Will it ever stop? You'll be a physical and mental wreck for the rest of your life, man. Going through with this will give you some self-respect, and you can hold your head up and know you have the power to fight people like Cecil.'

'You're right, of course. You're such a help, Facilitator. I'll do it. I'll do it. I'll go to Inverness – tonight.'

'Good man. Now, pay attention. You must leave a trail the cops can follow. Fill up with fuel as soon as you can, but only when you are definitely heading north. You want to show that your alibi begins well before the murder takes place. Use your credit card for fuel, use the card for shopping – a beer, whatever. Keep the slips. Make sure you're seen and memorised so you get a solid alibi. Plan on staying the week, although I reckon the cops'll find you and give you the news within a couple of days – long before that time is up. Only then come back. Be prepared for police interviews; you will be the number-one suspect, but it won't matter because you weren't here. You gotta have confidence in that. And you'd better start thinking – you will still have to carry out your side of the deal. I'll give you the details when you get back, but remember it must be done before the 26th.' Ferdy found that giving a date a few days earlier than the deadline gave a decent margin to correct any cockups, and Ivan was likely to make more than a few of those.

If he was even capable of fulfilling his contract. Ivan seemed useless, but he was the only person he could summon to deal with Simone – other than himself, of course. But that was out of the question.

CHAPTER SIX

Thursday 15th September

FERDY'S NIGHTMARE of Ivan breaking down and running to the police was cut short by the ping from his sub-surface office at 5.30 on Thursday morning.

For use during cases, he had rigged a beeper on the landing (it was loud and could be heard throughout the house) to sound if any of the present or past protagonists contacted him via the dark web. They might have urgent problems, something might have failed, they might want to call off the murder at the last moment, or the police clearly suspected them even if they had a sound alibi. There could be any number of things that needed urgent attention. After all, the lives and futures of everyone involved were on the line and mostly in his hands.

Ferdy rolled out of bed, put on a dressing gown and went down to his basement with that empty feeling in his stomach. A ping at this time in the morning? Something had gone wrong somewhere, somehow.

The message was from Millie – oh, God, she's been arrested. But no, the tone was anything but.

§

Hi, Mister Facilitator. Sorry it's so early, but I'm off in an hour to North Wales for some climbing. I wanted to get this message to you first.

Thank you so much for all you did. It's worked out exactly as I planned and there have been no repercussions. The main reason for my contact, though, is I wanted to say how much I enjoyed the experience. I found it liberating, I felt powerful and in control of life – mine and hers.

The excitement of the chase, of almost being caught, sent my adrenalin through the roof. I was so thrilled. And when that fat bastard got hold of me and I crushed his balls so hard he screamed, it gave me such a kick. God, that was so funny, I laughed for a week; I still laugh at it.

So thanks a mil. The experience has given me thought for the future.

Keep up the good work, Mister.

§

The tension in Ferdy's belly eased, and balance was restored. He typed, '*My pleasure. So glad all is good for you.*' But he did it as an automatic response, not because that was what he meant. In fact, he didn't really know what he felt. He was pleased that a client was happy, but an uncomfortable feeling about what this might mean in the future lingered in his mind as he stumped up the steps to the kitchen and an early coffee.

2

Sally's computer was ready. She arrived to collect it as Ferdy was making his third espresso of the day, so he made another and turned it into a flat white for her.

'Your machine's in the basement,' he said. 'I'll get it. Will you pay cash or card? With cash there'll be no invoice and we can ignore the VAT.'

'You naughty boy.' Sally grinned at him. 'Cash will be fine.'

In the basement, Ferdy wrapped the laptop in soft packaging, checked that his three computer monitors had gone to sleep and turned to leave.

Sally was standing behind him.

'*Ah*.' Ferdy started and was brusque. 'I asked you last time not to come down here. Please don't. Now go back upstairs, I'll see you in a moment.'

Sally looked hurt, said nothing, and left.

She was waiting for him in the lounge. 'I'm sorry. I didn't realise you're so sensitive about that.'

'Never mind. Just please don't go there again.'

'I won't, I promise. Why is your cellar out of bounds, so secret?'

'Erm ... er, it's private work I do for some people. It's to do with intelligence and I don't want to talk about it.' Ferdy knew his manner had been curt, but she was in the wrong. He had to get the conversation back on friendly terms. 'Is there anything you need computer-wise? I can get most stuff at cost.'

'No thanks. I suppose I'd better be going, let you get on.'

'Um ... er ...'

That wonderful smile. 'Yes, Ferdy?'

He fidgeted and studied his embarrassing feet. 'Um ... would you like to go for a drink or something?'

'Do you have a girlfriend, Ferdy?'

'No. No, I don't.'

'Then I'd love to. I wouldn't want to get involved in an existing relationship. I don't want the hassle of it. A drink is a super idea, but I've a better one. They show old movies in the town hall occasionally, and there's one I've been dying to see for a long time: Kind Hearts and Coronets. It's only on this week and I was planning to go on Friday night, tomorrow. Let's go together. Is that okay with you? We can have drinks and dinner too.'

This was turning out to be too good to be true. 'Brilliant idea. Tell me about the film.'

'It's a black comedy from 1949. It's about a man who is wrongfully denied his position in an aristocratic family. He's vengeful over it, so he decides to murder all those ahead of him in the line of succession – eight of them, all played by Sir Alec Guinness. The critics loved it and even placed it high up

the list of great British films fifty years later. I'm really looking forward to it. All those lords killed in different ways – it's
supposed to be very funny.'

CHAPTER SEVEN

Saturday 17th September

FERDY WOKE at six on Saturday morning. He lay supine, dwelling on what had happened the night before. A shy child, he'd gone to a boys-only school and so had little experience of girls until he was almost twenty. He found females to be odd, unfathomable creatures that made him nervous. He regarded himself as a quasi-virgin: not a real virgin, just an apparent one.

This almost-virgin status existed because at some party in London set up by his flat-mates and a corresponding commune of girls, he almost lost it.

One of the girls took a shine to him, (or rather to Felix as he was then), got him up to a bedroom and locked the door. After much fondling and groping and stroking, Felix followed his instincts and made moves to mount her. But she said no, she had her period. In compensation for winding him up for no reward, she proceeded to satisfy him manually in an embarrassingly short time.

As Ferdy, he wasn't sure where that eighteen-year-old experience left him on the scale of virginity. Indeed, was there even a degree of virginity? There wasn't any beating about the bush as regards pregnancy – a girl was either pregnant or she wasn't – no half measures. But did sexual satisfaction with a member of the opposite sex without penetration render his status as a virgin obsolete?

So was he a semi-virgin: a half consummated creature.

Or maybe a hemi-virgin? No, that's the Greek version of the same thing.

Or a peri-virgin? A man prowling the perimeter of virginity from within, searching for a hole through which to escape to the adult world outside.

Whatever, the debate was now over. Doubly over, in fact, because after the movie, in a series of events so confusing that Ferdy could not recall, their clothes had come off. Nervous as hell, he hesitated. Being as bullish as he felt might be too aggressive for her. Being too withdrawn might stretch her patience and she'd think him a wimp. He was saved by her taking control.

She had slithered over his body: her soft, silky skin smoothed his chest hair, her nipples, hard and distinct, traced their path up and down his torso, her hair tickled between his thighs. There was no doubt now – this morning – that he was no longer a virgin. To make absolutely sure, he brushed her long red trusses off his shoulder and let his hand – which seemed to have a mind of its own – wander down her chest.

The first time, he had been so focused on doing the right thing, without knowing what the right thing was, that he appreciated little else. He was more self-assured during the second round and became conscious of Sally's enthusiastic responses. He marvelled at her humming throughout, a steady contented sound which gained in pitch and broke in time with each thrust.

If Ferdy thought he might have been in love from the very first time he set eyes on her, he was now utterly convinced. He was besotted. He was her slave.

'There's a butterfly on your shoulder,' he said, reaching to touch it. 'It's a very good one.'

'Thanks. You won't have noticed last night, but I've another tattoo.' She flipped onto her front and pulled the sheet down. At the base of her spine was a scorpion.

'So there's a sting in your tail,' he joked, and bent to kiss it.

'Coffee?' he offered later, before climbing out of bed.

'Mmm …' Sally gave him a sleepy, satisfied smile and sat half up on her elbows. 'Ferdy, your feet, they're long, huge, actually.' She giggled. 'What's a little man doing with a big man's feet?'

His cheeks flushed. 'They've always been like that. I can't help it.'

'They must be an asset, make you more stable? What size shoe do you take?'

'Ten.'

'Ten? And you're five foot seven.' She laughed again. 'And they're hairy. Furry Ferdy. I'm going to call you Furry from now on. Do you shave them?'

'Of course not, they're not that bad. Look, do you want coffee or not?'

'Don't be miffed, Ferdy. I'm only teasing. If it's any consolation, they match other parts of your anatomy.' She laughed again and reached out a hand to touch him. 'Make the coffee, dear Hobbit. I'll come down.'

Ferdy switched on the machine and went around the ground floor opening the curtains. Why did she have to tease him? His feet were so embarrassing. It had always been the case that he would be teased by someone who got close to him. Maybe his fear of ridicule had contributed to his failure to have a relationship up to now. And, as expected, as soon as he did find someone, she teased him. She wasn't like those bullies at school, though. They were cruel.

'Pull yourself together, Felix,' a sports master had said. 'Learn to live with your flippers, make your own jokes about them. Get over them.'

Easy for the teacher, with his normal feet, to say, but not so easy to do. Maybe Sally's good-natured teasing would actually help.

The sun was low and hidden behind the houses across the road. Built in the 1930s, they all followed the same pattern: semi-detached and plain, except where enterprising occupants had made an effort. But now, their details were lost in shadow. No lights were on in the old crone's house, so she wasn't up. Maybe she'd died in the night. Soon, though, the sun would flood his lounge. With nothing interesting in the street, he went to the kitchen and spent some time staring out at his tiny garden. An immense feeling of satisfaction surged through him. A feeling of physical fulfilment: he'd managed a significant step forward in completing his manhood – if he died now, he would die complete – whereas yesterday … He was sure he had grown during the night (into his feet?) and he straightened up to match the feeling. But had it been good for her?

Sally came in and handed him an A4 envelope. 'This must have been hand-delivered last night. It was on the front doormat.'

Ferdy said, 'Interesting, but coffee first,' and turned to his machine. Facing away from her, he said, 'Last night … Um, I'm sorry, I'm not very experienced. In fact—'

'In fact, I'm the first.'

'Oh God. Was it that obvious?'

She took a quick step to him. 'Ferdy, it was lovely, it was fun, and I'm going to make sure it gets even lovelier – if you'll let me.'

'Oh God.'

Sally giggled and began talking about the film. 'I'm so glad we saw that movie. I've been dying to watch it. It's so funny. It's even funnier because it has all the quirks of a film made in the forties. All those murders and every one different. Right up my street – humour-wise, of course.'

'Which murder did you like best?' Ferdy wasn't happy talking about murder, it was too close to home, but after last night he didn't want to put any distance between them. 'You and that woman next to you were giggling at every one.'

'Ooh, I don't know. Maybe the bomb in the caviar? Imagine the mess. She agreed with me.' Sally laughed. 'And the admiral who goes down with his ship, saluting to the last. That's always been an image, but in the real event the victim won't hold out, he won't maintain a stiff upper lip, he'll panic like the rest of us. I love the whole concept of multiple murders, though, each one unique.'

Ferdy sat at the table, Sally held her mug in two hands and padded about the kitchen eventually stopping to look out of the window at the garden. Ferdy slit the A4 envelope and pulled out two photographs wrapped in tissue paper.

The blood drained from his face. His fingers trembled. He tried to hold them still, but they wouldn't stop. He flicked a glance at Sally. She was still sipping coffee at the window, her attention on a robin on the fence. It was often there because Ferdy fed it.

2

Sally put out a hand to him. 'What's the matter? Are you all right? You look like you've seen a ghost. What are you staring at? *Ferdy.*' She moved behind him and gasped. 'Oh my God. What—'

She rushed to the sink. Ferdy was vaguely aware of her retching. His eyes were locked on the image.

It didn't stare back. It couldn't, because it didn't have a head.

The body was seated at the base of a large tree. Its legs were spread and laid straight out. The torso was slumped forward so the severed neck faced the camera. Half a vertebra was visible as well as little circles of severed arteries and veins. Blood had streamed down the neck and soaked the back and front of the man's T-shirt. Where was the head?

Ferdy was hesitant. But curiosity overcame him. The second picture was of the head. It was nailed higher up the tree by a crossbow bolt through the right eye socket. How had the murderer done that? The left eye captured Ferdy. It was vengeful, it was saying, 'Ferdy, this is your doing. To every action, there's a reaction.'

Sally was behind him again. 'Oh God, this is awful. I can't look. What does it mean? Why did you get these? Is this a threat, Ferdy?' She put her hands on his shoulders.

Ferdy had his suspicions, but he couldn't tell Sally. 'I don't know what this is. Let's watch the news. Maybe there's a clue there.'

But there wasn't.

He had wanted to do something cheerful during the morning, but the photos had put a damper on that idea. Instead, they moped around before turning on the TV again at midday. This time, a few sketchy details of a gruesome murder were reported. A dog walker had found a headless corpse in a park.

Ferdy knew the area, which was some four miles to the south. The park was large and open for the most part, but a plantation on the eastern side separated it from the main road. The pine trees had been grown close together, making it dense and dark inside. It was easy to become disoriented in there, although a stroll in any direction for five minutes would take you to open ground.

The body must have been left near a path, or it wouldn't have been found – except by a dog. The victim had been identified from his driving licence and the police had already begun interviewing the men he had been out with the night before. The area had been cordoned off and there was an appeal for further witnesses.

Sally was close to tears. 'Why were those pictures sent to you before the news was out? I'm scared, Ferdy. Is this to do with your work? This is scary, you must get out of it.'

Ali had proven she was a vicious killer with no scruples. The message was plain: if he did not see that Simone was murdered in the next few days … Somehow he quelled his rising panic to think logically.

One thing was clear and urgent. Ivan must do what he promised.

After Sally had gone, Ferdy decided he had to get this whole episode over as soon as possible. The longer Ivan had to dither, the more difficult it was going to be to force him to go through with it. He phoned the little man, emphasising his

South African accent. He spoke at a slow pace with clear separation between his words. 'Cecil is dead, my friend. It's time you come back and finish your half of the contract. It's got to be done some time in the next three days.'

'B-but you said we had until the 26th. What's happened? I've got to prepare, I can't do it on such short notice.'

'You've had three days to get your act together, Ivan. Grow up. There's been a change of plan, so be in the cemetery at two tomorrow morning. That's Sunday, right? That will give you enough time to drive back and get to the church – say nine and a half to ten hours. The cops won't know you back, and you can check in with them later in the morning.'

CHAPTER EIGHT

Sunday 18th September

A STRONG breeze caused Ferdy to shiver as he waited for Ivan in the cemetery. Because of dense cloud cover, it was darker than the last time. Spits of rain patted his face.

The gate gave its familiar squeak, and hesitant steps crunched the gravel. Ivan's voice quavered, 'Hello?'

Ferdy could almost smell the man's fear. He would be useless unless he could be put at ease. 'You made it in time. Well done, Ivan, my friend. How was the traffic?'

'Terrible in places. I didn't think I'd make it at all. I got lost trying to find a way around a blockage, and I nearly had three accidents. I couldn't stop thinking about what I have to do and I lost focus on the other cars. I'm very tired.'

'Huh. Never mind. What's important is that you here and you safe. Relax, Ivan, it's going to be easy. Now, my friend, the cops is looking for you, 'cause you Cecil's partner, so you'll have to see them as soon as possible so they not so suspicious. You must report to them in the morning. This woman Simone has to be dealt with quick-quick, say at eight tonight – in about eighteen hours. Did you prep yourself? Are you ready for this?'

'I'm scared, sir, but I'll try.'

'Trying isn't good enough, Ivan. You have to do it or … well, you know the answer to that, you agreed to the terms.'

'Are you going to kill me, Facilitator?'

'I don't want to, man, I don't want to – genuine, man, it's messy. But I will if you don't comply with our agreement. The other party is another story. I can't control him. You have seen how Cecil was killed, or if you haven't you soon will. The other party is a very angry person, and if I don't do it then he will.' Ferdy laughed. 'I believe his method gets you a short coffin.'

2

One of Ferdy's expenses (which he couldn't claim off income tax) was a collection of mobile phones. He had his regular phone for day-to-day use just as anyone else would have, then he had four cheap pay-as-you-go phones. For a contract, he would allocate one of these to each client and give it a special ringtone. He also bought a selection of SIM cards which he would change in each phone depending on how many calls were made. Because the phones themselves could be identified through their IMEI numbers, when the job was over he'd throw them away (sorry, environment) and buy two more for the next assignment. The other two cheap mobiles were spares in case excessive use by one client necessitated a change.

This swapping of instruments and SIM cards reduced the chances of Ferdy being linked to a murderer. When he started the business, he twice got confused as to which phone to use for each client, so he marked the instruments with different coloured tape – in this case, red for Ratel and yellow (appropriately) for Ivan.

Ferdy tried to keep the communication to messages on the dark web. At first he considered using WhatsApp, which has end-to-end encryption, so at first glance it would seem safe. Then he read how WhatsApp itself keeps a record of the source and destination of messages, although not the content. This meant that if an investigation into his affairs was taking place, the police would see that he communicated with Ivan, a suspect in a murder. That would definitely be unwanted attention. But there were times of crisis or haste when an actual conversation had to be held.

The stress was getting to him. Thank God Sally was around, because he had to behave normally in her presence or face her probing questions. Without her, he would succumb to the pressure and make some stupid mistake that could lead to his own death.

He was oscillating between two extremes. On the one hand he was subjugated by Ratel – a nerve-wracking experience with his own life very definitely on the line. On the other hand he had to deal with Ivan, who also required close attention. But that was because the little man was unpredictable. There was no telling what he was going to do next: say he couldn't go through with the act, plead for help, or give up and start crying. And every time he needed help, he used his phone. It was dangerous and against the rules.

Ferdy was in his kitchen chopping up a small chunk of cheese into even smaller pieces to feed to the robin, which was on the fence outside watching him. It was there every day, ever hopeful.

The yellow phone vibrated and pinged. What did Ivan want now?

'I cant do this, Facilitator. I just cant. Im so sorry,' he wrote. *'Please dont kill me. I know i said you could but now i face it i cant take it. Will you kill me? Ill do anything, but dont ask me to kill this woman and please please dont kill me.'*

Ferdy could almost hear the tears dripping onto the phone. He didn't answer. This useless character had given him a major, life-threatening problem. So let the little sod wallow in his misery for a while.

'Facilitator, are you there?'

An hour later, Ferdy sent, *'Get off this channel now. Look on my website for a new number to phone.'*

Ferdy barely had time to replace the SIM card on one of the mobiles. He switched it back on, and it immediately rang. 'Oh, I'm sorry, Facilitator, so sorry. I forgot the security measures you said. I'm sorry, I can't kill this old lady. I suppose you will kill me now. I don't want to die.'

'*Ja*, you were happy when someone else was going to kill Cecil for you, but you can't do the same thing for him. How you think that person feels with you letting him down? You need to remember, Ivan, the other party is very, very angry. You saw what he did to Cecil. You want the same treatment? I might kill you first, but if I take pity on you and leave it to the other guy …? Perhaps you should decide not whether you should be killed, but how you should be killed.'

A pause followed. More silent weeping was probably taking place at the other end of the line. There was certainly a sniff.

'I must hide. I might give myself up to the police. That would involve you.'

'Where are you going to go, Ivan? Remember I know everything about you. You don't know my real name, you don't know my address. You only know a few phone numbers which are deleted soon after we've spoken. On the other hand, I know a hell of a lot about you. I know where you've been on holiday and who your friends are, for example. I could pass that information onto the other guy, and he would deal with you himself. So don't be dumb. It's best we keep this between us. Think, Ivan. You have to do this. There's no way out. You have two hours to decide. I want a positive answer by six this evening.'

'Oh, God.'

Ferdy put the phone down. It rattled as it touched the table. He took a deep breath. Was he being firm enough? The trouble was, he felt the same way as Ivan did. There was no way he could kill Simone, or anyone else for that matter. His business worked purely because it was based on bluff and bullying. The threat of death was what kept his clients in line. They believed him when he said he would hunt them down if they chickened out.

But now he was faced with a different animal altogether. He couldn't bully Ratel. She was far stronger than him, because she was undoubtedly a psychopath and had no scruples. A person who has no feelings, who is cruel without concern, who will kill without a conscience, will always dominate someone who values their moral position.

He would have to tell her what progress was being made this evening. First, though, he had to have Ivan's answer. If he wouldn't do it, then Ferdy would have to get rid of Simone himself. Simone would be very difficult for him, but he would have to do it – or end up like Cecil.

The robin was watching him through the window – *Come on, hurry up. I'm hungry.* If only life were so simple.

3

'Sunday night is Indian takeaway night – my treat.' Sally was at the kitchen table, sipping at a glass of Merlot and glancing through Ferdy's restaurant menu. 'I feel like a good spicy dish, don't you?'

'Brilliant,' said Ferdy. 'I'll have a lamb Madras – it's always good.'

Sally struggled to give the telephone order, because there was so much background noise in the restaurant kitchen, but eventually made herself heard. She asked to have her card details read back to check they were correct.

'They said about forty minutes.'

While they waited, after Ferdy had tossed a couple of cushions out of the way, they snuggled together on the sagging couch and watched the news without any great interest. The politics was 'same old, same old'; there were floods and an earthquake. Russia was sabre-rattling, Trump was shouting weird stuff, France was being difficult and China was being inscrutable. On the local front, the police were no further forward in solving the particularly gruesome murder and decapitation of two days prior. However they had issued an appeal for witnesses, having released CCTV footage of a person they wished to interview.

The grainy clip showed a figure in a hoody walking across a petrol station forecourt to the convenience store. As the person was almost directly below the camera, she looked up at it showing no sign of concern – a picture of innocence, in fact.

Ferdy jerked upright. '*God*. That's you.'

Sally stared. The presenter was still talking in the background, the image still on the screen. 'It looks like me, but it can't be. Look at the time stamp. That was three nights ago. I was here with you.'

'Of course you were. But she's the spitting image of you. Okay, the picture's blurry and grainy, but she's definitely very like you. This isn't funny. Someone could point a finger at you because of that.'

'Yes, but you would be my alibi.

CHAPTER NINE

Monday 19th September

FERDY HAD been worrying since he woke early on Monday morning. Actually, he had been in that state since Sally mentioned the previous evening that he was her alibi. The world seemed to be closing in on him. Full police involvement – meaning interrogation, a search of his house, confiscation of his computers and possible arrest – was just around the corner.

As if trying to make up for the total absence of sex during his eighteen years as a semi-virgin, he never missed an opportunity now, and it seemed that Sally was just as keen on helping him catch up. Not last night, though, his mind was on what the police would do, and he only fell asleep around midnight, waking at three.

He had eased out of bed just after four and gone to make coffee. He peered out of the kitchen window, leaving two steam marks on the glass. He saw nothing; it was still dark outside. He didn't hear Sally come downstairs a few minutes later. But then he failed to hear her moving about most of the time, she was so quiet. She put a warm hand on his neck.

'*Ah*. You gave me a fright sneaking around like that. Why aren't you still sleeping? Would you like coffee?'

'Yes please. I woke when you got up and couldn't stay in bed alone. Why are you so jumpy? Does going to the police worry you?' Sally always seemed to see straight through him. It was unsettling.

'I don't want them here. You see them in the TV dramas: "Mind if I look around?" or "Can I use the bathroom?" and they're off on a sneaky prowl around the house.'

'So what? You've nothing to hide.'

Ferdy hesitated. He didn't want to discuss the cellar again, but Sally was giving him that intense searching look she had when waiting for an answer. 'I've told you, the basement is out of bounds. It's classified. They can't learn that it exists.'

'Oh, don't worry. They're not going to come home with us. They'll take my information and let us go.'

'Maybe.'

He plodded back upstairs and went to the window. The street lights lent an orange glow to the Scotch mist that enveloped the road. It had been there since midnight and according to the met report it would stay that way until lunchtime.

Everything dripped. Life was full of gloom, and so was Ferdy. He crawled back into bed.

Not long after eight, a police car parked beneath a tree in the road below. The officers were just getting out when Ferdy saw it. Wishing his heart would stop thumping every time a threat popped up, he tried to calm himself before they crossed the street. But they didn't. Instead, they knocked on the door of the nosey old crone opposite. It was opened so quickly, she must have been watching them.

Ferdy had never met her, nor spoken to her, but he instinct-ively disliked her as much as he was sure she hated him. A few days back, she had been sweeping her path when she stopped to talk to her neighbour. That involved a fair amount of pointing in Ferdy's direction, followed by an emphasising gesture and a '*disgrace to the neighbourhood*' attitude. At least, that's how Ferdy interpreted it – *cow*.

Now, she stood in her doorway in her flowery apron and those ghastly blue furry slippers with her arms folded across her ample but sagging chest. Even from his position across the road, Ferdy could see the defiant, tight-lipped expression on her face. She didn't invite the officers in out of the wet – they probably had muddy boots. Leaving one hand in place, she pointed down the road with the other, and then to Ferdy's house.

Both officers turned to see where she meant. Ferdy ducked away from his window and moved to the back of the room, where he was less likely to be seen.

The woman had gone inside and closed her door. The officers were near their car, talking. One made a phone call, then they got in the vehicle and left.

'*Damn, damn, damn.*' The last thing Ferdy wanted was the police knowing he even existed, but now this nosey bloody cow had reported him – well, Sally, probably – as a result of the TV coverage.

Sally had mastered the coffee machine and was making their second round when Ferdy came in. He told her what the busybody over the road had done.

The grind had finished, but Sally didn't move. She stared at Ferdy for a while, her fingers to her lips. 'Um … I think it's best to be upfront with them,' she said. 'As soon as we've had breakfast, I'll go and find the inspector on the case and show him that I may look like his suspect but I'm not her. I want to forestall any reports that get me hauled in every five minutes. There shouldn't be a problem, especially if you come with me and provide the alibi. I think the movie tickets are still in my coat pocket. That'll help, and there's the waiter in the restaurant and, of course, the woman I chatted to during the movie. That'll account for every minute of our night.'

'Maybe. We don't know what time the murder happened.'

To be in a case file, even as an alibi for an innocent person, was, to Ferdy, waving his murderous activities directly in front of police eyes. But there was no way to avoid supporting Sally. 'Of course I'll come with you,' he said, but he had turned away to avoid her seeing his face.

'You know there have been several brutal unsolved murders around Britain in the last year? There's a rumour going around that it's that contract killer. The one who calls himself Ratel. I'm sure this one will enhance that theory. I mean it's got to be professional, hasn't it? No clues at all in any of them. And one, I think it was about nine months ago, also involved a crossbow.'

'Really?'

'Yes. What's the matter Ferdy? Why are you wearing a face like a boot?'

'Am I? I dunno. All this talk of murder, it's upsetting.'

2

Sally's insistence that they wouldn't be detained was probably right, but Ferdy wouldn't be mollified. At the police station, he kept silent, letting her take the lead when she asked for the inspector in charge of the case. 'We have evidence,' she said.

A few minutes later, a young man in blue slacks and a white long-sleeve shirt without a tie appeared. He frowned and gave Sally an intense look. He barely acknowledged Ferdy. Did he recognise her from the CCTV, or was it because she was so pretty? 'Detective Sergeant Murphy,' he said, holding out his hand. 'Detective Chief Inspector White is not here. You have evidence in the murder case, I believe? Let's go to an interview room.'

Murphy tapped on a window as they passed and signalled to someone to join them. Ferdy traipsed along behind. He had thought his heart had already sunk to its lowest point, but now he felt like a condemned man on the way to the gallows.

'This is Detective Constable Murdoch. Have a seat,' said Murphy, waiving towards a couple of chairs at a cheap Formica table. 'Please give us your names and addresses for the record.'

Murdoch was a tall, skinny young man dressed in jeans and a dark grey T-shirt with some logo on it partially hidden by his leather jacket. He was carrying a laptop computer.

Sally and Ferdy both said their names and Sally gave her address.

'And Mister Fellowes, are you at the same address?'

Ferdy hesitated. Sally said, 'Yes.'

Ferdy was petrified of falling foul of the police. If there was any bother later and they discovered he lived on his own, that would be the end of him. He'd never been to Sally's house, but how could he reply? Whatever story he told was going to dig a hole for himself. 'Actually, I've another address.' He gave it. 'But Sally's right, I'm mostly at hers.'

'Good, thank you. Now what can you tell us?'

'Can you bring up that CCTV footage you put on the news that shows a woman you want to speak to?' Sally said.

Murdoch raised a finger in acknowledgement and tapped on his keyboard. 'Here.' He swivelled the computer around so that they could all see the screen and set the clip to play. The woman looked up at the camera.

'Pause it … Do you recognise her?'

Both officers stared at the screen and then looked up at Sally. Murdoch's head gave a slight jerk; Murphy's expression didn't change, he merely stared.

'I came here to tell you that that person looks just like me, but she isn't, and I can prove it. I don't want to be identified and harassed when this has nothing to do with me, so I want to be up front to stop any future attempts to treat me as a suspect.'

Murphy stared at her. 'I understand, but I'm still going to have to ask you some questions. What proof do you have that that is not you? She looks identical. And where were you on Friday night between the hours of eight and ten?'

'Well, first, the proof that she is not me is that I wasn't there, which lies in my answer to your second question. Ferdy and I went to see a classic movie called Kind Hearts and Coronets in that little theatre in the town square, then we had dinner at Mi Casa. The film ended at 8.30, I think, so we were in the restaurant by a quarter to nine – it's close. Here are the movie tickets.' She passed them across the table and tapped one. 'Our seat numbers are there. There was a woman sitting next to me, and we were laughing together all through the film. If you can find her, she'll verify that I was there all the time. You can check with the restaurant staff as well. Oh, and it was my treat, and I paid with my credit card. We left after ten, which is a long time, but they had a singer and a dancer for entertainment.'

DS Murphy let them go, saying he would be in contact if there were any inconsistencies or developments that concerned them. 'I can't promise you won't be harassed by members of the press, the public or trolls over this. That's out of our hands. I should make you aware that your alibi will be checked, and that alibis provided by family members, friends or partners are questioned.'

Ferdy's gut cramped in a brief spasm. Although he'd spoken the truth, the fact that the police were going to check the information was frightening. How far would they go? Would they come to his house?

3

Sally had gone home after their visit to the police station. She said she was falling behind in her work and had to catch up. She'd be back by lunch the next day. Ferdy felt the loss, even if it was only for about twenty-eight hours.

Later in the morning, Ivan cracked. After much weeping and wailing and the baring of Ferdy's teeth, he had said he would do it; he definitely would.

Ferdy sent a message to Ali that Ivan was reconciled to doing the deed, and Simone would meet her end before Friday, ahead of schedule.

Almost immediately, his phone rang.

'This has all the signs of a complete fuck-up, Ferdy. You've had difficulty with that little creature from the start. He doesn't have the guts of a mouse. He's indecisive and weak.

He will not be able to kill Simone. Somehow you have to ensure that old crone dies. *Do. You. Understand?*'

Ferdy swallowed. 'It will be done, believe me.'

'I don't. And, if she lives, you and that failed specimen of a human will not.'

Ferdy shivered. He tried to recover. 'It's time for you to go away. She will be killed soon.'

That was met with silence, and for a moment Ferdy thought the call had dropped. Then, 'You do *not* tell me when it is time to do anything. Is that clear? I make my own decisions, and I may or may not tell you. You're best advised to keep your focus on Simone. That's all that matters.'

It was Ferdy's turn to keep quiet while he calmed himself. He opted for a change of topic. 'Your photo was shown on TV. Everyone knows what you look like.'

Ali's laugh was harsh and humourless. 'Yes, and don't I look like your girlfriend? It's quite funny really: she'll get the recognition and blame on social media while I walk around free. I've learned to be very good at disguising myself. It's a vital tool in this business.'

A sudden dread ran through Ferdy as he imagined what could happen if Ali posed as Sally in her escapades. 'Whatever happens, you won't harm her, will you? She's not involved, and doesn't have a clue what I do or what's going on.'

Ali gave a snort of laughter and hung up.

Ferdy climbed the steps from the cellar on weary legs. In the lounge, he collapsed onto the sagging couch, feet on one arm, his head on the other, and stared at the ceiling from a position akin to lying in a hammock. Ali was right, this had all the indications of a gigantic fuck-up. There was no way Ivan was going to be able to kill Simone, he simply wasn't up to it. So all this was his fault, wasn't it?...No, not entirely. Ferdy had to admit he should have rejected Ivan's participation from the start. He knew all along that the man was too weak – as was he.

To protect his conscience, Ferdy pretended that the organisation of murder was a completely innocent activity. He would never actually kill someone; he wouldn't even kill a cockroach. It wasn't that he was religious – he couldn't be religious doing what he did – it was purely that he was human, and normal humans did not go around slaughtering each other.

Meanwhile, he was slowly coming to terms with the fact that he was going to have to take care of Simone himself. It was going to be difficult, though, very difficult.

4

'I've made up my mind.' Ivan sniffed then coughed into the phone. 'I know I said I'd do it, but I just can't, Facilitator. Will you kill me now? You can't kill me, I'm going into hiding. I—'

'*Ivan.* We are not going through this again. We had it all out yesterday. I'm getting bleddy tired of all this whining from you, man. Pull yourself together. Act like a man, and *stop bleddy crying.*' Ferdy paused to let that sink in. 'I'm going to give you one more chance, man. We will do this together. You will kill this woman. I'll be there with you to help if necessary. If you fail, I'll kill you right there. That is a promise, Ivan. I'm sick of your nonsense, and I'm not going to suffer because you failed me. Do you understand?'

'Y-yes. Thank you, sir. Thank you for understanding and giving me a break. I won't let you down.'

'No, you won't. All right, Ivan, my man, the sooner we do this the better. I'll meet you tonight in the churchyard at eight, okay? Bring gloves, a balaclava or a scarf and wear the gimp suit or wetsuit I told you to buy. And remember to burn it when it's over. You must not leave any trace of DNA. Is that clear?'

'I didn't have to buy it, I've got a gimp suit. Cecil's friends wanted me to wear it. They had a game—'

'I don't wanna know, man. That's not my business.'

5

Out of sight on the bench in the cemetery, Ferdy watched a couple, hand in hand, amble along the path and disappear between some graves to his right. These meetings he had in the churchyard were usually much later, in the early hours of the morning, so that no other party would hear what was said. But this time there was to be no discussion. This was a rendezvous to commit a murder, to make sure Ivan did what he had agreed to do and to ensure that neither of them was subject to the punishment of a psychopath – hopefully. The gravity of the situation weighed on him. He was going to witness Simone being killed, and he might even have to help her on her way. This set him miles out of his comfort zone, which so far had never released him to get his hands dirty.

As usual, he was early, well ahead of Ivan, which allowed him to savour the peace and come to terms with what had to be done in the next couple of hours. He glanced up at the overcast sky. Low clouds reflecting the town lights scudded across from the south-west. It had better not rain. It would not be good to leave water from shoes or dripping clothing on the carpet of the old-age home and possibly give forensics something to play with.

Another squeak from the wicket gate announced his reluctant partner in crime. The skinny figure took hesitant steps down the path, trying hard not to scrunch the gravel.

'Good grief,' breathed Ferdy.

Ivan was dressed in black shorts beneath which were black tights, advertising the muscle-free outline of his skinny, knobbly legs, slightly bowed. A bulky black jersey hid his slight frame and a length of black material was wound round his head like a Tuareg.

Ferdy did not comment, but Ivan was obviously embarrassed. 'All my clothes are brightly coloured except these.'

'And the tights? Who wears tights, man?'

'Well, I had them … I mean, they're useful for …'

'I don't wanna know. Where's the gimp suit you said you had?'

'It's in my car, but it's torn … a bit. I'm wearing the tights because the slit is – here.'

'*Jees*, Ivan. I said I don't wanna know.' Ferdy was not having his car seen anywhere near a murder site, even two blocks away. 'We take your car, man. Where's it?'

Five miles in Ivan's scruffy, ancient Datsun Sunny was not an experience destined to calm Ferdy's nerves. His door took two hard slams to close, there was severe rust below the door sill that could be seen even in the dark, and it made some hideous noises. The squeaks and minor rattles were just age, but the occasional heavy metallic clunk from somewhere up front was alarming.

A stink of onions and meat pervaded the interior. Shifting a McDonald's burger punnet and an empty yogurt pot to one side with his foot, Ferdy put a protective hand out to the dash. Ivan was driving erratically, alternately accelerating and braking for no apparent reason. He seemed to see corners when already part way around them causing him to jerk the wheel and throw them both to the side.

Ferdy had to calm him down or there would be a disaster in the critical moments ahead. Ivan hit a pothole. A hard smack of metal on metal shook the car. 'How old is this thing, Ivan?'

'I think it was made in 1970 or about then, why?'

'Has it had a MOT?'

'Um … No, I don't think so … What's that anyway?'

'The annual roadworthiness inspection. If you get caught, they'll slap you with a thousand-pound fine. You got a licence?'

'No.'

'*Jesus*. Insurance?'

Ivan shook his head.

'Look here, man, we are not taking this wreck anywhere near the old-age home. If the cops find it and check on it, they'll come after you, and you'll have to explain why you were in the area. Find somewhere to park round here, down a side street, and we'll walk the rest. It's only about a mile. You'll have to put your gimp suit on to minimise any DNA that escapes your clothes.'

Ferdy strode down the road with a fine drizzle dampening his face. Even though he was a short man, his pace caused Ivan to trot occasionally to keep up.

Simone's retirement home was a large old house set back from the street. At the back was a wide expanse of lawn dotted with bushes and flowerbeds. The space was dominated by two large chestnut trees whose shade sheltered the elderly on hot summer days. Or they could use the selection of benches that overlooked the garden, and wheelchair users could stick to the tarred paths that crossed the area. Two of the residents delighted in telling the hard-working and even-tempered gardener what to cut and where to plant – he ignored them.

There were twenty retirees who were charged a fortune for the privilege of living in the home. They were housed in private rooms on two floors, Ali explained in her instructions.

§

Simone's room is on the ground floor. Entry through her window is possible but there is a high chance of discovery. Go three windows to the right as you face the house. It's a sash window that leads onto the corridor and is easy to open from the outside by using a screwdriver to prise the window up at a point opposite the catch. The catch is broken, so the window can't be locked. Once inside, go down the passage, past the first door, and enter Simone's room through the second door on the left. Her name is on the door. Do not make a mistake over which door to open. Refer to the sketch of the layout to be certain.

§

Ferdy led Ivan round the side of the house and found a clump of laurel to hide behind. They studied the back of the building a mere twenty yards away.

'That's the window we want.' Ferdy pointed. His finger, he noted, was quivering uncontrollably. He gritted his teeth – he had to stay controlled and be in control, because Ivan was most certainly not.

The sight of the access to where he was going to do this terrible thing was another step along Ivan's path to embracing the devil. Ferdy guessed it was coming, and braced himself for the reaction.

'Let's go.'

Ivan whimpered and dropped to his knees. He wrapped his arms round Ferdy's thighs and, with his head to one side, cried, 'We can't do this. We can run away and hide. We'll find a place together and be safe. *Please, sir.*'

A similar scene in Kind Hearts and Coronets had made both Ferdy and Sally laugh. He quoted now, 'Please arise from that absurd position.' But, his nerves shredded, he forgot his South African accent. Not that Ivan noticed. He looked away and staggered to his feet.

Ferdy hadn't brought a screwdriver; instead he had an old army bayonet that had been passed down by his father. He didn't think his dad actually used the knife, but just kept it after the war.

As Ali described, it was easy for Ferdy to insert his bayonet into the crack at the base of the corridor window and lever it upwards. Once he could get his fingers under it, it slid smoothly upwards for six inches, then stuck.

A click of heels on the parquet floor echoed down the passage. Ferdy ducked and stepped sideways. Ivan froze. Ferdy grabbed his arm and pulled him down. Ivan squeaked.

Whoever was on the inside sounded off in a marked Liverpool accent, 'What fool opened this. We try and keep the place warm and some health guru wants icy air in here. It was that colonel, I'll bet. Full o' nonsense he is. I'm going to have words.' She slammed the sash down and stomped off.

Ferdy peered over the sill. 'She's gone. We'll try again.'

'Maybe we should forget it. It's too risky. I'm sure your client will understand.'

'Don't be bleddy stupid, man. Pull yourself together or you'll be chopped in two by the end of the week – believe it. Now help me force this sash higher so we can get through.'

'Oh, God.'

With the window wider, Ferdy pulled himself up to the sill and slithered through the gap. Ivan struggled to get up to the sill. '*Christ*,' Ferdy hissed, leaned out through the window and grabbed and yanked on Ivan's forearms.

'Sorry. Thanks, Facilitator.'

'You really are bleddy useless, Ivan.'

'Sorry.'

They crept down the corridor, Ivan so close behind Ferdy that he trod on his heel.

'*Jeez.*' Ferdy rounded on the little man, who backed away his hands raised in defence. At the second door, with its 'Simone' nameplate, Ferdy put his face to Ivan's. 'Silence. Not a fucking word, not a fucking squeak.'

'She will be drowsy, if not asleep,' Ali had said.

§

Simone has a fire in her room at this time of year. She has her supper in the dining room, then maybe reads a bit in front of the fire, but usually falls asleep in a short while. The staff check on her around ten and get her to bed. They do not normally visit before that. Your task should be completed and you should be out of the house around 9.30. Any time after that you might meet a carer in the corridor. Your act should be bloodless and silent. The bed has a number of pillows.

§

It was easy for Ferdy to bully Ivan. He did it to force obedience for their mutual safety, but also, by being aggressive, he found it kept his own dread of what they were about to do suppressed. And he had to suppress it – as the moment drew closer, so his inclination to give up and run grew stronger.

The door handle rotated without the anticipated squeak. Hot, stuffy air loaded with the odour of the aged and tainted with some herb or other assaulted Ferdy's senses.

The room was lit by the flickering orange flames of a glass-fronted gas fire. Facing the fire, its back to the door, was an easy chair over which a standard lamp provided light to read. To the left was a bed, and a cabinet with a glass of water and vase of flowers.

It was a moment before Ferdy noticed the head of wispy grey hair lolling to one side of the chair. A hard-back book about roses rested face down on the arm. A skeletal hand, its skin like parchment, held the book in place.

Ivan was behind him, his hand up to his mouth, his eyes wide. He was trembling. Ferdy lowered his head to listen to the old lady. Her breathing was steady. His mouth was dry, his heart pounding – surely she would wake at that noise. He stepped back and gripped Ivan's wrist, pointed at the bed and gave him an emphatic thrust of the head.

Ivan's face was a mask of terror, his lip quivering, but he nodded and tiptoed to fetch a pillow. Ferdy nudged him into position behind the chair. But Ivan had frozen. Ferdy took his hands and put them at opposite ends of the pillow while Ivan stared at him with a mixture of disbelief and horror. Ferdy glared back at him and, keeping his demonstration above Simone's head, showed him what to do.

But Ivan's wide, wet eyes just stared at him, and Ferdy could feel his own panic rising. This creature had to respond, he had to do what he had promised. They couldn't back out now.

While still glaring his insistence on action, Ferdy drew his bayonet. In slow-motion he raised the blade to Ivan's throat.

Ivan shook his head, opened his mouth as if to speak, but no sound came.

Ferdy pushed the point enough to dent the skin.

Ivan squeaked.

The bayonet nicked the skin, drew blood.

Suddenly Ivan brought the pillow down over Simone's face. He pulled hard, forcing the old woman's head into the chair back.

She struggled – with surprising strength. The book of roses thumped as it hit the floor. Her aged claws tore at the pillow. But Ferdy had insisted to Ivan that once begun, the killing had to be completed or they would be exposed and caught. Simone fought. She clawed at Ivan's hands. Thank heaven for gloves; without them there would have been blood. She squirmed and wriggled, but not for long.

Simone collapsed. The fight went out of her, her hands fell away, her neck relaxed.

Ivan stepped back, gasping for the air he hadn't taken in while the killing took place.

Ferdy took the pillow from him and put it back on the bed, the fresh side up. 'Open the door. Careful now. Check the passage,' he whispered, and put Simone's book back on the arm.

The corridor was clear. The window was still open and there were no signs of alarm from the inside the home. Ivan was in shock. So was Ferdy, but he retained some sense and forced the little man through the gap. 'Go to the laurel and wait.'

Ferdy wriggled out and reached up to bring the sash down. A figure appeared at the end of the passage. Had he been spotted? The carer knocked on the first door she reached. The window was stiff, but gave suddenly and banged shut. The carer stepped back out of the room and looked straight at Ferdy. The light was in her eyes, could she see him? She went back into the room.

He breathed, turned, and ran for the laurel. Ivan was clinging to a branch and spewing vomit over the lower leaves. It was too much for Ferdy. His guts rebelled, his stomach heaved. Ivan watched him.

'It happens every time to me.' Ferdy wiped his mouth as he lied. 'There's DNA from both of us in that lot. There's a hose over there. We can water it all down and maybe they won't see it. Go and get it.'

'I feel terrible, Facilitator.'

'You'll get over it. Now, Ivan, go home and totally destroy that gimp suit. You hear me? Don't cut it up, burn it until it's total bleddy ash. And then you'd better do something about that jalopy before the cops get onto you. I'm gonna walk home, I'm not going in that cart of yours again.'

When he was home at about 10.30, Ferdy poured himself a stiff whisky and sank onto his couch. He had not a scrap of energy left in him.

Ali called ten minutes later. 'Well?'

'It's done. Simone is dead.'

'Lucky you,' she said, and hung up.

CHAPTER TEN

Tuesday 20th September

AT 4.32 the next morning, Tuesday – Ferdy knew the time precisely, because he couldn't sleep – Ali rang. 'Simone lives.'

Someone big and heavy and hard as nails had just punched him in the gut. 'Wha—? What? Impossible.' All moisture left his mouth. He swallowed.

Silence.

'Hello? What did you say?'

'You heard. Simone is still alive. You and that sorry excuse for a human have fucked up.'

'I don't understand. I saw her collapse. How do you know?'

'I am not in the country. The home called me to say she had been attacked but had survived. You have a very limited time to finish the job. I don't care how you do it, but – and I'll be generous here – if she is still alive in forty-eight hours from now... remember Cecil. In any case, your friend Ivan's life is over. Maybe you should tell him that, make him sweat for a while.'

2

Sally was still away on Tuesday morning, but would be back in time for lunch, she said. Ferdy thanked heavens that she wasn't there to witness his panic. He missed her, even after such a short time, but her presence was also restrictive. It was impossible to talk freely on the phone, and he could not think out loud, which he was desperate to do while he paced around the ground floor, trying to keep his thoughts logical and in order. Kitchen, hall, lounge. Amble through them again in reverse. In the lounge: stare at the broken couch, dirty and uncomfortable. Must buy a new one. What's that got to do with not getting hung, drawn and quartered? Nothing. Focus.

With Sally's tendency to appear without warning, he checked the road side of the house, including a long look at the old crone's front window to see if she was watching him. Then he double locked the front door to make sure his love didn't return unnoticed. She'd have to ring the bell for him to open up.

He made a coffee without focusing on what he was doing and overfilled his mug. Slurping off the excess, he took it down to the cellar and called Ivan.

A shaky voice answered on the third ring.

Christ, we really are a couple of trembling twats. But at least I'm not as weak as Ivan. I need to take command here or we might as well go and offer ourselves up to Ratel. *'Here, take me. Plunge your blade into my guts. Twist it round, yank it out, let the blood flow freely. Thrust it into my chest again and again…'* No, I've got to fight.

'Hello?'

'Friendly warning, Ivan: I suggest you make tracks. *Voetsek.* Sorry – go away, get lost, vanish, and like greased lightning, man. *Simone is still alive.* You must have pulled the pillow off too soon.'

Ivan gasped, but said nothing. There was a clatter that sounded as if he'd dropped the phone, then sobbing.

Ferdy hung up and stared at his computer screen, slouching in his chair. There was much to see, but he saw nothing. He gave a vigorous shake of his head and brought up his messages, looking for something to take his mind off the disaster. One grabbed his attention. He jerked upright. The message should have been deleted, having been read, but he hadn't done so.'Of course. That's it, that's the answer. Thank God.'

The message had been sent five days earlier and he'd forgotten about it. Other than his perfunctory reply, he hadn't really known what to say. But now he did, and left his number. 'Contact me urgently, please. I have something you'll like.'

3

Within half an hour, Ferdy's phone rang.

'Is that you, Mister Facilitator?' The voice was female, light, lively and Welsh.

'Who is this?'

'You left me a message. Urgent, you said. It's Millie.'

'Oh, Millie. Are you back from Wales? You sent me a very nice note about how you enjoyed your visit to Mary's house. Would you like to do that again?'

'That's tempting. God, that was awesome. Yeah, I'm back, and to do it again would be fantastic. But tell me more about it before I say yes.'

'It's an old lady in a home. There's a deadline on this – pardon the pun. It will have to be done tonight or tomorrow night at the very latest. There are full and clear instructions. The danger is that you could be spotted by one of the care staff, but they're mostly women who will almost certainly not have your strength. Getaway is quick and easy.'

'Okay, I'll give it a shot. Do we meet?'

'No, no time. Can you be in Lady Mary Park by 9.30, or at least before it gets crowded at twelve?'

'I can make it by a quarter to ten,' Millie said.

'I'll leave a rolled-up newspaper containing the instructions in the rubbish bin at the south-east corner, by the cricket nets. Go there at 9.45 and collect it. Even though time is very tight, I suggest you recce the place tonight and do the deed after dark tomorrow.'

'Sounds fantastic. See you – sort of – in a moment.'

'When you've read the instructions, call me. Rushing these things at crash speed, as we are, doubles the risk. It's far better to take it slowly and examine every detail, but there's no time in this case. We don't have time for mistakes, so we just have to make sure we don't crash.'

The previous day's clouds had blown away during the night, leaving the air cool and crystal clear. Leaves tumbled and scattered before a strong breeze, which piled them up against the boundary fence. Pages Ferdy had salvaged from the newspaper he'd binned were almost ripped apart, but he scrunched them into a bundle.

He had only seen Millie once before: in the cemetery in the early hours. His memory was of a short, lithe figure that moved with a bounce. Now, on a park bench a hundred yards away from the cricket nets, he looked over the top of his tightly folded paper to inspect his assassin in the full light of day. He wanted an image to hold, because he had a feeling that this was not going to be the last time he had dealings with her.

A slim woman with brown pixie-cut hair approached the rubbish bin from the north. Her stride was quick. Determination radiated from her. Was she pretty? Ferdy was too far away to see. There was no hesitation in her actions. She gave an imperceptible glance around, approached the bin, pulling something from her pocket, lifted the bin lid and threw the object in. She withdrew her hand complete with a roll of newspaper and walked on. She had hardly broken stride.

Would he recognise her again? Without a doubt. Had she been watching for the man who would throw his newspaper away? Was she interested in who he was? Undoubtedly. If she wasn't, then she was stupid, and Ferdy did not think she was stupid at all.

4

Shortly before twelve, Millie rang. Her words tumbled out in rapid succession, her enthusiasm electrifying. 'Mister, I've read the instructions and it's great – straightforward. I've been there – it's not far away. I identified the window to get in as well. I'll go back tonight and double check everything by getting closer.'

Over-the-top utterances made Ferdy suspicious, because the outcomes rarely matched the words. 'That's great. Just remember, you're going to dispose of an old lady. Are you sure you're up to it?

'Abso-bloody-lutely. I'm so pumped up over it. So many missed opportunities in my life so far. I could have been doing this years ago and living the thrills.'

Millie's enthusiasm was bizarre, but encouraging for this task, at least. Even so, Ferdy was wary. Was she going to be reckless and do something stupid? One had to be level-headed to succeed while staying hidden and safe in this business, and Millie wasn't showing signs of level-headed-ness. 'Remember, Millie, your last episode could be described as an indirect killing. You didn't lay a hand on Mary. This time you're going to have to be very direct and hold this old woman while she struggles and dies. Are you sure you can do that? Because if you can't, you must tell me now, not later tonight.'

'Relax, Mister Facilitator, I'm fine, I'm in control. I've got it sorted.'

'Okay, if you're sure. Do you want me to come with you?'

Millie laughed. 'No, whatever for?'

Ferdy hung up.

Sally called down from the kitchen, 'D'you want to eat something, Ferdy?'

His steps up the short staircase were heavy. At the top he stepped into Sally's hug. 'You look exhausted, sweetie. What's the matter?'

'I'm fine,' he murmured into her shoulder.

She put a hand on his head and tilted it up for a kiss. 'You're sweating, Ferdy. Are you all right?'

5

On the nights when Sally was there, Ferdy had been leaving his primary business phone down in the basement. He didn't want them to be interrupted (if there was something to interrupt), nor could he have her listening in to his sensitive conversations.

They hadn't gone to bed when, at around eleven o'clock, he heard the dim ring of the phone in the cellar. He jumped up from lolling on the couch with Sally, said sorry, and went down the steps, closing the door behind him.

'Yes?'

'Mister, it's me, Millie. Great news. The old bag is dead as a doornail. No doubt about it. She's deceased, passed, kicked the oxygen habit and taken her last breath – a difficult one, I grant you. She gave up the ghost and shuffled off this mortal coil to become worm food. She bit the dust as she kicked the bucket——'

'All right,' Ferdy snapped. 'It's not a joking matter. You went into the home? I thought you were going to recce the place tonight for a strike tomorrow.'

'I know, but it was so easy, I didn't think it was worth another visit, which would have doubled the risk, of course.'

'Millie, thank you. That's truly a load off my mind. But please listen to me: you must slow down and double check your every move. Act with caution. Think: What happens if …? If you seize an opportunity without a proper reconnaissance, sooner or later you're going to be discovered.'

'Yeah, I hear you, but this was too easy. I couldn't lose the opportunity. As it happens, I did get tangled up with a care worker. Huge black dude. You hear all sorts of rumours about these guys, but it turns out his bollocks are just as sensitive as any man's.' She laughed at the memory, and was still cackling when Ferdy said thanks again and put his phone down.

CHAPTER ELEVEN

Wednesday 21st September

ON WEDNESDAY morning, Ferdy slunk out of bed, careful not to disturb Sally. In his cellar, he shivered. The house felt cold, the heating would have to go on soon. He selected the red-taped phone. This was a call he dreaded, given that Ratel's evil temper could sour any good news. 'Simone is dead,' he said.

'I know. At long last. Who did you get to do it? It wasn't you.'

'What makes you say that? Of course I did it.'

'Ferdy, we both know you haven't the guts to kill someone. That's why I have total control over you. I have no qualms or feelings about right and wrong. I will kill for very little reason. You will agonise over the morals of the deed and do nothing; that means you will always do what I want, because you are incapable of acting as I can. Now, who killed Simone?'

'Oh, just a previous client who was happy for the money. Are you still in Spain?'

'I never was in Spain and it's none of your damn business where I am. Be careful, Ferdy, I'm the one who asks the questions, not you.'

He swallowed. She was right: he was completely subservient to her. 'What about Ivan?'

Ali sighed. 'Jesus may have said, "Blessed are the meek, for they shall inherit the earth." Meek though he is, Ivan will not be inheriting anything.'

2

Ferdy had no regard for Ivan. In fact, he thought the little man a weed, the sort of individual who subconsciously sought to be bullied. Perhaps it was for attention, never mind the pain, insults and abuse. He also didn't like him for myriad reasons he could list if he could be bothered, other than that they were simply polar opposites, of course.

Ali/Ratel, was going to kill Ivan, and probably in a gruesome way. Why was Ferdy sufficiently concerned to want to warn him? Was it because they were united in their horror of killing? Whilst admitting he was a bloody hypocrite, Ferdy wondered if indeed he did have a shred of human decency in him.

Ivan's phone rang and rang, but there was no answer throughout the day. Had he managed to escape? Had he left the country? Was he already dead?

Ferdy's mind was on this as he tailed behind Sally through a crowd of shoppers. She seemed to sail along, people parting as she approached, while they closed ranks and obstructed him at every step. It began to rain. He raised his collar and zipped his jacket as high as it would go.

She wanted to buy a present for her cousin's daughter, and had dragged Ferdy to a toy and hobby shop on the high street. The store was supposed to close at seven. They got in at five to, earning a disgruntled frown from the cashier. Sally was intent on a scooter. She kept searching for one that was robust and had exciting colours until a quarter past. Eventually she was satisfied and gave the cashier a sweet smile along with her card. 'Sorry to keep you after a long day,' she said. And to Ferdy, 'Becky's only eight next week and I know she wants this. She'll love it.'

With Ferdy carrying the scooter, they shed the idea of cooking at home and found a pub for a pint and a pie.

CHAPTER TWELVE

Thursday 22nd September

SALLY SPENT almost every night and some days at Ferdy's house. She made it obvious she was very keen on him. Every now and again she teased him over his feet, and she loved to run her fingers through his chest hair while purring, 'My Furry Ferdy.'

She claimed his hairiness was indicative of his masculinity and that his long and hairy feet were proof of his virility. By this time, he'd got over her teasing and wanted to believe that it was an indication that she might be in love with him.

Perhaps she really was in love with him; Ferdy was certainly in love with her. And that humming she did and the way it increased in tempo as she neared her climax. Her pleasure sent him skywards, urging him on: faster, deeper, faster, deeper. *Go, Furry, go.*

But sometimes she didn't hum. She hadn't hummed last night, although she had shuddered and gasped at the end. Was she faking it sometimes? He'd heard some women did that. Even if they were trying to be kind, it was humiliating. But maybe she just felt quiet on those occasions.

If she didn't hum, did that mean she wasn't really in love with him? Should he ask her? Should he confess his love? Would doing so weaken him in her eyes? Or, if he didn't, would she think he was just enjoying the ride? He grinned at his unintended pun. So many questions. With such limited experience of simply being with women, let alone exploring emotions, he was simply at a loss.

It was almost eight o'clock on Thursday evening in The Boar's Head, which wasn't far from Ferdy's place. Inside, it was a warm and friendly: a polished wooden bar, shiny brass beer taps, a fireplace with a stack of logs on the side and, in the next room, darts could be played, although ringing the bull was more popular. Somehow, in contrast to many pubs which had failed in the downturn, this watering hole had prospered. Was it the clientele or the publican or both? Ferdy didn't know, but admitted there was a little magic about the place and he always felt comfortable, even though he didn't know anyone well.

He stepped up to the bar to order another round. The TV switched to the news. Its sound had been muted, but there were subtitles. Another murder had been committed the night before, and speculation that it was Ratel's work had been expressed thanks to the removal of some body parts. Ferdy gaped.

'Twelve pound sixty, mate.'

The barman, probably a student (he was new), rapped a coin on the counter. 'Hello. Excuse me, sir. That'll be twelve pound sixty.'

'Oh, sorry. Sorry.' Ferdy woke to the present and waved his card at the machine. He pointed at the TV. 'Awful.'

But the barman was already talking to another customer.

Somehow the photographer had got close to the body. The slight frame lay spreadeagled on its back, its white skin in stark contrast to the carpet of autumn leaves. The face had been pixellated out, as had the man's groin area.

Apparently, his face had been battered to a pulp and his genitals had been amputated.

There were no clues to the man's identity, but Ferdy knew who he was. Sally was staring at the screen when he reached their table. 'What's happened? The TV's too far away to read those words.'

Ferdy told her. He felt rather than heard the emotion in his voice. 'Poor man,' she said. 'Are you all right, Ferdy? You've gone pale.' Her face radiated concern. Her eyes flicked back and forth across his features as if searching for an answer.

'Yes, I'm fine.' He really had to learn to control his emotions.

Sally's doubt was obvious, but she looked back at the screen and gasped. The same CCTV clip that had been broadcast previously, that of the woman who looked like her, was showing again, as well as a still picture, possibly from another CCTV clip.

Voices at the table behind Sally:

'I reckon that's Ratel's girlfriend – bloody stunner.'

'Nah. That's 'er. That's Ratel 'erself. No reason why a woman wouldn't cut a bloke up like that.'

'Don't agree. A woman ain't going to be that vicious. That's his partner.'

'You need to grow up, mate, or you'll find you're missing a treasured body part one morning if you keep on shagging everything in sight.'

They laughed.

Ferdy said, 'Drink up. We need to get out of here.'

'What's the hurry?'

'Because that couple sitting at the bar are looking in our direction. Any moment now they'll call the police and we'll be taken away in front of this crowd. We don't need that exposure.'

'But we – I – haven't done anything, and the police know I'm not the killer.'

'They didn't say what time this happened last night, but we've got alibis for some of it. It won't stop the embarrassment of being taken away in my local, though.'

2

They walked back to Ferdy's house against a stiff breeze. He held back for a moment to admire Sally's hair streaming out behind her like a banner.

'I bet you the police will be round here shortly, looking for you,' Ferdy said as he turned into his front gate and dug in his pocket for his key.

'They know I didn't commit the other murder. They've acknowledged that I'm not the person they're looking for, so why should they bother us? You're really quite twitchy about this, aren't you, Ferdy?'

Silently, Ferdy acknowledged that 'twitchy' was inadequate for what he felt. To have the police snooping around his house was plain bloody nerve-wracking. Maybe he should close operations, shut down the business and store the computers elsewhere until all this had blown over. He would do it tomorrow. Out loud, he said, 'With good reason. All I'm saying is don't be surprised. They'll be back, and at the latest it'll be tomorrow morning.'

It wasn't then. It was ten minutes later that heavy knocking on the front door revealed Detective Sergeant Murphy standing behind another man. 'Good evening, Mister Fellowes. I'm Detective Chief Inspector White. You met my colleague here, DS Murphy, a few days ago. May we come in?'

Ferdy led them into the lounge. 'Can I get you something to drink: coffee, tea?'

'No thank you. Is Ms Kemp here? We went to her flat, but she was out. Is she here?' White was a short, wiry man, smartly dressed in a grey suit, a pale blue shirt with a Prince of Wales check, and a red patterned tie.

'We've just got in. She'll be down soon.'

'Good evening.' Sally padded into the room in oversize woollen slippers which showed off her calves. Murphy, who had said nothing up until then, straightened up and let a smile onto his face.

DCI White may have been impressed, but he refused to show it through a fixed, serious expression. 'Ms Kemp——'

'Sally, please.'

White nodded. 'Sally, we looked for you at your own flat. If we need you again, should we rather try here instead? You may have heard: there's been another gruesome murder, and just like last time we have additional footage of a woman who looks like you. So that's two video clips with this woman deliberately showing her face to the camera – and she's a spitting image of you. You must understand that we have to ask you where you were on Wednesday night between seven and nine o'clock.'

'Oh that's easy. We went to buy a scooter for my niece – my cousin's daughter actually – she's eight; then we went to a Wetherspoons for supper. I can show you the receipt for the scooter, if you like. But look, I came to see you originally to try and stop this questioning before it even started. You know it's not me, I've proven it twice now, so do I have to be checked on every time this sick individual kills someone?'

'I'm afraid so. We're duty bound to follow up on every bit of evidence, no matter how unlikely. If she keeps killing, then you'll see more of us – I'm sorry, but that's the way it has to be. One more thing: you have a sister, I believe?'

'No. I *had* a sister, but she died of hypothermia ten years ago. You can check on that, all the records are there.'

CHAPTER THIRTEEN

Saturday 1st October

NOTHING HAPPENED for nine days. There were no murders that could be attributed to a hired killer. A wife poisoned her abusive husband in Newcastle, a shopkeeper was attacked by a thief in Birmingham and later died behind his counter, and a drug-related stabbing of two youths blighted east London. But there were no horrific, sadistic mutilations of a corpse. It appeared, some joked on Facebook, as if Ratel was taking a well-earned rest.

The police were no further forward in their investigation in spite of several sightings of the woman in the video. The force had only said they wanted to interview her, that she was of interest, but that did not stop the public assuming she was the killer. Ratel had morphed from man to woman overnight, and transgender jokes began to circulate.

That she was an extraordinarily good-looking woman was universally agreed, and she developed a following. She didn't have her own page on Facebook, of course, but thousands of speculators produced wild and not so wild theories as to who she was and where she was hiding. Redheads became objects of suspicion, and doctored images spread like wildfire.

She was discussed at length on social media; one tabloid dubbed her 'Red Ratel'. Confusion reigned, and a quick survey showed that eighty-eight percent of the population had no idea what a ratel is. Pictures of the honey badger were quickly displayed, and the jokers changed its characteristic white top to red.

Ferdy was astounded at the speed of the rubbish spreading over the internet. If these idiots only knew what a vicious woman Ratel was, if they could experience the chill that Ali's voice sent through him when she threatened, their jokes would falter. But they would never know, of course. They, the keyboard warriors, are at liberty to express their warped opinions and hateful comments – cowards, all of them, spewing bile while sounding brave behind the shield of internet anonymity.

Ferdy could see that Sally was worried. She said she wasn't, and went about without apparent concern, but Ferdy insisted it was dangerous out there amongst the public. Some vigilante nutcase could attack her – stab her, maybe. She had been reported several times as a sighting to the police, and each occasion had to be verified. 'Were you in the supermarket on Tuesday at around ten o'clock?'

'Yes, I was getting some food and wine – especially wine. I need it with all this pressure.'

'Sorry, Ms Kemp, but we have to make sure it was you and not the other.'

'I know. I don't blame you, but it is becoming tedious. I wish you'd find her and stop this madness.'

CHAPTER FOURTEEN

Sunday 2nd October

FERDY AMBLED down the street, lost in thought. Drizzle accumulated in his hair, trickled down his neck and under his collar. He shivered. What was he going to do about Sally? Their relationship was going to go far, of that he was certain. But it meant he would have to give up this life of organising other people's murders, which was a shame because it was stimulating, gave him insights into some weird characters and brought him a decent living for very little effort. Sally would be horrified to learn what he was really doing. He would be cast out of her life.

So what could he do instead? It was time to give some serious thought to this.

He reached the corner shop. Outside, under an awning, was a rack displaying the day's newspapers. He stopped to glance at the headlines. His heart went into overdrive. Cold spread out across his back, down his arms and forward to cramp his belly.

'Red Ratel Kills Again' screamed the paper which had coined the name. Another had, 'Ratel Runs Riot'. What had this woman done now? What abhorrent deviance had she employed in this latest bloody slaughter?

He grabbed a copy of the Mail on Sunday, added a six-pack of Guinness, a bottle of wine and a block of Stilton, and went home to study the details of the story.

Sally was out when he reached the house – gone to source something for lunch, most likely. Ferdy was glad. He wanted to take control of his emotions before letting her see his reaction to the killing. He read the column. It wasn't long so he read it again. It was almost twelve o'clock when he switched on the TV.

Sally was at the door. Ferdy called, 'Come and see this, Ratel's at it again.'

There was a pause. Ferdy was about to repeat himself, then: 'Coming. I'll just put the shopping down.'

The picture was of a dense wood with a forensic tent set up under a large tree. Behind the reporter, a couple of nondescript white-overalled figures moved about in apparent silence, peering at objects and scratching around in the undergrowth like meerkats searching for insects. Another had a camera and was examining his (or her – it wasn't possible to tell) shots.

The reporter was explaining how the body had been found. 'I'm standing here in Magpie Wood, which is to the north of Newbury. The roar you can hear in the background is the M4 Motorway. The wood is popular with locals who are often seen walking their dogs, and it was a dog who found this body.'

He turned to the side, and the camera followed him as he bent down and petted the animal, a young black Labrador, which was sitting with its owner. The dog reacted by getting up and wagging its entire hind quarters, obviously pleased that someone recognised its outstanding achievement. Not so, its owner. This lady was pale and looked in need of a stiff drink.

'Can you tell viewers how you found this body?' The reporter asked.

'I was walking with 'Ugo like I do every day. We always take the same path 'Ugo was running in front like 'e always does. 'E went sniffin' under that tree. I went ter see what 'e were interested in, cause 'e were really excited, like. I came round the tree – it were on the other side, see – and saw it. I were lookin' down where 'Ugo was and I seen this body wivout a head and the dog lickin' its open neck. Blood and bones and pipes an' all.'

'That must have been quite a shock,' said the TV man.

'It were disgustin'. I nearly threw up, I tell you. I pulled 'Ugo away and then looked up, and facing me were this head stuck to the tree with a knife through its eye. It were staring at me, evil like, and I couldn't 'elp it, I puked, I couldn't 'elp it. It just rushed up from below and came out all over the body. It won't 'elp them much.' She pointed briefly at the forensic team. 'Sorry.'

Sally's lips were pressed so tight together they were white. It was only for a moment, then she relaxed.

'Are you all right?' Ferdy said. 'You look – I dunno – upset, cross even. That must have been pretty shocking for her.'

'I'm fine. I'm just angry at the lack of respect of this Ratel creature. If your business is killing people, then just do it cleanly and show the dead respect. He doesn't. He mutilates the corpse, which hurts the family and – well, it's inhuman.'

The TV crossed back to the studio. The newsreader said, 'That was Matt on the scene earlier today. Let's go over to the press conference which was held an hour ago.'

Senior members of the police team sat at a table facing reporters. A large badge of the force on the wall behind loomed over them.

The Commissioner was talking, giving assurances that this crime was focused and there was no danger to the public at large, and that the force was committing its most dedicated officers to the case. No stone would be left unturned. He handed over to the inspector in charge of the case.

DCI White had more presence than his superior. Again smartly dressed in a suit, and with an air of authority and a sharp voice, he commanded attention. 'A lot of speculation about this murder is already circulating amongst the public and on social media. I would like your, the media's, cooperation in keeping that to a minimum, please. Refrain from exaggeration and rumour, if you will, because it will not help towards a swift resolution of the case. There is much speculation that this killing is the work of Ratel, the contract serial killer who commits horrendous murders and has eluded police up and down the country. The reason, as I'm sure you are aware, is his practice of mutilating the body. Most murder victims are stabbed or shot or beaten and left where they died. Ratel's trademark is to inflict horrendous injuries after death. Often these mutilations are indicators of the victim's lifestyle. This particular murder bears all the hallmarks of Ratel, but we are keeping an open mind as to the identity of the perpetrator.'

2

The smell of last night's curry permeated the house. It hit Ferdy as he entered from the crisp, fume-laden air of the street. He'd made the chana masala himself, without great success, mainly because he only had enough spices for a dish half the size. Sally was unimpressed but polite enough to say nothing. The amount left on her plate, though, which he consigned to the waste food bin, was comment enough.

He left the front door open to clear the air and went through to the kitchen. His mobile phone rang – a hidden number. Oh God, he knew who this was. Why can't she leave me alone now her problem with her inheritance is out of the way?

'*Ferdy,*' Ali snapped. Her voice could cut steel sometimes. 'What the hell is going on?'

'What are you talking about?'

'This new murder. You must have seen the news. It wasn't me. Someone is copying me, and I'm bloody furious. I never repeat myself, and this was almost identical to the way I left Cecil – a knife through the left eye instead of a bolt through the right. And he did it over the weekend. I never kill on the weekend, because … Never mind. I want to know who did this, Ferdy. I'm at the top of this game and I'm not having some copy-cat topple me. If this creature can do better by being original, then fair enough, but not by copying me. Who is it, Ferdy?'

'Ali, I haven't a clue.' But although Ferdy did not know for certain, he could hazard a guess.

'You're lying, Ferdy. I don't like being lied to.'

Ferdy was scared of being confrontational with her, but he sensed she would respect a sound counter-argument rather than submission. 'I'm not lying. You can't expect me to know every murderer in the country, can you?'

'I suggest you find out, Ferdy, because if I can't find him and you won't tell me, a head is going to roll, and you should know by now that I don't make empty threats.' A loud pause while Ferdy listened to the thumping of his heart. 'I think it's time we met face to face, Ferdy.'

Christ. 'Yes. Of course. We should.' God help me.

Why is this woman being so unreasonable? Ferdy paced in and out of the kitchen and the lounge as he tossed the problem around in his head. He couldn't understand it. Everything had worked out to her satisfaction. Simone was dead, admittedly with some difficulty and delay, but the outcome had been successful in the end. In theory, there should be no need for further contact between Ratel and himself. In fact, it was highly desirable that they split as far apart as was possible for security reasons, but she was still pestering him from the shadows. There should be no need for her to involve him. Surely, as a professional killer, she was perfectly capable of dealing with a copy-cat without his help?

'Hello,' Sally called. 'I got us some lunch. Healthy stuff: pumpernickel, avo, tomato and cheese. I closed the door. It doesn't smell anymore.'

'Great. I just need to do one thing then I'll be with you.' He opened the door to the cellar, took a step down and closed it behind him. Waiting for his computer to come to life, Ferdy switched the SIM card in a spare phone and sent a quick message highlighting the new number.

CHAPTER FIFTEEN

Monday 10th October

FERDY WAS naked and about to climb into bed. In spite of his worries, he was ready for another night with the woman he loved. No matter what situation faced him, he always seemed to be ready these days. He stood looking down into her smiling eyes.

'Ferdy, standing there like a windsock in a light breeze isn't going to satisfy me. Get in here.'

His mobile rang. The wind dropped, and their anticipation subsided. He started at the noise, grabbed the phone and scrambled out of the room. Sally groaned before he closed the door.

'Millie, have you been practising your new skills?' Somehow the words 'murder' and 'kill' were uncomfortable to use.

'What do you mean? If it's what I suspect, then no.'

'Are you sure? You're in very dangerous territory if you have. I've had Ratel on my back and he's seriously pissed off. He's extremely dangerous, Millie. I strongly advise you to stick to using your own methods. Copying his will get you killed. I mean it.'

'I doubt it. If I want to operate in his way or anyone else's way, I will.' She laughed and sang, '*Anything he can do, I can do better. I can do anything better than him.*'

'Don't be stupid, Millie. This is far from a joke. The best I can do is deny any contact with you after Simone.'

Ferdy, still without clothes, went back into the bedroom. Sally was facing away from him. Without turning over she said, 'Finished? Shall we see if we can get a hurricane blowing to revive that thing of yours?'

CHAPTER SIXTEEN

Tuesday 11th October

FERDY HAD never had sex with anyone other than Sally so he couldn't tell if his post-coital behaviour and recent upbeat mood were a result of the act itself or because it was Sally herself who caused them. In bed with her, or in anticipation of being there, his worries fell away. He forgot they existed. He did realise this was both distracting and dangerous given that he was living on the edge with Ratel breathing down his neck, but he was infatuated. Sally, or the sex, had him under complete control.

She was an adventurous lover, urging him into a variety of different positions. 'Have you been studying the Karma Sutra?' he once asked, breathless. It was a stale joke, but she laughed anyway. Some nights she was submissive, giving him his way and humming with contentment. On other nights she took control, dictated their moves, and never made a sound.

Last night she'd been in her humming mood. 'Thank you, lover,' she murmured when it was over. 'To be fucked into sleep is simply the best.' And she'd clung to him, refusing to let him go until she passed out.

Bit by bit, Ferdy edged away without her waking and rolled onto his back. Half-conscious, staring at the ceiling, he felt a surge of self-satisfaction. No matter what else was going on in his life, moments like this were so wonderful that everything else paled into insignificance.

But such moments never lasted. The problems remained, and they seemed to be accumulating by the day. With Sally's almost inaudible breathing as background, he had a sudden feeling of being trapped by the weight of everything that was going on.

He lay awake for hours, considering how out of his depth he was, with all his efforts focused on staying afloat, treading water and not going anywhere. In a way, Sally was his life-vest, currently deflated. If he could pull the toggle by sharing his troubles with her, the vest would inflate, and he'd stay afloat and weather the storm. But he couldn't do that, and so she would be no help to him. Without her support, his energy would eventually be spent and the deep would claim him.

What should he do about Millie? To save his own life, he should betray her to Ratel. But that was as good as killing her, and Ferdy couldn't bring himself to do that. Organise people to murder others – yes. Actually killing someone – no. He'd proven that with Ivan and Simone, and playing that out had been hard enough. It was a petty distinction, but he was struggling to define a position to take. Eventually, it might boil down to doing whatever he had to do to save his own life.

The best thing for now was to escape, to flee from this woman who would kill him simply because he wouldn't tell her what she wanted to know.

Where to go?

Dawn was not far off. Ferdy went downstairs to make coffee. When he returned, Sally had woken. How could someone be so beautiful on waking? No puffy eyes or other signs of recent sleep other than tousled hair. An actress in a movie would wake with perfect make-up, her hair in place and her bra on, even though she was supposed to have had a night of unbridled sex, which never says much for her lover.

Sally, a real woman and bra-less, sat up looking fantastic. 'Mmmh. I smelled the coffee up here. It woke me.'

Ferdy proffered her mug and sat on the bed next to her. 'I have to go away.'

'*No*. Why? Where?'

'I can't tell you that, but it'll be this morning.'

'I'm coming with you.'

Ferdy would give anything to have Sally share his problem, but looking after her when he was being hunted by a psychopath was out of the question. 'No, you can't. It's not allowed. I'm sorry.'

'But—'

Ferdy held up his hand. 'It's out of the question. I'm sorry, but that's the way it is.' He took a sip of coffee. 'They won't allow it. But it won't be for long.'

'Who are *they*? I'm tired of all this secrecy. If we're a couple then everything should be shared. I want to be part of your life, not pushed to the side because *they* say so. I will support you. Four eyes are better than two, you know that's true.'

And so the argument began. It went on for another five minutes with no progress in either direction.

'I've had enough,' she said finally. If we can't be together, do things together, be open with each other, then it's better we make it a permanent split.' She threw off the bedclothes and stalked off to the bathroom.

Ferdy watched her impeccable naked form depart, jumping as the door slammed. A black hole grew in his stomach, its intense gravity sucking at his intestines. Vomit threatened. He wanted to come clean, to own up to everything, to explain that what he was actually doing was protecting her, but he couldn't. In any case, she had reached that point in the disagreement where she would no longer listen.

Ferdy plodded down the stairs. It might only take one slip, one catch of his heel on the step, and his problems could be over: he could fall and break his neck, in which case that would be that, no more worries; or he could be injured and lie in hospital for days, in which case the delay might cause Ratel to back off and Sally to rush to his side.

He reached the bottom step and the opportunity was lost. Down in the basement, he dismantled his office. The computer was backed up several times a day, so he deleted all the files from it. He packed his laptop together with his back-up drive and put it to one side.

Upstairs again, Sally was still in the bathroom. Ferdy pulled his little suitcase down from the top of the cupboard and began filling it with clothes, clean and dirty. It didn't matter, as long as he had enough.

Sally came back into the room, glanced at the case and then looked at him with red-rimmed eyes. 'So, you are going. I thought you might reconsider. I can't live like this with all your secrets, Ferdy. It's best we don't see each other again.'

'Sally—'

'No. Ferdy, I'm not going to have a fractious on-and-off relationship with you or anyone who can't be open with me. We would be fighting and forgiving the rest of our lives. I can't do that. It's got to be permanently on and trusting, no arguments like this, no repeats of this scene.' She stared him down.

'I… I don't believe it will be like this ever again. This is a one-off thing that will be over in a couple of weeks, if that. Can't you trust me that far? I'm committed to an agreement I made long before I met you. I can't walk away from it just like that.' God, the lie he was spinning. How the hell was he going to get out of this story when life returned to some-where near normal? 'I'll call you every day. Then, after the immediate issue is over, you can come and join me if you like. As soon as I can I'll come back here.'

'No. I see the pattern developing just as I've seen it before. I see what our lives will be like if we continue, and I'm not going to live like that. It's been great up to now, Ferdy. Let's remember that and part without arguing any more. Please don't call me.'

2

Ferdy had a half-cousin-in-law, Phoebe. Her husband, Henry, had died in a car crash eighteen months ago; after Felix had changed his name to Ferdy. He had hired a dark suit and gone to his funeral, where he met Phoebe for the first time. He got talking to her father over the drinks after the service, a larger-than-life and yet skeletal, hook-nosed man of well over six foot. A retired naval commander, he leaned over Ferdy like an eagle about to shred him to pieces. It was Phoebe who rescued him as she passed. 'Daddy, stop dominating the poor man. He's Henry's cousin, not one of your ratings.'

'Daddy' stood upright, looking down his beak at the smaller man. He put his hand on Ferdy's shoulder. 'Apologies. Can't help it with our relative statures. She's right, of course. She's always right.' He watched her greet someone else. 'Good girl. Strong – has to be in her job. She's got me round her little finger. This is all bloody sad, but she'll get over it and move on.'

Later, they had a chance to talk for a few minutes before someone else claimed Phoebe's attention. It was a brief meeting under difficult circumstances. Her sadness was evident, but beneath it Ferdy detected a cheerful, humorous person, who must have been a perfect match for his happy, exuberant cousin. He took to her immediately.

'It's good to meet you at last, Ferdy,' she had said with a slightly puzzled look. 'Henry told me about you, although I thought he called you Felix. He said you're a wiz with computers and if we ever needed help, you were the one to call.'

Ferdy didn't explain his name change. This day was not about him, so he let her comment go. His instinct had been to befriend and protect this currently vulnerable person, but that was neither the place and certainly not the time to encourage a relationship of any sort. Instead, he merely offered his help with anything should she need it. Little did he know that it was she who was going to help him in the future.

He had called her once since then to find out how she was coping, but that had been their only subsequent contact until this escape. He knew she and Henry had run a B&B in a village near York, and wondered if she still had it. If so, he wanted it for a month, if that was okay. She did, she said, and it was vacant following some renovations. He was welcome.

Ferdy had made this call while heading north up the M1 with no idea where he was going to go. All that was in his mind was to get away and out of Ratel's immediate view. He thought of Ali as Ratel now. The use of her real first name somehow gave her legitimacy, turning assassin into acquaintance – too personal, too close.

The village of Upper Windon lay on the side of a hill. To reach it, Ferdy had to turn off a B road, down a narrow, tarred lane which twisted and turned round the hillside, crossed stream courses, and was almost entirely encased by high hedgerows beyond which he could see nothing. There were short steep slopes up and down, and the surface was strewn with great clods of mud shed by massive tractor tyres. If he met such a beast, he would have a long way to reverse for them to pass.

The road widened where a Norman church stood at a junction. Shortly afterwards he turned right at a signpost into a single lane, which became a track and ended in a farm. The farmer had demonstrated his consideration for lost souls by creating a turning circle at the end of the track, accompanied by *No Entry*, *Keep Out* and *Windon Farm Only* signs – *Windon Farm* in black lettering and *Only* in red.

Uphill of the lane was a single row of houses, some semi-detached, some terraced, and the odd one stood alone. Downhill of the lane, the buildings were slightly larger for no obvious reason and mostly obscured by garden vegetation.

Phoebe's B&B was the last detached house on the uphill side, next to the farm fence. An old mud-spattered Mercedes blocked the entrance to the garage, so Ferdy parked his car behind a stone wall and hedge so it couldn't be seen from the lane.

Phoebe answered the door. 'Ferdy. Welcome. How are you? It's so nice to see you again. Bring your bag, and we'll have a cup of tea and a catch-up.'

She was an attractive woman, Ferdy admitted. Prettier than when he last saw her at Henry's funeral, which was not surprising; sadness hardly enhances beauty. She had no discernible make-up. Much of her dark brown hair was tied back in a long ponytail, but loose strands fell down on each side to frame her face. Her slightly sunken cheeks led down to a chin more pointed than broad. Hazel eyes smiled at him beneath untrimmed brows.

In tan cord jeans and boots, she towered over him, being almost six foot. Thanks to his time with Sally, though, he had much more confidence now. His nervousness around women had retreated. He made to take his shoes off.

'Oh, don't worry about that,' she said. 'As long as you're not dripping mud everywhere, shoes are fine.'

CHAPTER SEVENTEEN

Saturday 15th October

FERDY DECIDED not to take on any new clients until his life settled down. Fortunately, he didn't have any at the moment anyway. To keep himself occupied in the village, he walked a lot, something he had never done before. Much to his surprise, he found the activity therapeutic. The thoughts cluttering his head would clear with the exercise, at least until he got back to the village. Sometimes the walks were long, sometimes short. Throughout, his mind seldom strayed far from Sally – although, when it did, it was to make sure he returned in time for Phoebe's visit.

Sally had told him not to call her. Ferdy obeyed, but it was a huge frustration. He itched to speak to her and to hear her voice. He imagined the way her lips moved as she spoke – always on the verge of a smile and enhanced by the tiny parentheses of lines bracketing her mouth. Her eyebrows would lift and her eyes sparkle with enthusiasm – he loved that. And her hair: long, red, silken locks he could stroke for hours.

Without actually saying anything, Sally had ensured that Ferdy kept his house clean and tidy, because he was too embarrassed not to. It was becoming a way of life, but it was not yet so ingrained that he didn't need to think about cleaning. Now, here, in someone else's house, he felt compelled to be diligent.

Not only was Phoebe a distant part of his family, but she was also a nice person, and he didn't want her to think ill of him. Which was why, when she came round every day to check that there were no problems with the house and that Ferdy was comfortable, he did his best to show he was a model tenant. For her part, she was an excellent landlady, but was that all there was to her visits?

It was still early. Ferdy had run a vacuum cleaner through the kitchen and adjoining dining room. He hadn't used the lounge, so after doing the hall and clearing an old cobweb Phoebe must have missed, he put the device way.

He was thinking on what route to take on his walk, when Phoebe arrived lugging a heavy bag of salt for the water softener. Ferdy knew how she liked her coffee by then and began to make her one. She slit open the salt bag and eased out a block. 'Do you have a girlfriend, Ferdy?'

This was quite a direct and personal question, and he hesitated over the truth for a moment. 'I didn't have for a long time. I was just too busy, I suppose. Then someone happened and until I came up here everything was going smoothly. Then … what is it today, Saturday? On Tuesday she called it off, for reasons I can't work out.'

'Oh dear. Poor Ferdy. It's all part of life, I'm afraid. Are you sore?'

He didn't reply for a while. It wasn't comfortable having a conversation about his deep feelings with someone he hardly knew. But with Phoebe it was easier than it could have been. 'Yes. The trouble is I don't know if she means it. What about you, is there a man in your life?'

'No. When Henry was here we entertained ourselves and went out a lot: pub meals, local plays, village fêtes, game fairs and such. Alone, I don't really feel like it anymore. Sometimes I do, but normally not. This village and others around us are mostly composed of old folk and couples. The young leave for money and fun in the cities these days – except the dedic- ated farmers – thank goodness for them. There's no one of our age to hook up with. Although,' she said with a short laugh, 'I think the farmer at the end of the lane, Joe Small, fancies me. He's a grumpy old thing, but he softens up when I'm around, and I've caught him watching me. It's quite funny really.

'I don't mind being alone, it's preferable to having someone like Joe to look after. I'd feel sorry for his wife, but she's just the same. What's demoralising is the lack of suitable entertainment. Meanwhile, I have to make some money out of this place, so I'm a bit stuck – for the moment, at least.'

Ferdy nodded. He didn't know what to say. Was she dropping a hint or simply stating facts? He felt sorry for her, but he also felt sorry for himself and imagined the two of them as lonely souls in the same boat. There was a sense of kinship with her, and he looked forward to her visits. She was pleasant company and her presence distracted him from his thoughts of Sally, boosting his morale during the short times they were together.

2

Phoebe left to go shopping. With her departure, Ferdy's melancholy returned. He had sworn he wouldn't call Sally, but he desperately needed to talk to her. Did she still mean what she'd said? Was it really over?

He held his breath as the phone rang and rang until the rings stopped and he gulped in air. Did she not hear it? Was she not there? Or had she looked at her mobile and refused to answer?

He was on the point of trying again when his phone lit up.

'*Ferdy*. I'm so sorry.' Sally sounded as if she was almost in tears. 'Please forgive my stupid reaction. I know you're duty-bound to do whatever it is you're doing, but I was so disappointed it didn't include me. I was being selfish and I'm sorry. Can you forgive me?'

Tears welled up in Ferdy's eyes and he struggled to hold his emotions in check. It took a few seconds too long.

Sally's swallow was audible. 'Can we go on as before …
please? Can you forgive me?'

'Of course,' he said, and went on to lie that his work was
almost over and that it was a lovely place, and why didn't she
come and join him and have a little holiday in the peace and
quiet for few days. She would leave in an hour, she said,
which meant she could be there by about five.

In fact, it was closer to six when Sally parked her car in
front of the garage. She produced a cooler bag containing a
bottle of Dom Perignon. 'Don't say anything, don't do anything. Just take me to bed – *now*.'

3

They'd finished the champagne. With Ferdy's head on the
pillow and Sally shaking the last drops into his open mouth,
he and the bottle had much in common – drained.

In the kitchen, he opened a Cabernet Sauvignon and was
heating spaghetti. Sally switched on the TV to see the news.

'*Oh God*. Ferdy, come quickly. There's been another
murder.'

That familiar shiver ran up his spine. Not again. The TV
only showed the building where the crime had taken place,
blue cordon tape around the front, and the odd police officer
and forensic experts coming and going. It closed with a different CCTV shot of Sally's look-alike. This time, she not only
looked directly into the camera, but also smiled and waved.

'God, she's got a cheek. It's as if she's teasing the police, challenging them to catch her. Where were you when this happened? Do you have an alibi?'

'I must have been on the road, coming here, but no one saw me. I didn't stop at a services.'

'Haven't you got a dash camera? That will show the road at the time of the murder. They could identify it and you'll have an alibi.'

Sally looked doubtful. 'As long as that recording hasn't been overwritten by later footage.'

'Let's look at it. Get the card and I'll stick it in my computer.'

'Oh, not now, Ferdy. I'm exhausted. I'm also starving. Let's eat and go back to bed.'

Ferdy kept two phones close to him, his normal one for general use and the red one. Ratel was too important at this stage of his life to miss a call from her. And he suspected that she would continue to talk to him and threaten him until she could get nothing further from their relationship.

But why? She was more than capable of solving her problems on her own. She didn't need him. There must be another reason, and whatever it was, it was bound to be appalling.

The ping of a WhatsApp message almost interrupted his preparations. but he thought it was on his normal phone and ignored it.

'Aren't you going to look at that?' Sally said.

'Food's more important than social media. We need to eat.' He strained the spaghetti, poured in the sauce he'd concocted and dished it into two bowls. When he finished his plate, he opened his phone. It wasn't that one. His stomach lurched; it must be from Ratel.

Four photos were on the red instrument. The first showed a man in an upright chair, his ankles strapped to the front legs and his wrists to the arms. Naked, his skin was pale with thick, dark chest hair, tattooed forearms and thighs, and a number of bangles on his right wrist. A dark blue balaclava hid his expression, but it wasn't a stretch of the imagination to picture the misery behind it.

Ferdy studied the image for few seconds before moving on. The head was tilted back, the body arched. His palms faced up, the fingers curled, angry talons desperate to tear himself free. There was nothing to grip but empty air.

Never had Ferdy seen a still photo bring so much trauma to life. He could literally feel the man's helplessness. He shared his terror. Was this to be his own fate? Was this what Ratel had planned for him? There was no doubt that this was a message.

From Ratel to Ferdy, with love.

Ferdy shook his head as if to rid it of such thoughts and studied the detail. In each of the man's arms a needle had been inserted. A connecting tube led to a small plastic ball valve, and from there down to a clear container between his legs.

The tube above each valve was red, below it was clear.

The next photo was a close-up of a large needle, probably 16 gauge, taped down over the man's vein. A woman's fingers gripped an open valve, and the tube downstream was red. There was no appreciable difference between the red of her nail varnish and the colour of blood – was that deliberate?

Ferdy shot a quick glance at Sally. He didn't want her to see these images. She had her back to him and was busy loading the dishwasher.

The third shot was a close-up of the bucket. The graduations on the side showed a capacity of ten litres. It was almost half full. The final picture was of the man slumped forward, wasted and colourless. The tubes, above and below the valves, were empty but for a crimson trickle.

The poor man, whoever he was, had literally experienced his life flowing out of him.

Only the murderer could have sent those images – and only Ratel knew the number of the phone that Ferdy had dedicated to her.

CHAPTER EIGHTEEN

Sunday 16th October

FERDY FINISHED cleaning his teeth, dried his face and studied it in the mirror: a lack of sleep, his eyes haunted above dark shadows, uncontrolled strands of hair sticking to his wet forehead, and a mouth that struggled to smile at his reflection. All summed up in one word: haggard. 'I feel hunted,' he said out loud. 'Well, it's true, isn't it?'

The positive was that Sally was back. There'd been apologies and forgiveness on both sides and the inevitable physical endorsement of their feelings with broken sleep. It almost felt like normality had returned, but it hadn't. Ratel still lurked in the background and Ferdy didn't have an effing clue what to do about it.

He wandered over to the window to admire the scenery. From the upstairs bedroom, he could see across the fields that descended to a little stream. On the opposite hillside, dry-stone walling partitioned the land into lush pastures of differing size and shape with not a right angle in sight. Little white blobs of sheep and larger brown lumps of cattle dotted some fields. A solitary farmhouse with a huge barn lay halfway up the slope. Above that, under an uncluttered blue sky, the distant moorland could be seen with incredible clarity. It was enough to cheer even the most depressed of spirits.

A movement below the window snatched his attention. Sally was just visible in the garden talking to someone out of view around the corner. She smiled often, and Ferdy smiled with her. Her pleasure was his pleasure.

A man in a flat cap and a green fleece gilet led a pair of horses along the lane, the clop, clop of their hooves sharp and clear in the crisp morning air. Sally turned to look, and Phoebe stepped into view. She gave a little wave to Sally and hurried off to catch the man.

For a reason he couldn't explain, Ferdy's stomach suddenly felt empty. Seeing Sally and Phoebe talking happily confused him. But why? Sally was his girlfriend, and maybe, hopefully, would become more than that. Phoebe he hardly knew, although there was an undeniable connection between them, even though nothing had been said. He had told Phoebe that his relationship with Sally was over; now she knew it obviously wasn't. He felt the need to explain the situation to her. Why? He owed her nothing, but he had to admit the potential was there –she was a lovely person, and he would like to know her better. 'God, don't complicate my life any more, please.'

2

'I ran into Phoebe in the garden,' Sally said. 'She seems very nice.'

'Yes.' Ferdy cleared his throat.' She's a good host.'

'She said what a lovely man you are. Of course, I could have told her that. I could also have told her what a demon you are in bed, but I thought that was going a bit far having only just met her.'

'Just a bit.' Sally was joking, of course, but the possibility of her saying something like that to a decent person horrified Ferdy.

'I'm not sure, but I think Phoebe recognised me. My whole alibi thing will have to be done again up here.'

'If they do come to interview you, you can tell them to contact DCI White. He'll explain. And you've got your dash cam footage.'

'Oh yes. I forgot about that, I must get it.'

'Where are your keys? I'll get it for you now.'

'Oh, not now. There's no hurry, I'll get it later. Let's rather go for a walk.'

CHAPTER NINETEEN

Monday 17th October

IN FERDY'S experience the weather worked to spoil everything for humans. As a general rule, it rained over the weekend while the sun shone brightly on a Monday. This Monday, however, the rule was broken; it was miserable. Sunday's brilliance had vanished overnight. Low cloud, drizzle and a stiff breeze drove the wind-chill factor into single digits.

He stared out of the window at the gloom for ten minutes before waking up to the fact that he was achieving nothing. Sally appeared in a dark green dressing gown and furry slippers. She switched on the TV to see the eight o'clock news.

Another murder had made the headlines. 'This is ridiculous,' she said. 'Can't the police do anything?'

The reporter on site was saying that this was the same modus operandi as Ratel's work two days ago. But he said there was speculation that this was a copy-cat killing as it was not as clinical as the famed murderer's. For one thing, there were no valves to control the blood flow in the second murder, meaning the man would have bled out without the killer having any control. With the original, the murderer could have adjusted the speed of death (perhaps to taunt the victim or get information). The tape used to strap the man to the chair was different to the original as well.

On the other hand, some pundits on social media claimed that it was indeed Ratel deliberately working to a different standard in order to confuse the police.

Ferdy bit his lip to hide his dismay, his anger and his fear of the consequences. Why the hell couldn't Millie curb her crazy psychopathic urges? Who was the victim this time? Had she been contracted for this job, or had she selected some poor innocent sod just for the hell of it? He wouldn't put it past her.

His mind was a jumble of frightened thoughts, but he tried to speak rationally. 'Whatever the cause, the police are certainly confused. I don't think they've got a clue. Ratel is far too clever and has covered her tracks well. I think it's a copy-cat. Ratel likes to tease the police by appearing on camera afterwards, the copy-cat doesn't do that – can't do that unless he or she can pass as the beauty on the CCTV. I wonder how Ratel views her imitator; sparks could fly, in time. We'll have to wait and see if the police get any leads out of this murder.'

Ferdy knew that Ratel was going to be apoplectic over this and was dreading her call. He had no doubt she would ring. For some reason he didn't understand, Ratel wanted to keep him under her thumb. She knew perfectly well that there was no obvious rationale for Ferdy to know who the imposter was, yet she insisted, almost on pain of death, that he tell her. He was going to have to advise her of his suspicions to save his own neck – but not until he'd warned Millie again.

CHAPTER TWENTY

Tuesday 18th October

FERDY WOKE slowly on Tuesday morning. All this sex was wearing him out, he decided. Why is there always a negative side to the positives in life? He gaze drifted up the pale olive wall to a corner of the ceiling. A dust-covered cobweb stretched across it. The web vibrated gently in a draught. What had the spider hoped to catch up there?

He was lying on his left side and switched to admiring the glossy auburn mane strewn out over Sally's pillow. How did it come about that this fantastic woman had entered his mediocre life? Why did she actually take to him – to him, a nothing person, really? He reached over to bring her closer.

She murmured her contentment and wriggled backwards to firm-up the contact.

Ferdy tensed. Fear shot through him as if he'd touched a live wire. His approaching hardness subsided.

It wasn't physically possible for the arm that lay on his chest to be Sally's.

'Sally,' he whispered in her ear.

She rolled over to face him, green eyes soft and gentle. 'I'm not Sally, Furry Ferdy – I'm Ali.'

A tremor ran through his body. He couldn't control it. Here he was, naked, in bed with Ratel, the country's most cold-hearted killer ever. Inventive, vicious, and with an extremely short fuse, she dangled his life by a thread as thin as that spider's web.

Carefully, as if a sudden action would be his last, he turned over to look into the soft, green and apparently gentle eyes of Sally – identical.

'*Oh God*. Are you going to kill me?' Ferdy's voice quavered. Was that an echo of Ivan saying the same thing?

They didn't answer, but sat up on either side of his out-stretched legs and faced him. Two beautiful women, completely naked. A symmetrical duo with pale, porcelain skin, their pert left breasts hidden behind auburn tresses. On each right shoulder was the tattoo of a butterfly, and at the base of both their spines was their private joke, their sting in the tail – the scorpion.

They moved together, tucking their inner legs between his and working their toes under his buttocks with a caterpillar motion. A warm, moist contact imprisoned each of his thighs. Any normal man would have burst at the seams with the feelings running through Ferdy. But not him, not when he knew their exploring fingers were stained with death.

His back was arched with tension. He strove to relax and felt his muscles ease. Curiosity took over. 'Which one of you have I been sleeping with?'

They laughed, the same titter from both sides. 'Both, Ferdy. We share everything. We brief each other on your little quirks, likes and dislikes, so we can pass as the same woman.'

'If I'd known, I'd have spotted a difference. Which one of you hums?'

'Both of us,' said Ali.

Sally looked at her. 'I don't. I didn't know you did.'

Ali frowned. 'That's annoying. What else have we missed? How did we not know this?'

'We've never put ourselves in this position before. We've never shared a man. What else have you noticed, Ferdy?'

His eyes flicked from one to the other and back again, straining to see a difference. With, as he saw it, the cloud of death hovering over him, he was pathetically eager to please them.

Both pairs of eyes had lost their warmth. The sense of fun the pair had put into their teasing had vanished. Ali leaned towards him. 'What else, little man? It's important.'

Sweat broke out on Ferdy's forehead. 'Nothing. Honest. No, wait. Your smile lines are more pronounced, Ali, and I think you have more freckles, Sally. There's no way I could notice if you weren't both together at the same time.'

They looked at him in silence – stares devoid of emotion.

Ferdy glimpsed his future in those eyes. 'Oh God. Which of you does the killing?'

As quickly as their playful mood had switched off, so it came back on. The smiles returned and Ali twirled a finger in his chest hair. Sally's hand lay on his stomach.

'We both do. We take it in turns, and the other one fabricates the alibi by being seen somewhere distant, using the credit card, on camera, in a pub or hotel. The possibilities are endless.'

'Stupid,' he said. 'Stupid. Why didn't I see this? Identical twins, the obvious conclusion. Why haven't the police seen it?'

'Ah, well the police are at a disadvantage. You see, our parents died in a car crash when we were twenty-two. That same year, Ali was assaulted.'

Ferdy had been looking at whomever had been speaking, Sally on his right or Ali on his left. Now he focused on Ali, his shock somewhat diminishing in favour of sympathy for her. What level of mental damage does a woman experience following a physical attack? In the long term it would probably be more than any physical damage, much more. It would impact her in ways he doubted he would ever understand.

After a period of silence, as if she had been debating whether to tell him about it, Ali said, 'We'd been at a party. I hooked on a guy I thought was pretty cool. Sally was fooling with some other bloke and didn't see anything. We, this creep and I, went outside. We walked down to the river and went into the bushes. He, … he lost control of himself. Today I'd have destroyed him, but then I was inexperienced and didn't know how to fight effectively.' She paused, looked out of the window and pursed her lips … 'When he'd finished, I think he came to his senses and realised he was going to be in deep trouble if I lived. He dragged me to the water and pushed me under. It was freezing, but I didn't notice, I was fighting to stay alive, to breathe. I went unconscious, and I suppose he was in such a panic, he thought he'd killed me and so left me for dead.'

Sally took over. 'I don't know how long she was in the water, but she was found by someone, we don't know who, and dragged out. She was obviously suffering from hypothermia, so they got her to a house hoping to get her warmed up. They found a doctor, who must have been an idiot. He determined that she was sufficiently warmed, but couldn't find a heartbeat. That's the criterion, the patient must be warmed before the doctor can declare they're dead because the heart rate can be so slow when the temperature's low. We don't know exactly what he didn't do, but he said she was dead and signed the certificate.

'The people, the rescuers must have also thought she was dead, because they left to organise things, tell the police or something. Whatever, that was when I found her, and she was breathing. It wasn't that warm in the house. I managed to get her to my car and got the heater on full blast. Eventually, she regained consciousness and I got her home.'

'The police couldn't find me,' said Ali. 'We hit on the bright idea that with one of us declared dead, we could get away with all sorts of nonsense. We simultaneously had this idea that a life of crime would be great fun.'

'Surely the police had to ask where you'd got to?'

'They must have imagined the man had stolen my body to destroy evidence. The doctor said there were bruises on my face, so it was obvious I'd been attacked. They opened a case on it, but they must have given up by now.'

'What about the man, did you find him?'

The twins looked at each other and smiled. 'We're grateful to him, really. It took us around five years to find him. He was our first, he set us on this career. Without him we wouldn't have had half as much fun.'

'So, Ferdy, the police are not aware of me as alive. They know the twin sister named Alison is dead. It's in their records,' said Ali. 'You'd be surprised how many people are certified dead through clerical errors or a lack of obvious signs of life. Once I'd got my senses back and Sally had confirmed that I was officially dead, we hit on the plan to keep it that way and thereby operate as a team with one of us always totally innocent of the crime.'

The pair looked down on Ferdy with apparently sympathetic eyes.

'What are we going to do with him?' said Sally, as if he wasn't there.

'He knows a lot about us now. He could be dangerous to have around.'

Ferdy's voice came out as a squeak. 'I won't tell anyone. Honestly, I won't. I promise.'

'He knows who we are and how we operate. He's a danger.'

'True. Whose turn is it?'

'Yours. But when you think that we've both been so involved with him, I reckon we should make an exception and have a one-off joint operation. How shall we do it, what little twist does our Ferdy deserve?'

'*For crying out loud*. I swear I won't tell. I promise.'

'Take it easy, little man. All our victims have died quickly. The desecration has been at the customer's request and is always inflicted after death. It's the media that wishes the public to think they died in some ghastly fashion and in great pain.'

'Hang on, Sally. He's given us good sex, hasn't he?' Ali's hand slid under the blanket and seized Ferdy's penis. 'Ooh, it's not as big as I recall. Sal, the poor little thing has shrunk for some inexplicable reason.'

From her side, Sally's hand found his testicles. Her sharp nails cut into his scrotum. 'That's true. Perhaps we should enjoy him a little longer before disposal?'

'Agreed. In fact, now that the need for deception is over, there's no necessity for one of us to sleep alone anymore. We can all go to bed together from now on.'

'I tell you what: we'll keep him as long as he can keep up with us.'

'We'll keep him alive until we're certain there are no other differences between us.'

Both of them squeezed, and Sally's nails must have drawn blood. Ferdy's back arched and he gasped. 'You … you're not really going to kill me are you?'

'We don't have plans for that, Ferdy.'

'Answered like a politician, Ali. We're teasing you, Ferdy. You haven't given us too much of a reason – so far. We're quite fond of you actually.'

Both hands relaxed, but did not release.

2

Ferdy tried to shift his position; the pressure of their hip bones on his thighs had become painful. But his efforts came to nought. The women both ground their hips a little to enforce the discomfort while smiling sweetly at him.

'Right Furry, it's time for the T's and C's – the Terms and Conditions of our future relationship.'

Ferdy swallowed. This was it. He was about to learn why Ratel had been maintaining contact when their relationship should have been over. And, as sure as Earth wasn't flat, everything they were about to say was going to be bad news.

'You run a comfortable little business ensuring that people get rid of others who get in their way without being connected to their murders. Good idea, clever. We run a successful bespoke assassination firm which pays well, but there are two of us to share the income, and those that can afford our fees are few. We need more business, and you can provide it. You'll be our agent, and we'll pay you a commission.'

The twins alternated in explaining their plans for his future.

'Ratel is going to disappear. No more murders will occur under that name, and dark-web communication will be stopped. Instead, we'll work through your website. You can offer bespoke services with charges that depend on the method.'

Ferdy's jaw dropped. Figuratively, of course, because he was lying down. 'You can't do that. I'll be exposed for your hideous crimes, which will have nothing to do with me.'

Sally squeezed and dug in. Ferdy arched, gasped and subsided.

'Actually, Ferdy, we can do what we like, because either you follow our plan or you cease to exist.'

'Ferdy, our love, look at it this way: we get less exposure, but you get more. That will enhance your business and will also make your life less stressful, because if you get another dreadful coward like Ivan trying to worm out of his side of the agreement, we'll do his job for him.'

'And see that he bothers no one again.'

'You see, Ferdy, dear, your reputation as a thoroughly reliable instrument in the murder business will be enhanced, because we will be beside you—'

'—And behind you.'

'All the way.'

'This combined operation will muddy the waters for investigators while we enjoy our favourite occupation—'

'—Playing with people's lives.'

Both of them increased the pressure on his genitals a little. He squirmed.

'Now that we've told you, there's no escape, Felix – sorry, Ferdy Fellowes.'

Nails stabbed into him. '*Aagh.*' He looked up into two sweet, warm, smiling faces whose mouths would not melt butter. A damp sheen on his forehead chilled in the draught.

'Sorry. Just emphasising our point.' The pressure subsided.

'There's another benefit, too, Ferdy – unlimited sex.'

He groaned.

They laughed. 'And we'll look after you. We'll see to your grooming. For example, Ali will cut your hair, it's getting too long. And I'll brush your chest hair every day.'

'And I'll look after your outstanding feet. Your foot hair has to be combed daily, Ferdy. Imagine the reaction if you were in an accident and taken to hospital. The entire staff would come to see your extraordinary feet.'

'They might fight over who should give you a bed bath – to see if the rumour is true.'

'And if your foot fur were messy and tangled, those pretty nurses would be turned right off. No, we can't have our partner looking unkempt and grubby.'

'My feet are not that bad.'

'Not to you, maybe, you're used to them. To a stranger …'

'Lastly,' said Ali – or was she Sally? Under the pressure, Ferdy had lost track of which side of him each had taken. 'You're going to tell us who it is who is trying to steal our business. Who is the creature who hasn't the wit to be creative and find his own methods to kill? Who is the copy-cat?'

'I don't know why you think I can help. I would if I could, but I don't have a clue. You have to believe me.'

'Ferdy, think before you make unwise utterances. You should know by now that we don't have to do anything we don't want to, least of all what you tell us. You may not know for certain, but you have your suspicions – not so?'

'No, honestly. I don't know, and I understand my position is… I understand the danger I'm in. Look, give me a chance to find out. Please.'

The twins cocked their heads at each other and nodded. Ali said, 'All right. You have twenty-four hours to come up with a name. And if your suspicions are wrong, we promise not to harm anyone if they are not the copy-cat.'

'You know, Ali, I met Furry's landlady in the garden on Sunday. She seems very nice. Pretty lady: Phoebe. She likes Ferdy. She said what a lovely man he is, and she's glad he came here and met her again. I had this feeling that there was something brewing between them, that if we weren't around they might have a thing going on. Maybe they already have a thing going on. They were together a few days before I came up here.'

'No, no, there's nothing between Phoebe and me.' Ferdy suddenly realised that with this arrangement of theirs, there could never be another woman for him. The poor creature would always be a bargaining chip and always in great danger.

'Methinks the lad doth protest too much. Think about it, Ferdy. We'd hate to harm Phoebe, but if you won't cooperate we may have to. Our plan needs you; it doesn't need her.'

Ali waggled Ferdy's withered penis from side to side. 'Changing gear for a moment. There's one other minor detail.'

'What could that be?' Sally said with obvious feigned innocence.

Ali flashed wide eyes at her prisoner and grinned. 'Both of us, Ferdy, are *pregnant*.'

'*No*.' He didn't have time to consider what that meant. It wasn't possible. It could not be. Life would not be so cruel to him, surely.

'Oh *yes*. Just think: you're going to be a daddy, a double-daddy. Isn't that good news? Ferdy, *the man*, will have proved his worth. And you'll have two pretty little redheads to gurgle at and play with. You can buy them toys and watch them grow. You can take them to school and pick them up, and people will say what a good daddy Ferdy is. What would you like them to be, Ferdy: two girls, two boys, or one of each?' Ali had been gently stroking his penis as she spoke, but something had shut down and the blood would not flow. Was he so inadequate that he couldn't respond?

At last they withdrew their hands. Ali held up hers. 'Look, Sally, I've drawn blood.'

'Does it need a plaster?'

'Maybe, but how will that affect his erection?'

They erupted in a fit of laughter.

'I want to be the one to pull the plaster off.'

They were teasing, of course, but their humour had an ugly tone, and he wouldn't put it past them to act on their joke. This had to stop. His life had already begun to become one of misery. It was going to get worse, and there was only one way he could think of to solve the problem.

3

Ferdy stayed supine for half an hour after the twins left him. There was so much to take in, he felt paralysed. His life was an absolute disaster. He wiped a solitary tear from his eye.

One of them called. 'Don't you want breakfast, Furry? Come on.'

He didn't respond. If the twins really were pregnant, it would be an absolute catastrophe. He felt boxed in – as if he was at the bottom of a well with high, crumbling walls: bricks, stones and debris crashing all around him, and his only way out blocked by two monsters. To stay alive, he had to appease these creatures, but they had never been known for leniency.

At best they might be good mothers. If that were so, they would take care of their kids and he would have a limited role to play. Even so, at some stage there was going to be a conversation like:

'You're my daddy, and my mummy is Sally. But you're also Petula's daddy, and her mummy is Ali. How can that be? All the other boys and girls have their own daddy, they don't share one.'

'It's complicated. I'll tell you one day, but not now.'

If the twins continued in their chosen career, then a different conversation might be:

'Where are you going, Mummy?'

'To kill someone, darling. I won't be long.'

'Why?'

'To make some money before I go shopping. Daddy will look after you until I'm back.'

Another possibility didn't bear thinking about, but he did. Psychopathic behaviour can be hereditary. Not always, but there were known examples. If these kids were to inherit their mothers' traits, Ferdy would have an unmitigated disaster on his hands. His mind wandered into another depressing fantasy:

'Mummy, how do you use a garrotte?'

'I'll show you, darling, then you can practice on Daddy. He won't tell anyone.'

If they were bad mothers, then care for the innocents (all are born innocent, we're told) would rest with him. He would have to provide food, shelter and care, things he was mentally ill-equipped for when it came to children. For a start, he didn't make enough money to provide for one child, let alone two.

What was the way out? If the twins were to die, that would solve his problems, but it would also kill the babies, and in the scrambled mind of the master murder facilitator who had almost lost the ability to tell right from wrong, that wasn't acceptable. On the other hand, allowing the unborn kids to die with their mothers would prevent future deaths if they grew up as psychopaths.

God, what a debate. It was insane. Ferdy couldn't believe he was having to make a decision like this.

There was another way out of the baby dilemma: wait nine months before having the mothers killed. *No*, they would be serving him up as cocktail sausages at their baby shower long before then.

There was also the possibility that the twins were lying. It would be just like them to string him along. Cruelty was part of the game.

But hang on. There might still be way out of this nightmare. A figure high up on the collapsing brickwork of his imaginary prison was unfurling a rope ladder.

There was no time to lose.

CHAPTER TWENTY-ONE

Tuesday 18th October

FOR FERDY to make a phone call when he was going to be under almost constant surveillance by the twins was not easy. Fortunately, the mobile signal in the house was poor and only by going up the hill behind could a connection be guaranteed.

'I have to supervise another project,' Ferdy had said, telling them he wanted to make a call.

'Oh yes, what's that?' said one.

'A case a bit like yours was, actually. Sarah wants to get rid of a cousin who stands to inherit the family wealth. If he goes, then she will be the principal beneficiary.'

'If you have trouble, you know who to call to solve the problem, don't you?'

'Don't I ever.'

Both the twins laughed. 'That's our boy.'

'I'll also make some calls to see if I can identify a Ratel imposter.'

'You do that,' was the reply. 'You do whatever you have to do to find him. But remember, Ferdy, don't run away or do anything silly, because Phoebe is just down the road, well within our reach.'

Blood drained from his face with that comment. They would have seen it go pale and confirmed they'd found a chink in his armour. Armour? He had none. He didn't even have a shield.

At the back of the house was a motorbike, a scrambler, leaning against the kitchen wall. So that was how the second one had arrived last night. Those bikes make a fearful noise, yet he hadn't heard it. She must have pushed it along the lane.

The uphill plod alongside the dry stone wall taxed Ferdy's under-exercised legs. He was halfway up, but the woods he was heading for would not come closer. A low sun brightened the scene, but its warmth was too weak to penetrate his jacket. Half of last night's rain still clung to the grass. Heavy, soaked trainers and saturated socks iced his size-ten feet and squelched with every step. He knew what they looked like: white, hairy and water-wrinkled, his perpetual embarrassment.

He stopped to catch his breath and tried to make sense of these two extraordinary women. Ali and Sally were separate individuals, of course. But, as a collective, when they assumed the same mantle and he was unable to tell who did what, they were Ratel to him.

His misery knew no bounds. His first real love had conned him into believing her own affection equalled his. She/they/ Ratel had deliberately led him to think there was a future for them as a couple, a life of unending bliss for him, a novice in romance. Ratel had fooled him, betrayed him and thrown him out with not one iota of compassion. On top of that, they were brutal killers who showed no remorse whatsoever. His shame at being taken in by them meant that, at least for now, he would not be able to face another person. If he met a stranger, a new customer, or even a friend, he was going to drop his eyes or turn away – he knew it.

Miserable he might be, but he was also conscious that although this situation was weakening him, viewed in perspective, the threat of death and being ordered around by not one, but two, killers would have a negative impact on anyone, wouldn't it? He wasn't a superhero, but he wasn't abnormal either.

Ratel did not hold all the cards, though. Ferdy had a hand he could play, and doing so could well end this nightmare. He could not live the rest of his life wondering if each day was his last because they had decided to be rid of him for some trivial reason. It was the only solution, but it was fraught with danger. The risks were so high as to be almost unacceptable – and not only to himself. The alternative, though, was to give up, live in misery and die prematurely – also not acceptable.

At that moment, Ferdy had zero self-respect. But that hadn't always been the case. He had plenty when he was in control of things, when he told his clients what to do and threatened them with death – then he revelled in his short-term power. But as soon as someone stronger and more ruthless came along, he collapsed. That trait had to stop. He had to regain at least a semblance of dignity. But how?

In view of the danger, any gains he might make would be minuscule. No matter, if he gave himself a point for every win, no matter how small, then, as the points built, the more confident he would feel and the more able to take the risks needed for victory.

He managed a grin and gave himself one point for deciding to take action.

Looking back down the hill to the village, he saw no one. He wouldn't put it past Ratel to follow him. They weren't on the path he'd taken, but they could be out of sight on the sunny side of the wall. He tramped on. Having got his breath back, the wood appeared closer. Why the cover of the trees should give him confidence was a mystery, but they would be a place to disappear, a place to calm himself, a temporary shelter from this cruel life.

Five yards into the forest, Ferdy once more checked that he was not being followed before sitting with a heavy thump on a fallen tree. He dialled Millie.

She pressed the answer button but didn't speak to him. Instead, she continued with a discussion at her work. 'James, this is your responsibility, no one else's. Do your job.'

A distant voice. 'But Ms York, this is going to offend them—'

'I don't give a damn, James. Offence is not a word in my vocabulary. This is necessary. Do your job or I'll have your resignation on my desk by close of business. Do you understand?'

James's reply was inaudible.

Eventually, in a warm voice that gave no indication of her just-released anger, '*Mister*. Hello. What can I do for you?'

'Millie, we've got a very difficult and dangerous situation on our hands. We need to discuss it securely. I'm restricted on time, can we do a WhatsApp call now? It'll be encrypted.'

'Sure. Give me two minutes to secure things before calling.'

Ferdy drummed his fingers on the log while he waited.

He tapped the audio call icon. 'Millie, Ratel is furious with you. She's going to kill you. She's pressuring me to tell her who you are. I've said I don't know, but she insists, and she going to kill me if I don't tell her. You have to protect yourself before I'm forced to tell her.'

'O-kay,' Millie said slowly. 'So, Ratel really is a woman, that one on TV?'

'Yes. Millie, I know her. She's never going to give this up. You will never stop being her target, and she's very good in every aspect of what she does. There is only one solution in my eyes.'

'You want me to kill her?' A slight rise in tone at the end – was there a smile behind that answer?

'Yes, and I've a good idea how you can do it. But my calls are going to be limited. They're treating me with great suspicion and querying my every move. I'll give you the address in a moment. You should get up here as soon as possible, because if they get bored they're liable to change their hideout.'

'What do you mean, they?'

'That's the difficult part. Ratel is actually two women, identical twins. You kill one and the other is going to go berserk.'

'This is getting exciting.'

Was Millie salivating at the prospect of killing psychopathic twins? 'I'm warning you, she/they are every bit your match and have much more experience. It will be difficult and extremely dangerous, Millie.'

Ferdy gave her a description of the twins' car and registration, and what clothes they might be wearing. 'They always wear identical outfits, and they don't have much of a change with them. They will never be seen together, so only one will be a target at any one time. Which is ideal, as only one will be able to offer up any resistance. Let me know when you're here, and I'll supply you with the final details when you're ready to act.'

Was Millie's recruitment worth one point or two?

PART THREE

CHAPTER TWENTY-TWO

Thursday 20th October

EVER SINCE Millie York had ripped her stepfather's testicles from his crotch, spat and sworn at her mother for not protecting her and stormed out of her home forever, she had lived off, and later partially on, the grid. After a week spent sleeping on a park bench, she found help and a bed at the YMCA.

The charity set her on a path to the future, for which she was always grateful. Eventually, though, the help given to this fiercely independent girl became suffocating, and she left to forge her own future. From a mattress in a commune to a spell as a miserly banker's mistress, she built her life. The banker saw to her everyday needs, but that was all. The only way to improve her situation was through shop-lifting for essentials and sometimes more expensive items.

When her mother died, Millie didn't bother going to the funeral. Even when she realised she'd been left a comfortable sum of money, she merely shrugged and opened her first bank account. Some of that money went into off-grid accommodation: a camper van and a canal boat. At last she could live a life free of a mortgage and regular energy bills. Her expenses were incidental and variable, such as mooring and parking fees and occasional fuel and grocery costs. As free as she wished to be, she could change her location on a whim, and often did.

Now, in Upper Windon on Thursday morning, Millie parked her little camper van in an open field behind the hedge so it could not be seen. She was used to doing this, it was why she'd bought the van in the first place. When on a climbing weekend, she would often 'park and climb', as she termed her practice. There was always the risk that the farmer would find the van and lose his rural cool. Once, Millie had been forced to mollify the man with a ten minute inspection of her sleeping arrangements – an insignificant sacrifice that saved her vehicle from being bulldozed out of the gate.

She sent Ferdy a text, 'OK', and made herself a mug of tea.

Half an hour later, Ferdy appeared in the field. She was surprised to see what a scrawny little man he was (although he was wearing outsized shoes). Somehow, she'd expected a tougher-looking brute, a bouncer figure, to be an organiser of murders. She could easily twist his head off if she felt like it – but no, they were allies, and she owed him for her current feelings. She was content with her life at the moment, everything was going her way: the company was all hers, and her new-found passion for ridding the world of useless people had got off to a good start.

'Millie?' said Ferdy, looking up into the van.

'Mister Facilitator. Yes, it's me.'

'Millie, I don't have a lot of time. We can sort the first one out tomorrow morning. I heard them discussing leaving at nine to go and get some food for the weekend. Only one will go; the other will stay out of sight. This is what I suggest …'

CHAPTER TWENTY-THREE

Friday 21 October

AT FIVE past eight the next morning Millie took a brisk walk down the lane towards Windon Farm, just as she had done the previous night. It had not rained for almost three days, and with the traffic, light as it had been, the lane had turned from mud to dust.

Then, under the waxing moon, she had listened to the sounds of a hamlet almost asleep. Someone was still having a late barbecue, its distinctive odour carried on the smoke drifting across her path – suddenly she had been hungry. Unashamedly, she peered into people's windows where the curtains were open, but some lights were already off as she passed. People were going to bed. It was cool and, but for some faint music that drifted from just audible to barely discernible on variations of the breeze, generally quiet.

When she'd reached the end house she had seen an old Vauxhall blocking the drive. The twins' car, the Volvo XC90 SUV that Mister Facilitator had described, was in the road facing the way out. The lights were on in the house, but the curtains were closed. Millie stepped into the driveway and took note of the hedge and the space behind it. The garage doors in front of the Vauxhall were closed. White paint peeled off their edges, and the hasp and staple were almost rusted through. No chance to hide in there: the doors would creak and be likely to fall off. She walked past the signs and into Windon Farm. A huge combine harvester stood just inside the gate. From behind it, she could still see the Volvo and down the lane – ideal.

The night had been clear, but now, in the grey light of Friday morning, a heavy overcast announced that typical November weather was just ten days away. It wasn't yet raining, but it was going to.

Millie strode past the Volvo and through the farm gates. Praying that the farmer had long ago left for his fields, she waited behind the combine. She pulled off her gloves and adjusted the balaclava which was rolled up into a beanie.

It wasn't long before Mister, looking weedy beside a taller woman, appeared. The woman – was she Sally or Ali? – was above average height with long blonde hair. She must have dyed it, wasn't it supposed to be red? Or was she wearing a wig? Without knowing why, Millie guessed she was Alison.

The pair stopped at the front of the car, discussing some-thing. Mister was facing Millie but showed no sign of seeing her. He had positioned Ali in just the right place, in front of the left headlight. Millie pulled down her balaclava and trotted forward. Quick and quiet, she closed on the car in seconds. Their voices were audible, the discussion was about something he wanted her to buy. He was describing it – blue box, about two inches high, and you'll find it amongst the eye products.

Millie reached the driver's door. Mister had already unlocked it and left the key fob on the dash. In a second, she sneaked into the seat, didn't close the door because of noise, and had started the engine.

The woman, Ali, whipped round. With one stride she'd gone from the left side to directly in front of the car. Millie gunned it. The heavy vehicle leaped forward. Mister jumped back. Ali fell out of sight. A front wheel bumped over something. Then a back wheel hit the body.

Millie slammed the gear into reverse – bump … bump. Her door, unfastened, swung open. She slammed it shut. Mister was at the window, yelling at her, '*Stop, stop!*' He hammered on the glass with his puny fist. He yanked on the door handle, but it had locked itself. He pummelled her window, screamed at her as she ran back and then forward again, crushing the life out of the woman.

Enough. Millie pulled the gear selector back into Drive and accelerated down the lane. A dust cloud followed her. The engine was screaming and, in the mirror, Mister was running after her, waving and shouting. It was hopeless. He gave up, hands on knees, bent over and gasping for air.

A hard braking before the tarred road and the car skidded to a stop. Millie tucked the vehicle up against the hedge, ignoring the scrape of branches. She jumped out, took the key fob and threw it across the lane, before running up the hill to her van. She was laughing – it was so easy and so thrilling – and so much fun.

2

A piercing scream shattered the peace. The village had yet to come to life, but it did then.

Ferdy, further up the lane, was still doubled over, struggling to get his breath back. He looked up. Was she dead?

'*No, Ali, no.*' Sally was kneeling by her sister. '*Ali.*'

Ferdy summoned courage and ran back. He stared over Sally's head at the once beautiful woman. But those looks had deserted her. Grazed, distorted and punctured by gravel, her face was pockmarked with blood, her head misshapen. A crimson mess flowed out of her nose and across her cheek. Tangled to the side was a blonde wig. Tufts of that gorgeous auburn hair had been ripped from her scalp. A sandy tyre tread pattern crossed her T-shirt, and the lower half of one leg lay at an impossible angle.

'I know CPR,' Ferdy said. 'Let me in.'

'*You stupid little twat. Look at her: Ali's been crushed. How can you do CPR, you idiot? My sister, Ali, my sister.*' She stood, her arms by her sides, her fists clenched. Tears streamed down her face. She turned and, eyes on fire, lashed out. The punch slammed into Ferdy's face and sent him reeling. He tripped over his own feet and fell back against the hedge.

The commotion roused the residents. People, mostly elderly, were hurrying as best they could. A few younger ones ran. Two dogs were ahead of them, but kept their distance.

Sally reached down and grabbed Ferdy by the collar. Pulling him to his feet, she lowered her voice and hissed, 'You little rat. This is your doing. You betrayed us. You got that bloody killer here and helped him do this. You're *dead*, Ferdy Fellowes. You're walking dead.'

Someone said, 'Call 999.'

'Is she dead?'

Sally had dropped to her knees beside her sister again. She stayed quiet. Ferdy's voice came out as a croak. 'Yes.'

Another said, 'Keep those kids back.'

Sally motioned to Ferdy. 'Help me, I feel a bit weak.'

He hesitated, but stepped forward. Surely she wasn't going to kill him now, in front of this growing group of villagers.

'Put your arm round me. Move out of earshot.' She leant into him, her cheek, wet with tears, against his, her lips at his ear. 'Listen, Ferdy, and listen carefully. To leave Ali is going to kill me, but the police are coming. I can't wait here; everything will unravel and you'll be implicated as well. You stay and tell them what you did and how you tried to stop that driver. Of course, you have no idea what this is all about. I shall go, but we'll meet again. If you cover for me as I say and tell me who that was and where he is, then you can forget what I said just now. Do you understand?'

He breathed out. 'Yes, I'll do my best. I promise.'

Sally left him and plodded, head bowed, up to the house. Ferdy watched her with mixed feelings. She stumbled at one point, and he almost took a step forward to help. At least one element of her/their character still captivated him, in spite of her betrayal and murderous personality.

Ferdy glanced at the expanding group of onlookers. Some had hands to mouths in horror. Others, who could not face the scene, had turned away. Phoebe had arrived and stood at the rear, staring in disbelief. She raised her eyes, meeting Ferdy's, and stepped forward. She gripped his elbow. 'This is awful, I'm so sorry, Ferdy. Are you all right?'

'I'm okay. We'd ended it, but still this is unbelievable.'

'What …?' Her voice tailed off.

'I have no idea. This man came out of nowhere and just ran her down.'

A light motorbike started, issuing a sharp crackle that smashed the silence and shook the crowd out of its stunned condition. The driveway was almost blocked with people. The rider, in black leathers and a full helmet, gave a couple of demanding blips of the throttle. A path opened and the scrambler took it. Then it was gone with an unwelcome roar and a trail of dust.

'Who was that?'

'I don't know. Only Sally and I were here.'

The first signs of rain could be seen to the west.

CHAPTER TWENTY-FOUR

Monday 24th October

FOR THREE days, Ferdy tried to contact Millie without success. He was desperate, because as time passed with no progress he was certain the top of his head was going to blow off. Although all this was frustrating, he was pleased that, with one half of Ratel out of the way thanks to his initiative, he could add a point to his scale of confidence.

The police had questioned him, of course. He admitted that Sally (who was actually Ali, now dead) had been his girl-friend, but they had agreed to part ways. He had no idea why anyone would want to kill her. No one in the village knew anything at all, except one or two people who had seen her at the B&B. Phoebe had met her, but there was nothing in that, so the police had left empty-handed – for the moment, at least.

Meanwhile, he spent some time with Phoebe when she came round to check on the house and have a coffee every day. Phoebe was familiar and was easy to get on with. But he had difficulty explaining his attitude to other people – anyone he came across. Although not an introvert, he became overly shy, could not look others in the eye, deliberately cut conversations short and was sometimes brusque to the point of being plain rude.

Initially, he felt that the loss of Sally, as he thought collectively of the loving side of Ratel, was the cause; then he realised it wasn't the loss of the women who had betrayed him, but his shame and embarrassment at his own stupidity and immaturity at his age.

Phoebe asked no questions and made no comments on the murder, even though it had been an extremely traumatic event. Villagers had been upset, children had been shushed away from the site, and two women had burst into tears, but Phoebe seemed to take it in her stride. Ferdy found this odd and realised he knew very little about her life prior to marrying Henry. Had she been in the police, for example? Or maybe she saw action in the army. He expected, and dreaded, some input from her, but, in its absence, he was grateful. Without saying as much, by behaving normally, she was offering a helping hand as he struggled to put the crisis behind him. His problem was, there was more trouble to come, and he knew it wasn't going to be any better.

Ferdy finally made contact with Millie on the Monday evening. 'We need to lure her into a trap,' he said. 'If she learns where you are, she'll come to kill you. You should be prepared for that and strike first.'

'Or, I could hunt her down.'

'Ideal, but she won't tell me where she is, and if I ask she'll smell a rat immediately.'

'I suppose. I'm mobile. I live out of a canal boat I own, and sometimes my van.'

'As the chief exec of a company?'

'Why not? It may not be conventional, but I don't know why one has to be conventional to be effective. The boat suits my attitude to life, and I'm still efficient at work.'

'Okay. So, do I tell Sally you're living in a van, or a boat? We should only declare one, I think.'

'Of course. The less she knows the better. Tell her I live on the boat – that'll leave me with a faster, more manoeuvrable getaway vehicle if I need it. The boat is part of the plan being forged in my tiny brain as we speak. Unfortunately, it's moored some distance away at the moment, and it'll take me two days to move it. Once it's in place, I'll send you the current location via WhatsApp.'

'Two days! Where is it?'

'I've got to drive up there, bring the boat back via various canals at walking speed, and then go back on public transport to fetch my van – yes, two days.'

'That's a pity,' Ferdy said. 'Because we can't waste time over this. Sally's unpredictable; I've no idea what she's going to do next. She might snap unless she gets an answer out of me before you're ready. Please hurry. I'll come down tomorrow. We can sort details when you've got your boat back.'

2

Ferdy's heart was pounding as he picked up the phone to call Sally. A bit like having to plunge his warm body into icy water to show others how brave he was, he had to do it but couldn't summon the courage to jump. A long time was spent rehearsing his lines before he managed to press the buttons.

'Sally, I've found him. You were right, he was a client of mine, but from a long time ago.'

Ferdy put her curt reply down to her distress and rage at Ali's death. 'You've known this all along, haven't you?'

Ferdy gulped. '*No*. No, I haven't. He called me to boast about his achievement. I told him he had to stop, but he said if you don't like it then you should try to stop him.'

'Likes a challenge, does he? Where is he?'

'He lives on a narrow boat most of the time, but not always. I don't know where he sleeps when he's not there. Maybe he has a girlfriend and stays with her. He tours the country's entire canal network, moving frequently for security. They tell me he's nervous of reprisals from his wife's family after her murder. They, the family, are convinced he had arranged it, although he's never been charged for it.' Ferdy was surprised and not a little ashamed by the ease at which his lies could flow.

'Where is he?'

'I don't know, exactly. He's supposed to be moving south from the Midlands. Please give me a day or so to find where he stops, then I'll have information you can use.'

Sally hung up, leaving Ferdy adrift. Would she grant him that time?

CHAPTER TWENTY-FIVE

Thursday 27th October

STUPOR WAS too strong a word to describe Ferdy's dazed state, but after only two beers on his tired brain on Thursday afternoon he was definitely thinking slower than normal. The constant threat he was under lessened if he drank a little, and maybe a little more.

The map of Millie's position had come through on Wednesday night. In case Sally reacted before they were prepared for her, Ferdy put off phoning until after lunch on Thursday, when he was back home in his own dismal little house. Dismal, because now that he had experienced that pretty and quiet hamlet in Yorkshire, he realised that rural life was more appealing than urban mass housing. And why was it, he questioned as he looked down his wet, gloomy street, that rain up there was more easy to accept than it was in the suburb?

Ferdy opened the red phone and punched in Ratel's number.

'Well? Do you have answers for me?' were Sally's opening words.

'He's arrived, and the good news is that he's moored quite close to here.'

'What's the name of this boat? How is it identifiable?'

'It's maroon and black with gold lettering for the name in some fancy font – Polly, which was his wife's name. Fifty-five feet long with solar panels and a bicycle on the cabin roof. He usually moors for free anywhere along the towpath, but he can't stay any more than two weeks or he'll be charged.'

'Where?'

'I'll send you a map image after this. You'll have to walk along the towpath from the pub on the right of the map until you find the boat. I can't be more specific than that.' Ferdy stopped himself from asking when she would go in search of the boat. She would be highly suspicious of any questions related to her revenge – yet he had to find out something that would give Millie a helping hand. 'How are you going to do it this time?'

There was no reply. Had he gone too far?

'*Don't* ask questions.' Her voice was husky, and didn't come from his phone.

Ferdy almost lost control of his bladder. He turned.

Hatred had distorted her face. Gaunt, skeletal almost, it had lost all its beauty. Her luscious hair, now lank and rain soaked, hung straight, unwashed and sticky. Only her blood-shot eyes had any life, it seemed. They glared with an intensity Ferdy imagined was one of the last things her victims would have seen. And now, he was the recipient.

He swallowed, but his mouth was dry. '*Sally*. What …? How did you get in?'

'You gave me a key.' Her jeans were ripped at the knee. That was fashion, but the dark stain on the right leg could only be her sister's blood.

'Oh, yes …' Then because he couldn't think of anything else to say: 'Did you look up the boat's position?'

Sally said nothing. She merely looked at him as if he was a complete idiot. 'You haven't sent me the map yet.'

Ferdy had read somewhere that you should never look a wild animal – a lion, say, a bear, or anything that would eat you – in the eye. The beast would see you as aggressive and attack. He dropped his gaze.

'Ferdy, you are going to do exactly as I say. Nothing less and nothing more unless something goes wrong and you can rescue the situation. Understood?'

Ferdy looked up briefly, met her eyes, nodded and looked away again.

'I, Ratel, cannot afford to be seen frequently in the area before a death takes place. So you're going to watch that boat and report back to me when that man is there. When you're convinced that he'll be spending the night on board, you'll be my lookout. You will fetch and carry as I say and generally be an extra pair of hands.'

Again Ferdy nodded. Then he plucked up courage and said, 'You've never needed help before, why now?'

'Because, Ferdy, I want you involved, I want you to share the blame in this man's murder for my own protection – if I let you live.'

2

Sally had left in the same silent way in which she'd arrived with the parting words, 'Be careful, Ferdy, or your end will be earlier than expected.'

Ferdy wanted to ask when that would be, but his nerve failed him. As someone who dealt in death, in happier times he had often debated whether it would be a good thing to know when he would have to pay Charon to ferry him across the Styx (he would need the correct sum on him, as no change was given) or whether to let death catch him by surprise.

But, he argued, if he knew when he was going to die, he'd decline rapidly. He'd be unable to sleep, he'd lose his appetite, physically he'd weaken and mentally he'd lose all will – he would give up and, in losing the will to live, that would be the end.

On the other hand, if he didn't know when the fateful day would come, he'd have no time to get depressed and deteriorate. He'd be able to live his life (such as it was) to the full up to the last moment.

Once Ferdy was certain that Sally had left, he called Millie. 'I'm to tell her when you're going to be there for the night and to act as a lookout and be a general dogsbody. Remember, she thinks you're a man. I don't have a clue what she'll think when she sees a woman on the boat.'

'I could be the girlfriend and therefore innocent – if we get that close.'

'She has no scruples. If you're associated with the man and are in the way, you're dead.'

'We're not going to get that close, so I'm not worried.'

'What are you going to do? How will it work?'

'I haven't decided yet. What I want you to do first is to tell me when Sally is coming, step by step. That's vital. Then you keep watch on things. Tell me her movements, tell me if third parties are nearby, tell me what she wants you to do. I need to think something through, and I might want you to act as a decoy.'

'So she shoots *me*?'

'No, Mister, of course not. I need you. Besides, I wouldn't betray you. I give you my word on that.'

Ferdy wasn't too sure how much her 'word' meant, coming from someone who enjoyed killing people. His mind became stuck in first gear – revving like mad with little result – but somehow he forced himself to change up. 'We need a set of signals. I'll have my phone on silent, I can't have it ring and alert her. The quickest thing is for me to text you. That'll be silent. Say 1 for she's on her way; 2 for a two-minute warning; and 3, arrival is imminent.'

'That's a good idea. I won't reply, you can assume I got the messages. When it's over, I'll need help with the body. We can't leave it near my boat, I'll have to move it in the van.'

'All right. Whatever it takes to get this done. When will you be ready, when can I say you'll be on board for the night?'

'Not tonight, or tomorrow. It's too short notice. Let's pencil in Saturday. I want the time to prepare something.'

Ferdy closed the call. His panic was on the rise again. His situation was dire. Here he was, helping two women to each kill the other one. One thing was certain, one of those women was going to die. If it was Millie, then Ferdy was as good as dead himself. If it was Sally, then there was a reasonable chance that Millie would leave him alone (that was what she claimed, anyway). Somehow, he had to continue his support for Millie while convincing Sally he was helping her even as he betrayed her – *Christ, how did he get into this situation?*

There were others to think about, too. Phoebe had already been dragged into the mix, although she probably didn't realise it. He needed to think about her safety as well.

It was getting to be too much to handle. Depression and physical deterioration in the face of death were creeping up on him.

He awarded himself one point for setting things in motion with Millie, but should he knock a point off for his defeatist attitude?

CHAPTER TWENTY-SIX

Thursday 27th October

GRIEF ENGULFED Sally. Little else entered her thoughts. Ali had been killed – her sister, her twin sister, to whom she was so close that they were effectively the same person. Sally was Ali and Ali was Sally. At the same time as Ali was being forced into that icy water all those years ago, Sally had been short of breath without knowing why. When Sally, as a child, had broken her left arm, Ali had difficulty using hers until Sally's cast was on. Half of her had been ripped away, half her heart and half her mind had been shredded.

But mixed with the grief was rage. She boiled, a pressure cooker at its limit. Something had to assuage her anger. And the ultimate focus was Ferdy-fucking-Fellowes. There was no doubt that although he didn't kill her, he'd planned and facilitated Ali's death. He was going to die and, unlike Ratel's other murders whereby the mutilations had been carried out after death, Ferdy was going to suffer before his demise.

But not yet. He still had his uses.

The rained had stopped, but a gentle breeze passed down the street. It was too light to blow the sodden autumn leaves around, but it was enough to send a chill through Sally as she walked back to her car, some three blocks from Ferdy's house.

A group of young men were drinking and clowning around ahead of her. Two of them sat on a low wall, two lounged against it. One of them saw her coming, some quiet words were exchanged, and they moved to block her way.

Sally made no effort to bypass the group by stepping off the pavement. She stopped, her path obstructed by a man a little taller than her. Jeans, faux-leather jacket with studs, and cap on back to front. He hadn't shaved in a week.

'We got a looker here, lads. Fucking smashing, she is.'

Her pressure cooker was about to blow. It was all Sally could do to keep it under control and in a firm, but calm voice, say, 'Get out of my way.'

'Sure, but there's a toll to pay, darling. One kiss and you can be on your way.'

Sally managed a smile. 'All right. Just one, right?'

'From each of us.'

The group laughed.

'I'll 'ave a blow job instead,' chirped a shaven-headed yob with narrow eyes and tattoos on his scalp.

Sally turned and gave him a smile.

The first one pouted and tapped his lips. Sally moved into him, her eyes smiling, her mouth open, her arms extended to hold his head. Inches away from contact, her neck and back rigid she drove upwards. Her forehead smashed into his jaw. Before he hit the ground she delivered a flying kick to his groin.

Kisser screamed and doubled up.

The others gathered behind her. She turned on them. Two were wary. Their six-inch blades pointed at her in a 'Don't come any closer' attitude rather than a 'Back off or we'll stab you' threat. Tattooed-brain was different. He radiated aggression. His knife was long, at least a foot. He raised it. Sally stepped closer. He began with a slash. Sally blocked it and stabbed two fingers into his eyes.

He shrieked.

She kicked him in his undefended groin, and he went down. Then she wrenched the knife from his grip and drew the full length of the blade through his throat. The other two yobs took one look at the fountain of blood, and ran.

Sally returned to the kisser, who was on his knees. She kicked him onto his back, stood over him and slashed the knife down between his legs.

He screamed again, briefly. Then cried.

Sally picked up his cap, used it to rub her fingerprints off the knife and tossed the weapon at him. Striding off down the road, she felt considerably better. The cooker was off the boil, but it was still superheated.

CHAPTER TWENTY-SEVEN

Friday 28th October

BOOM, BOOM, boom. The beat resonated down the street from the Pride-flagged doorway. Millie approached, outwardly flaunting an eagerness and confidence she did not feel. This was not her bent, but it was in her plan.

At the door, under an awning, stood a bouncer, a large grim-faced, shaven-headed man, who studied her with cold, indifferent eyes as he compared her driving licence photo to her face. The few raindrops on his scalp glistened in the entrance light. He handed the card back and nodded, giving a slight inclination of his round head towards the open doorway.

Inside, the club was an assault on the senses. Laser beams flashed off a rotating globe to dazzle and invite flicker vertigo in the sensitive. Music demanding ear-defenders to prevent early-onset hearing loss foiled any possibility of rational thought. A mass of gyrating bodies crammed the floor in an uncoordinated tribal dance. Arms and legs flew about in a wild rhythm, hips were thrust in sexual innuendo. It was more like a mixed martial arts free-for-all than a club.

Millie negotiated her way around the edge of the throng to the bar. Two men, a hand on each other's upper thigh, occupied stools and watched the action. At the end of the bar, behind a man yelling his order and facing out towards the dance floor, sat a chubby woman in her mid twenties. Scarlet hair, heavy mascara and black lipstick. Ripped, skin-tight jeans covered her sturdy legs, and her well-filled T-shirt proclaimed, 'Misandry is a Response'. Beyond her, a female couple gazed at each other as they sipped a single brightly-coloured cocktail through individual straws. The lone girl met Millie's look when she was fighting her way through the crowd. Every time Millie glanced up from dodging a flailing arm, their eyes locked.

'Whew, that's a battle,' Millie said. 'I need a drink. You want another?' She sat beside the woman, putting her back to the crowd.

'Yeah, why not? White wine spritzer. I wus drinkin' pisco sours, but I'm getting pissed, so I'll ease orf a bit.'

Millie smiled. 'I'm Sonia.'

'Celia.'

Millie reached over to Celia's T-shirt and let her hand rest on her shoulder and trace a path down beside her breast.

'Love your slogan – so true.' Her hand fell to rest on her own thigh, but her little finger was touching Celia's.

Three drinks later, they were getting on fine. They had danced until Celia ran out of breath, which didn't take long. Then they verbally decimated half the male population and invented unpleasant ways to deal with the rest. Celia was slurring, but her eyes were intense as she captured Millie's. 'D'ya wanna fuck?'

'Thought you'd never ask.'

Millie helped the woman off her stool without falling. She held her hand and led the way. 'My van. It's a few steps down the road. Everything you want is there.'

CHAPTER TWENTY-EIGHT

Saturday 29th October

MILLIE HAD driven the van to a secluded parking area just off the main road on Friday night. Lovers who had nowhere else to go to fulfil their needs, or those who got a thrill from performing with nature as a backdrop, used the spot regularly. Neither were to Millie's taste, but her camper provided seclusion, and the drumming of the rain on the roof enforced a closeness between them; two fragile humans in each other's arms as they sheltered from the forces outside. Besides, as she kept reminding herself, it was a necessary ingredient in her plan.

Millie had a healthy appetite for sex. She made little distinction between men and women, but there were times when she definitely preferred one over the other. Last night's choice would have been to have a man. She couldn't explain why, it just seemed more appropriate in the circumstances. But hey-ho, this liaison had a purpose far beyond her need for sexual gratification.

She gave Celia's nipple a good-morning tweak, kissed it and rolled out of the bunk. Somewhere on the floor was her scarlet G-string. She was conscious of Celia watching her as she found a T-shirt to slip on.

Moments later, her little stove was lit, water was on the boil and the cramped space smelled of coffee.

'Toast? Or you want an egg? You need some protein after last night,' Millie asked.

Celia giggled. 'Yeah, I need my strength back. You've a good bod, Sonia. Wish mine were wiry like yours.'

Millie laughed. 'Don't worry. You're very comfortable. Shall we join up again tonight?'

'Can't get enough of a good thing – sure.'

'We'll go to my boat on the canal. There's more space, the mattress isn't as hard, and it's private. No noisy bonkers will be shagging in the car next door.'

2

Ferdy had taken a brief look at Millie's boat on the previous two nights, even though he knew nothing would happen until Saturday. Hopefully, the action should prove to Sally – if she was watching – that he was doing what she had told him to do.

On Saturday morning, Millie called him to say they were on and she would be on board.

A warm front hung over the area: a thick mass of low cloud that completely shut out a full moon and delivered a steady drizzle. After six that evening, when it was dark, Ferdy went to the canal, but only as far along the towpath as he needed to, to see Millie's boat. There was movement, a shadow in a lit window. Without bothering to inspect further, he called Sally. 'It looks like tonight's the night. He's on board.'

'Wait for me in the car park. I'll be there in about four hours; it's too early now. In the meantime, you make sure he doesn't leave. I don't want to go there for nothing.'

Four hours. Ferdy grumbled at the wait, but he'd suffer anything to have this nightmare over. He hurried back to the shelter of his car.

Sally was there before ten. Beneath her hood, her face was wet from the rain. Her mouth was set in a thin pale line while her eyes glinted like pinpricks of ice. She sniffed. 'Is he still there?' She was wearing a dark jacket and carried a small backpack – what was in there? Even so, she looked as if she had put on weight. Impossible, and highly unlikely, in the short time since he'd last seen her, though.

'Yes.' Ferdy swallowed. A climax was approaching. He wasn't sure he wanted it to; he was scared both of the actual event and of the fallout if it went wrong. Yet he had to get it over with.

'Follow me. How far is it?'

'About half a mile, a kilometre maybe.'

'Right. When we get there, you will stop about thirty yards from the boat. I'll indicate where that will be. There will be no talking, not a sound. Understood?'

Cough. 'Yes.'

'You will keep quiet until I have spoken. After that, there will be no need for silence. Got it?'

'Yes.'

Sally pointed to a position behind her – she might as well have ordered him to *Heel* – and set off along the towpath.

Ferdy had prepared the first text on his phone, so all he had to do was bring it to life under the cover of his jacket and press send. A figure *1* then winged its way through the ether so Millie knew her killer was coming.

Sally turned round at that moment. She took a step towards him.'What are you doing?'

'I'm just making sure my phone's sound is off, that's all.' Hearing the tremble in his own voice, he clenched his jaw. For Christ's sake get a grip or you'll as good as commit suicide, he warned himself.

'A bit late. What else have you forgotten?'

'Nothing. I left it on in case you called me, but it's all good now.' What was his excuse going to be if she caught him a second or third time?

They marched on, splashing through the odd puddle or squelching through a mud patch. Once again, Ferdy was struck by how bulky Sally was. A vest, that's what it is; she's wearing a bulletproof vest.

CHAPTER TWENTY-NINE

Saturday 29th October

THE BOAT was warm and cosy with the little wood burner alight. Flickering orange patterns danced around the cabin sides – reflections of its flames. Only a dim side light added to the illumination, and Sting crooned about fields of barley at a low volume.

Celia was lying back on the boat's bench seat with her second stiff gin and tonic in her hand. Millie still nursed her first one, and hadn't taken more than a sip. She looked at the reclining creature, resembling Rubens's 'Sleeping Angelica' with a few more clothes, smiled, and raised her glass. Whatever this buxom lass was expecting from her tonight wasn't going to happen. Very far from it, in fact.

Millie's phone vibrated once – 1 – Sally was on her way. That would be about a seven-minute warning. Make it five to be on the safe side. Millie's watch read eight minutes past. She stood, turned, and smiled. 'I'll make us something to eat, then we'll open bottle of wine to enhance the mood.'

'*Christ*. My mood's fuckin' up there right now. Leave the grub till later, Sonia.' Celia grabbed Millie's hand and tried to pull her down.

'No. It's good to put things off, to tease ourselves. It increases the passion, makes it all the more worthwhile.' Millie's grip almost crushed the intrusive fingers.

Celia pulled her hand back and looked up with a pained expression. '*Ow*. That hurt.'

'Sorry, didn't mean it,' Millie mumbled as she glanced at her watch. 'I need to pee first. I go outside after dark so as not fill the Portaloo too quickly. Help yourself to another drink, I won't be long.'

As she reached the cabin door, her phone buzzed again – 2 – two minutes. She stepped out into the drizzle and closed the door as quietly as she could. A jerry can of diesel threatened to obstruct her movement around the cockpit. Millie would move it to and from her van as required. She was never likely to run out of fuel in either transport, but her can ensured she wouldn't – it was her security blanket. Now, she pushed it out of the way. In case of what? It didn't matter, it felt better to have the space clear.

Earlier, she had moved the boat a short distance to a place near where the canal made a gentle turn. Because of the vegetation, the corner created a blind spot in the towpath about forty yards from her mooring. Once on the bank, she ran a few paces back towards the corner and snuck into the bushes where she'd stashed her kit.

2

Sally led Ferdy at speed along the towpath. His short stride compared to that of her long limbs had his little legs pumping like a steam locomotive in trying to keep up. Whenever he dropped back, he had to trot to catch her. They were going much faster than when he had paced it out, so he had to update his estimate and managed to send the second text – 2 – without Sally knowing.

She reached the bend and stopped. Ferdy closed up to her, panting. She took his wrist in an unyielding grip, which stopped him sending the third text: – 3 – arrival imminent. She led him forward, round the bushes, until they could see the boat. A few more paces and he was released. She signalled him to wait. In the dim light her eyes and the sheen of mist on her forehead gleamed for a moment until she turned away.

Ferdy, rooted to his spot, was trying to quell the butterflies in his stomach and forgot about sending the third text. With trepidation, he watched Sally sneak forward. She reached the boat and, taking great care, transferred her weight to the vessel. With such a small boat, any sudden change of weight, up or down, would create a movement of the hull that the occupants couldn't help but notice.

A hand touched Ferdy's arm. He jerked back and stifled a cry to a barely audible gasp.

Millie. She didn't speak, but pushed ahead of him. In her hand was a short bow, already nocked with an arrow.

Apparently, Sally was satisfied that no one had detected her boarding, because she stood and faced the cabin doors. Her right hand held something shiny and was ready to rap.

Millie raised her bow and took aim at Sally's back.

Ferdy shut his eyes but, prepared to be horrified, opened them again.

Sally turned to check behind her as Millie released the arrow.

'*Aaaargh,*' she cried. Was that pain or rage, or both?

Sally slumped out of sight behind the panels on either side of the doors with the sound of a sack of potatoes hitting the deck. Millie pushed Ferdy in front of her and ran for the boat as a 'You all right?' and a 'What's goin' on?' came from inside.

Sally was on her side in front of the doors, blocking them. The arrow was sticking out of her upper arm. How far in had it gone? She was struggling to get a grip on the shaft. 'Ferdy, what the fuck are you doing? Where's that bastard? Pull this fucking thing out of my arm, I can't move it. It's locked my arm to my vest. *Fuck*, it hurts.'

Celia pushed on the doors from the inside, but they were jammed by Sally's body. She banged on them. 'What's goin' on, Sonia? *Lemme out.*' BANG, BANG.

'*Shut up, you stupid cow. Jesus. Ow.*'

Ferdy hesitated. This was a decisive moment. An opportunity to finish this nightmare by ending Sally's chances of survival was staring at him. She was his greatest threat. He had already sided with Millie to get rid of Sally. But the trouble was, Ferdy was more frightened of Sally than he was of Millie. And here she lay wounded in front of him, yet he was unable to summon the courage to harm her. With her strength and will, she might overcome him even though she was disabled.

On the other hand, he could help Sally to rid the world of her rival psychopath. That would surely convince her not to kill him. He could also stand up and walk away, leaving the two killers to sort out their differences. But if Sally won this battle, he would still have her to reckon with.

Ferdy made no decision. And in not choosing a winner, all he could do was help Sally with her arrow. He gingerly poked around the wound, pulling on the jacket to clear the material away. 'It's gone through your bicep. I don't know if it's damaged the bone.' He grabbed the short shaft with both hands.

'*Jesus*, Ferdy. Pull you little drip, *pull*.'

'Are you ready?' Ferdy pulled. It could wiggle, but would not come out. 'The barb on the arrowhead is caught between the armoured stuff and the seam at the edge. We can't free your arm without taking the vest off or unscrewing the head from the shaft.'

BANG, BANG. The doors rattled. '*Lemme out!*'

He was leaning over Sally when Millie leaned over him. All Sally could have seen was an extra silhouette above her. It was enough. In one movement, ignoring her pain and restricted left arm, she sat up and lunged past Ferdy with a long knife.

She hadn't the reach to make a deep cut, but it was enough. Millie fell back. Her head hit the low steel gunwale with a thud.

'Ferdy, will you get this fucking thing out of my arm.'

Celia thumped the door again and again. 'What's going on? Let me out. *Help*.'

They ignored her.

'I can't, it won't move.'

'Then break it.'

'*Help*.' BANG, BANG.

'It's aluminium. It won't break, it'll bend. And it'll hurt.'

'*Jesus*, Ferdy, it's already sending me through the roof. Work it until it breaks. Stop whining and *do* it.'

Ferdy bent the shaft one way and then the next, over and over. As he did so, the arrowhead dug into and lacerated the flesh under her arm. Sally's teeth were bared and clenched. She grunted with every twist. Eventually, the shaft broke, leaving a three-inch stub. But the arrowhead itself was caught in her stab vest and she was effectively one-armed.

'Right let's deal with this bastard.' She struggled to her knees and crawled to Millie. 'It's a *woman*. Ferdy, you said it was a man. I've been looking for a man. You betrayed me, you little shit.'

'*A woman?* Oh God. I'm so sorry. I assumed it was a man, everything pointed to it being a man.'

Sally shook her head. 'Help me now and I'll leave you alone, but this is the last time, Ferdy, the *last* time.'

'You've said that before,' he muttered under his breath.

3

Celia didn't stop her pleas to be let out. Occasionally she had spurts of hammering on the door, but they were getting weaker. She began to cry in fear and frustration. Sally ignored her, and Ferdy was too scared to do anything other than what he was told.

'Drag this bitch so she blocks the door,' Sally said. 'I don't want that wimp in there to get out and complicate things.' She searched around the cockpit area and spotted Millie's jerry can. She picked it up, hefted it for weight and undid the cap to sniff. 'Aha.'

'Clear the roof of this thing, Ferdy. *Aah*,' Sally grunted.

'The bike's easy, but the solar panels will take time,' he stammered.

'Just do the bloody bike. Ditch it in the canal. There'll be enough space.'

Ferdy began to undo the lashings that held Millie's bike in place. Why the hell did he have to do this? It was a waste of time. With the racket this woman in the cabin was making, it was only a matter of time before some people came to see what was going on. And with Millie stabbed, perhaps dying, the last thing Ferdy wanted was to be found at the scene. He needed to get away from this disaster as fast as possible. But Sally was to be obeyed.

He undid the last strap and gripped the cycle frame. Its weight surprised him, but it was an old-fashioned bike with a basket for your shopping and a chain-guard so your slacks didn't get caught, not a modern, light, carbon-fibre racer. It was an effort to drag it off the cabin roof and heave it into the water.

Who the hell was that woman making such a noise in the cabin? She was screaming questions, 'Who's there?' and 'What's going on?' Then begging, '*Please* let me out.' Was she some innocent, or a relative of Millie's? And who was this Sonia that she was pleading to? Whoever the woman was, she was a complication that didn't seem to worry Sally. And what was in her plans for Millie, what for him? James Bond would have turned the tables on her ages ago – but Ferdy accepted he was no Bond.

Sally was still at the steering position, standing over Millie. 'Ferdy, get this bitch up onto the space you've cleared.'

'I'll try, but I don't know if I can lift her up there.'

'Stop being so bloody negative. Of course you can.'

Celia started banging on the cabin door again. 'Let me out. Let me out.' BANG, BANG.

Sally kicked the door. 'Shut up, you. It's not your business.'

Celia wailed and sobbed.

Ferdy half dragged and half lifted Millie from the cockpit floor to the roof. He got her over his shoulder, put her bum on the roof above the doors and toppled her over backwards. He winced at the thud as her head fell back on the steel plate. Sally used her one good arm to help. 'Ugh, aagh,' she moaned with the effort. Once Millie was half on the wet roof, it was easy to slide her forward until only her lower legs hung down over the cabin doors.

Ferdy felt something sticky. His shoulder was soaked – black in the darkness. 'She's bleeding.'

'Least of her problems,' Sally muttered, and produced some cable ties from her backpack, which she handed to Ferdy. 'Fix her wrists to the handrails. I want her spread out on the roof.'

Horror crept into Ferdy's mind. It didn't swamp him suddenly, it entered little by little, taking over his thoughts. 'Wha-what are you going to do?'

'You'll see, but this witch will forever regret killing my sister. Forever won't be long.'

4

Millie was regaining consciousness. Ferdy tied her right wrist as instructed, but the rail on the other side was too far away. A mounting for a boat hook would have to do, even though she was not spreadeagled.

Behind him, Sally had opened the cabin doors. 'Who the fuck are you?'

A high-pitched squeak came from below. 'I'm Celia. What …? *Oh my God, you're Ratel.*'

Ferdy glanced in the cabin window to see Sally lash out with a flat hand. Poor Celia reeled back onto the settee clutching her cheek. Wide-eyed, she stared at Sally in disbelief. Not for long. One-handed, Sally yanked her up and propelled her out of the door.

Celia's head bobbed up between Millie's knees as she left the cabin. 'Wha—?' A violent shove flung her to the stern and over the guard rail to flop into the canal with a splash worthy of a breaching whale.

In Millie's ear, Ferdy whispered, 'I'll free you as soon as I can. Lie still.'

There was no reaction. Had she understood? He looked at her wound. It was oozing blood. What was Sally doing in the cabin?

Holding the handle of the jerry can with one hand and the flat side resting on top of her forearm, Sally raised her elbow and poured diesel over the woodwork and furnishings. She called, 'Get out, Ferdy, get out.'

He retreated as far as the stern rail. In the cabin, Sally laid a trail of fuel and backed out of the doors. She lit the diesel and watched the line of little flames as they travelled down the steps to meet the soaked furnishings.

The fire took hold. For a short while a cushion was burning on its own. A few seconds later, the fire flared, engulfing the cabin with a whomp.

Sally gave a nod of satisfaction and jumped for the bank, where she stood back and watched. Ferdy stared, stupefied, as the flames rose higher and higher. Black smoke was filling the cabin. The heat coming out of the doors increased. The rain hissed as it hit the cabin roof, and steam rose.

Millie was conscious. She screamed and squirmed and screamed.

Ferdy shook himself into reality, and glanced around. Sally had disappeared, but she could be nearby.

Celia was wallowing in the canal, struggling to climb out.

A pop sounded from the forward end of the cabin; the roof had buckled upwards.

Millie was frying.

There was no way Ferdy could imagine himself as some sort of hero – ever. But, without thinking, he leaned down and picked up Sally's knife, which was lying at the door. She must have put it down to use the jerry can and forgotten to collect it, which was unlike Ratel. The stress must have been getting to her.

The searing heat from the cabin side singed Ferdy's leg. Further forward a window blew out with a bang and a splash as it landed in the water.

The knife was razor-sharp. Ferdy worked his way forward outside the cabin. The steel was already too hot to touch, while through the window was an inferno of orange flame and swirling black smoke. He leaned forward, holding onto the rail with one hand, and thrust the knife between Millie's wrist and the cable tie. It parted. She rolled over onto her side, pushing herself up off the roof to minimise contact. As quickly as he could, he worked his way around to the other side and slit that tie.

Millie shot upright – anything to get away from that steel roof – and slid off and into the cockpit. She wobbled, then stretched for something to hold onto, before Ferdy grabbed her. He led her to the side and jumped ashore, extended a hand and pulled her after him. She slithered on the bank and went waist-deep in water. He hauled her out. 'The water will cool those burns, but there's a huge chance of infection. Can you stand it – the pain?'

Millie nodded, gritting her teeth.

'Help me.' Celia was wallowing in the water, her breasts floating ahead of her like water wings.

Ferdy saw that she hadn't the strength or the agility to climb out. He said to Millie, 'Stay here, don't lie down. I'll just get this woman out and be back.'

The cabin fire was raging, casting a flickering orange glow across the canal. Noxious smoke drifted in their direction. Two more windows blew out, and the paint was bubbling off the sides.

Ferdy knelt and held out a hand to Celia. As soon as she grabbed it, he pulled, but she was heavy and their grips slipped on wet skin. She fell back, creating another tsunami on the canal.

'Come on,' Ferdy yelled at her. 'I've got to get to the hospital.'

Eventually, he got her out, and she stood shivering on the towpath. Her hair was sopping and stuck to her face, her soaked T-shirt clung to every mound and fold of her body, her mascara had run – she was a caricature of misery.

'Go. Go home. You saw what happened tonight; I suggest you keep quiet about it or you might become a victim.'

Celia cried and ran off down the towpath.

Ferdy watched her disappear round the bend. 'I did a first-aid course once. Let me see your back. Here, I'll help you get your top off.'

With Millie biting her lip, they raised her T-shirt. The fire was dying out and had not spread to the fuel tank. Even so, there was enough of a glow for Ferdy to see Millie's back. The orange flames lent colour to the area, but it was clear that her main injuries consisted of red first-degree burns with some blistering indicating second-degree damage. He couldn't see any broken skin. He couldn't help noticing how hard and muscular she was. Not an ounce of fat filled out her torso.

'How's your wound? … It's still bleeding. Take your shirt off and hold it against the cut. Come on, we need to get you to hospital.'

'No, I can't go there, it's too dangerous.'

'No it's not. What's more dangerous is internal from that knife wound, and the extent of your burns, plus infection. You can't be treated outside a medical environment. Come on, let's get to my car. I'd carry you, but I don't think I'd get too far.'

It was a slow, painful walk with Millie clutching her shirt to the cut, but she made it. Ferdy held the car door open. 'Lie on your side across the rear seats.'

'*Jesus*, my back's on fire – thighs and bum too. What am I going to tell the emergency staff?

'Yes, that's a problem … Why not say you were mugged by a knife-wielding yob. You staggered into your van, knocked over a paraffin lamp, which started a fire, and you got burned as you were getting out? Is that too unlikely?'

'It's stupid; they won't believe it. *Ooow*. I'll think of something.'

'Let me know so I can back you up.' Ferdy was amazed at himself. From being a little man who stayed out of trouble and took orders from others except when he was running a project, here he was taking charge of the situation and being decisive. Needs must, but he had never thought of himself as a leader, more a nervous wimp. Surely, he could add to his positive points score after tonight. He'd been scared, yes. He'd been frightened silly, but he'd taken decisions and acted on them. He felt good about that. More positive points. He'd work out how many more, later.

'Who was that other woman? What was she doing there?'

Millie's voice was hesitant and weak. 'Oh, Celia. She was just a decoy. A body to make Sally think I was on the boat when I was actually behind her.'

Ferdy closed his eyes for a moment. *God*, how callous can these people get?

The car hit a pothole. '*Aagh*. Where did that Sally go?'

'I don't know,' Ferdy answered as he scanned the road ahead for more potholes. 'She ran off. She couldn't do much with only one arm of any use. But she's alive, and we've definitely not seen the last of her.'

CHAPTER THIRTY

Sunday 30th October

WORKING WITH only one arm was a pain in the proverbial. Working with an arrow through the other arm was beyond a joke. When that arrowhead had cut a centimetre into Sally's side and worked deeper into the wound with every move-ment she made, the stinging pain compounded her vicious view of life.

Their workshop, the place where she and Ali had together created tools and aids for the sole purpose of killing people in novel ways, was in the old garage. They'd had so much fun in there, imagining the methods, tweaking the designs, actu-ally producing the implements of destruction and collapsing with hysterical laughter as they rehearsed their macabre plays. The results of their workmanship could be as elaborate as an alteration to the firing mechanism of a rifle, or as simple as cutting and preparing a specific length of rope for a hanging.

With only one tiny window, the garage was dim. Sally put a bottle of Reyka Icelandic vodka on the workbench and switched on the light. That useless weed Ferdy had been unable to get sufficient grip on the arrow to unscrew the head. She herself, with one hand, had found it impossible. She needed a third hand – but there were no humans she knew who could, or would, help. A set of vice-grip pliers would have to do.

With some difficulty, Sally had to lower her body and twist her torso to put the stub of the arrow sticking out of her left bicep into the bench vice. She leaned over sideways until the stub was between the jaws, and tightened the vice with her right hand reaching across her body.

She tried to take a huge swig of vodka. With her head tilted to one side, half the spirit flowed from her lips and onto the bench.

With the pliers in her right hand, she eased them below her armpit between her upper arm and her body. Feeling where the shaft ended and the head began, she clamped them onto the metal point. Sweat beaded her face and dripped onto the bench. Cramp threatened in her side from holding the contorted position with the shaft in the vice. She gripped the pliers and turned to unscrew the arrowhead.

At first the turn was stiff. As it loosened she could take off the pliers and unscrew the head with her fingers. But the point had already punctured her flesh, so every turn widened the wound like a drill embedded in wood.

'Right, now for part two of the problem.' She took another swig of vodka and eyed her next move. She had to pull herself off the shaft while staying in line with the arrow for the best and least painful result – and it had to be done in one swift movement. No stopping, or she'd probably faint.

Quickly, before the vodka affected her judgement, she lined up. She held her left arm into her body with her right hand and took a deep breath. Then she jerked herself away from the vice.

Anticlimax. The shaft slid out of her arm quite easily.

She took a deep breath, then a deep slug from the bottle. With the stab vest, complete with the embedded arrowhead, shed and on the floor, the distraction of that sharp, cutting point was over and her mind could turn to revenge.

Given their trade and the ever present possibility of injury, the twins had built up a good stock of medical supplies. Clutching her bottle, Sally opened the chest. Antibiotics just in case, a good clean of the wound, and dressings for both sides of her arm with a bandage. What else was there to do?

Drink. Drink to fantasise. Drink to forget. Drink to calm down and so to plan with care. Drink to sleep.

2

A philanthropic chap in an Audi waved his parking ticket at Ferdy. 'No sense in wasting the hour left on it,' the man said, and grinned. 'The fees here are far too steep, they encourage cheating, the robbers.'

'Thanks, good of you. Brilliant.' Ferdy scanned the car park for CCTV and parking attendants before putting the ticket on the dash. He locked the car and headed for the hospital reception.

With a belly wound and a burned back, Millie was committed to lying on her side. Ferdy dragged a chair round the bed to face her. 'Sore?'

'I was, but they've given me something I might get addicted to.'

'Have they asked how you were injured?'

'Yeah. I told them your idea. I don't think they believed me, but the police will want to talk to me because of the stabbing. I won't be able to help them, of course.'

'Did they say how long you'll be in here?'

'Wouldn't – *ow*– commit. Several days.'

'We've got to do something about Sally,' Ferdy said. 'As long as she's alive, we're both as good as dead. You, stuck in hospital, are particularly vulnerable.'

'Except she doesn't know who I am or even if I'm in hospital.'

'Assume the worst. She's far from stupid. She knows you've suffered burns and been stabbed. The plus side is she's got a badly damaged arm. She may wait until she's fitter, but by then her trail to you will have gone cold. I reckon she'll at least try to find out who you are as soon as possible, even if she doesn't act.'

'I'll keep an eye open.'

'With your back to the door? … Anyway, I must go up to Yorkshire. Sally thinks I fancy my landlady there. She might hurt Phoebe in order to force me out into the open.'

'Do you?'

'What, fancy Phoebe? She's very nice, I like her, but … No, it's not that. Even so, I can't let her suffer because of me.' He stopped, then added in a softer tone, 'I've done enough damage. I can't let anyone suffer.'

'Ferdy, will you do something for me? I've lost my boat, and you chucked my bike into the canal. I've got the van, but the bike is an essential extension of that. Will you retrieve it, please? You know where it is, so it should be easy enough.'

Ferdy restrained a sigh. 'Sure. I'll go there now. I'll hose it down and put it on your van. But I must leave for Upper Windon early tomorrow. I can't afford to waste time on the bike, provided it's working.

3

Cleaning her wound was a painful process that had Sally grunting and squirming, as the antiseptic she used stung like hell. She placed a sterile pad on each side of her arm to cover the entry and exit wounds and held it in place with a bandage. The antibiotics she had were mild and meant for general infections. Whether they would be strong enough to ward off anything serious, only time would tell. She swallowed the first pill and put the remainder of the course in her backpack.

Dressing her left arm with her right was not easy. When it was over, Sally sat back and took a deep breath, letting the pain die away. She mulled over the whereabouts of the copy-cat and the treacherous little rat who was with her.

Even though the fire had not reached the aft of the cabin, over which the copy-cat was strapped, and the paint had not yet begun to burn, the surface must have been scalding hot; the rain had been hissing off it. That bitch must have been badly burned; she had certainly been screaming with pain. The sensible thing to do would be to seek medical attention as soon as possible, and Ferdy would help her, without a doubt. There was only one hospital in the area, so it wasn't a matter of choosing the closest one.

She was tired, mostly from the stress of her beloved sister's awful death, but tension from the canal episode and being shot with a bow and arrow certainly compounded the feeling. She was so tired, in fact, that she needed to sleep before taking any action. She set her phone's alarm for 3.30, which would give her a bit less than four hours. She'd recovered in less time than that before.

Nurses started their early shift at seven. That was going to be a busy time, with those going off duty handing over to those coming on. Sally had to be in and out of that hospital by six. It was an ideal time, as the night shift would be tired and less observant than the newcomers.

CHAPTER THIRTY-ONE

Monday 31st October

ONE THING the twins had not duplicated was their transport. They owned the Volvo, and they also owned a red Fiat 595 Abarth, a powerful little car which they reckoned was excellent for nippy getaways. They would swap the cars between them depending on what the action was. So, with the Volvo now held by the police and under forensic investigation, Sally could use the Fiat.

It was a little after five on Monday, ten days after Ali's death and two days after she had been shot on the boat. Darkness would reign for another two hours at least, especially with the dense cloud cover; although it was now dry, Saturday's light rain having broken into occasional showers.

Sally avoided the Pay and Display car park and left her Fiat in the road outside the hospital.

When she (or was it Ali?), had told Ferdy that she was a master of disguise, she hadn't been joking. They had plenty of props to use. She was dressed now in black trousers, a green blouse and a white lab coat with a stethoscope poking out of the pocket. An ID card, stolen from a previous hospital visit, hung from a lanyard. It was a cliché of a disguise, used in every movie and TV medical drama, but it was valid nonetheless.

Her left arm throbbed and ached. She kept that hand in her coat pocket, partly to act as a sling, but also to cover her weapon.

There was no point in making herself obvious, so she skirted the front entrance to the hospital and went round the side. A door marked 'Staff Only' led to an unlit passage with a storeroom to the side. Ahead was another door to a deserted corridor. Overhead signs with little arrows showed the way to Oncology, Paediatric, X-Ray and Intensive Care.

Two nurses were behind the desk of the ICU. Both looked tired.

Sally put on the best contented face she could manage and smiled at them. 'Long night?'

One nurse groaned audibly, the other said with a laugh, 'Trouble all round. End of shift in sight, though.'

'I've come to see the woman with the burned back. Margie something, I think it was. I've forgotten. Where is she?'

'Oh, that's Millie York. I heard about her. She's not in here, she's in the High Dependency Unit next door. Are you taking over?'

'Oh, no. I'm a paediatrician. We have a mutual friend and I'm delivering a message.' She tapped her pocket.

'Next ward down, third bed on the right, Doctor.'

2

Morphine did not completely dampen the pain from Millie's burns. On that frying pan of a cabin roof and desperate to get away from the heat, her back had arched so much that the main points of contact were on her shoulders and thighs. Except when she had been freed and was getting off, and her bum and right forearm were scorched. They weren't bad burns, just painful ones.

Now, an uncomfortable but bearable hot sting ran across those areas. The ache from her belly wound was nothing in comparison. They had told her what damage had been done by the knife, and that the surgeon had repaired something and sewn her up, but she had been so woozy at the time she couldn't remember what it was. All she had to do now was be patient and she would recover in time, they had told her. Meanwhile, she was condemned to lie on her side.

Millie was an early riser in any event. Even drugged she was awake by five having slept enough. Later in the day she would sleep some more. Dim lighting in the ward was supplemented by the glow of lights and screens from various bedside monitors, ventilators and other devices. One patient was on a ventilator. The sound of air rushing through a tube and the *click-thump*, *click-thump* of the machine was relentless and irritating. If she were more mobile she'd switch the bloody thing off. Instead, she lay staring at the window and its pale blinds. When dawn broke, the light would show through them and the day would begin. She'd only been there for some twenty-eight hours, and for some of those she was unconscious, but already she was bored.

She closed her eyes again. She felt nothing, heard nothing – rather, she sensed another presence. This wasn't the bustling of a nurse checking her machines. Ominous warning signals skittered through her nerves. She opened her upper eye to a slit.

The blade of an ugly knife was descending to her throat. In slow-motion it came. In slow time her mind grasped the danger. She rolled. Her back screamed at her. She didn't care. Both her hands clamped onto the killer's arm. Her climber's grip paralysed Sally's right wrist. The knife dropped and thumped on the floor.

A nurse looked up from behind the desk. '*Hey.* What—?'

Millie's grip was steel. Sally's yanking and struggling had no effect. Millie saw her grab at an equipment stand with her left hand, saw the woman's face twist with the pain. The stand was up in the air and swinging at Millie's head. She twisted away, but her grip relaxed. Sally tore her arm free, turned. The nurse was almost there. A punch to the poor woman's nose sent her flying, and Sally was out of the door and running.

Millie, panting and agonising, lowered herself to the floor and watched helplessly as the white-coated figure vanished out of sight. She looked down at the nurse who was struggling to her feet. Her inclination was to stand and watch, but it would look better and might even pay dividends if she helped, so she reached out a hand.

The nurse got up on her own. 'Are you all right dear? Did she cut you? Let's have a look.' This, in spite of the stream of blood pouring from her own nose.

Hospital security arrived, called by the other nurse, presumably. Questions; helping hands ushering Millie back to bed, more questions; it was all too much for her to handle. She was used to being in charge, making decisions, organising people, but no one seemed to be taking control in the aftermath of this murder attempt, certainly not her. Then the police came with their questions, and the direction they took after one of the nurses said that the 'paediatrician' looked just like the photo of Ratel focused Millie's mind on getting the hell out of there.

Get clothes, get phone, get out. She couldn't leave the hospital in a gown and had no idea where her clothes were – and they were soaked in blood anyway. She lay and watched the chaotic activity on the ward until an older nurse in a slightly different uniform came in and took charge, ordering non-essential people out.

All the strength drained from Millie. Her arms would not rise, her legs would not move. She felt as if her body was collapsing into a flat thing – a sort of gingerbread girl was the image in her mind as consciousness deserted her

3

They had re-dressed Millie's burns and checked on her stomach wound. 'You need to take it easy, dear. The doctor put you back together inside, but you could pull the stitches if you over-exert. Try not to move in a way that will put any strain on your tummy muscles. A couple of the blisters on your back burst in the struggle, so you've open wounds there, but they're shallow, and more painful than serious. Still, we must watch out for infection. Doctor will be around later.'

Millie slept for an hour. The shift change had not yet happened. She needed to act before it did, because after that many more people would be about, from cleaners to nurses to doctors – and later, the police. Always someone checking on something.

The ward desk was visible from her position. Whoever was manning it was away for the moment. Millie eased herself off the bed and stood to see how she felt – weak and woozy, as expected. That was the cocktail of drugs and painkillers, for sure. There was no other reason to feel useless, though, therefore she could overcome it and get on with what she had to do – the drugs would wear off with activity.

Millie walked towards the desk and the door. Carefully at first – mustn't fall or make a noise. Muted conversation and a burst of laughter came from a small room behind the front desk. She cleared the ward and set off down the corridor. At this time in the morning there were no visitors and little movement. No one stopped her and asked where she came from or was going. The front entrance was empty.

It was still dark outside, and wet following a light shower. Low cloud, reflecting the orange carpark lights, scudded past. She splashed through a puddle. Icy water soaked her legs – if only that were on her burns. Ahead was the car park, demarcated into small areas by low hedges. A woman stood at the back of her old Mercedes estate, the tailgate up. She bent and reached into the car.

Millie picked a rock from the beneath a hedge. 'Hello,' she said, conscious that her loose hospital gown and bare feet would trigger a reaction.

Without standing, the woman turned her head. Her ponytail swished to one side. She straightened up, concern on her face. 'Can I help you? Shouldn't you go back inside? It's cold out here.'

Millie shook her head.

The woman smiled. 'My name's Kate. Let me put this away and lock the car and I'll get you back inside. Just a moment.' She turned her back.

Millie slammed the rock down onto the blonde head. The bleeding began before the woman hit the ground. Millie dragged Kate further behind her car and began to strip her of her clothes. Another vehicle entered the car park. Millie watched it, but the driver found a spot closer to the building. The wail of an approaching ambulance was unsettling, but she knew it was bound for Accident and Emergency, not here.

Undo Kate's belt, yank off her skin-tight jeans with some effort. Scarlet knickers beneath. Should I? Yuck, no, I'll go without. Unbutton blouse, remove it. Bra? No. Too big for my little tits.

Millie shed the gown she was wearing and tossed it into the back of the car. Naked in the chilly air, she looked down at the woman without feeling, before slipping into her clothes. Kate was probably a size larger than her, so her blouse and jumper fitted over her dressings without pressure, and the jeans were a little loose, but comfortable.

'Kate, you look very undignified in your bra and panties. Better cover you up.' Millie forced the unconscious body into the hospital gown. 'More importantly, they might dither around thinking you're me for a short while, and I need all the time I can get.'

The Mercedes started at the first turn of the key.

4

Tiedness almost overcame Millie before she reached her van. The drugs and painkillers, plus the excitement of Ratel's attempt to kill her, and then her escape all had their effect.

She parked Kate's car half a mile from her van and walked the rest of the way. A wash, clean underwear and a short kip were needed before she undertook a trip north.

But her nap wasn't short. It lasted most of the rest of the day, leaving her feeling much better afterwards. Only the unrelenting burn on her shoulders and lower body reminded her of her miserable condition.

CHAPTER THIRTY-TWO

Monday 31st October

FERDY HAD rented Phoebe's house for a month, not know-ing at the time how long he would need to hide from Ratel. There were still another seventeen days left in the rental agreement. Had Phoebe found any other tenants over the week since Ali was killed? It was impossible to tell how long it would take for whatever was going to happen to be con-cluded, and he might need to extend his stay.

He left home early, hoping to avoid the morning rush hour. It was more than a five-hour trip to Upper Windon, giving him plenty of time to think about the twins and the two other women – all so different from one another.

Sally and Ali were beauty personified. They had such exquisite bodies, just gorgeous. It was all he could do to keep his fingers off their silken skin. Had he fallen for their sensuality, or had they enraptured him because he was so inexperienced that he had confused prettiness with niceness? One of them had taken his over-extended virginity, which was enough to make any man fall in love, at least for a while. The point was: they had used sex and their beauty to dupe him into loving them. They then had used his gullibility to further their business.

A nagging concern was the possibility that Sally really was pregnant. What on earth was he going to do about that if she triumphed over Millie?

Avoiding the rush hour was only a dream, he decided, as the traffic on the A34 and later the M1 was already heavy with trucks. Lost in his thoughts, he settled back to accept the pace set by others. The odd shower left the road wet in patches. The wipers swished intermittent strokes to keep the windscreen clear as moisture built.

Sally and Ali occupied his mind for some time before he considered Millie, comparing her to the Ratel twins, or rather the one that was left. She was a professional hit-girl. No, that must be politically incorrect: a girl is a young person. Hit-woman, though, which was accurate, sounded ridiculous. So did hit-person, even though it was PC; and you couldn't say hit-man, because she wasn't a man. What about hit-person with a cervix? *For heaven's sake.* Hit-girl, then. Was it even necessary to avoid offence when discussing a murderer?

Millie wasn't professional, she killed for her personal satisfaction, for fun. Aside from the contract she'd held with him, Ferdy didn't believe she'd done a hit to order. She'd taken victims off the street, so to speak, purely to taunt Ratel.

Even if he'd known nothing about her, she would still have been a hard person to like. Why he was comparing her to Sally and Ali he had no idea; they were poles apart. The gorgeous auburn-haired twins had attracted him, even if they were ruthless killers. They could pretend to love and be loyal with devastating effect, whereas Millie was a relentless cold fish.

Millie's form was athletic, slim and hard. He knew that because he'd seen it while assessing her injuries. It matched her face, which, although not unattractive, was always serious. Come to think of it, he'd never seen her smile. No hint of fun resided in that persona. Nevertheless, he couldn't help feeling sorry for her: immobilised in hospital, in pain, and anticipating Ratel's arrival at any moment.

And Millie was on his side, of course (for now, at least), whereas Sally wanted to kill them both.

Ferdy was dwelling on this problem as he merged on to the main road north, the M1, near Northampton. He wandered too far right into the next lane. A truck horn blared; so loud and so close, Ferdy jumped. He shook off his preoccupation and accelerated away from that driver's rage, ashamed of himself.

He was shaking; that had been close. Gradually, he settled and his thoughts turned to Phoebe. Whatever attractions the other two had, they were evil, both of them. On the other hand, Phoebe seemed to be a genuinely good person. With little evidence to support this view, he just knew it to be so. He felt more confident when he was with her, perhaps because she was supportive. She had shown empathy over his split with Sally, and she had, in her innocence, helped him immediately after Ali was killed.

He liked her, he was pretty sure she liked him, and it felt comfortable when they were together. Any progress beyond that never entered his head. Ferdy was so disillusioned with 'love' that he felt he would shun any affection for fear of further hurt. Besides, there was still a very rocky road to be navigated – a road strewn with opportunities for life and death. And life had to come first, because love wasn't much use without it, surely?

Ferdy was comfortable that he'd found a genuine friend, (although he'd thought that when Sally had turned his life around). Whether Phoebe would think the same after they'd spoken was uncertain, to say the least.

2

His heart was pounding as he entered the lane through Upper Windon. A potentially disastrous conversation had to be had with Phoebe. She was the very last person he wanted to alienate. He needed a genuine friend, not just a friendly serial killer. He had been trying to think how to sugar-coat his story, but there was no way out. Don't lie, whatever you do, don't lie, you'll only dig a deeper hole for yourself. Either she accepts your honesty or she tells you to go away. Whatever her decision, you must respect it.

Ferdy had left the rain behind somewhere to the south, but the overcast was dark and threatening. It matched his mood.

Tempted to pass Phoebe's house and carry on to the rental, he took the plunge and decided he had to get this over with sooner rather than later. Delaying the agony would not make it better.

Phoebe's face lit up as she answered the door. 'Ferdy. This is nice. Come in. Are you back for a while?'

He followed her and made to close the door behind him.

'Give it a push, or it'll spring open again. I must get it fixed. So much to do.'

This was the first time Ferdy had been inside her home and, in spite of the potentially disastrous discussion ahead, he was curious to see how she lived. Was the rental modelled on her own house? Or did she have a different lifestyle to her guests altogether?

From what he could see from the hall, the physical layout of the two houses was similar. A large kitchen and dining area lay to the right and a lounge to the left. But it was the personal items that were of most interest. An old and rather tatty Baluchi rug lay at the foot of the stairs. The hall table had two photos of her husband Henry, one where he was holding a horse and another looking down into a single scull where he was resting his oars and grinning. He must have won, Ferdy thought, unsurprised. Cousin Henry had been very focused when it came to sports.

Next to the table was a rack holding a collection of walking sticks. One or two were plain, but most were beautifully crafted, with handles of bone, antler, wood, silver and bronze.

'Henry's,' Phoebe said. 'He had a passion for them and would hunt for unusual ones wherever we went. How long are you going to be here this time?' she asked again.

'I don't know. We need to discuss something.'

'Okay. I was about to make supper. I don't think you've any food in your house, and it'll be easy to make enough for the two of us. Will you stay?'

Ferdy's honesty policy failed him. He was so scared of her reaction that he wanted to refuse and leave immediately. 'Love to. Thanks.' She might kick him out before they ate, anyway.

A small TV sat on the counter. An advertisement with fluffy obese bears was on the screen. Ferdy had seen it before, but couldn't remember what the product was. It made a lot of noise. Phoebe turned the volume down. 'Wine's in that cup-board, and glasses in that one. I'll chop onions. What have you been doing with yourself?'

'Phoebe … This is very difficult. Phoebe I think – and please correct me if I'm wrong – but I think we both recognise there's a good connection between us. It's one of those things that is very hard to define, but we like each other and, well I for one imagine there could be a future in all this if we let our relationship develop.'

Phoebe stopped chopping. She wiped the onion tears from her eyes, which were soft and smiling, her lips amused.

'There's no need to be so nervous, Ferdy. You're right, let's be honest and admit our feelings. We're both past the age of being silly about these things. We mustn't waste time. But we need to learn more about each other before jumping to conclusions too soon.'

He sighed with relief, even though he knew it was a temporary respite. 'I need to tell you something. You're not going to like it, but please hear me out. Our lives depend on it.'

The smile fell from her face. 'Tell me.'

'I have never killed anyone, I promise you. But I have facilitated several murders.'

He told her everything, about his business, about the twins and Ratel, about Millie and the awful events on the canal. He was completely honest about his role in all this. Phoebe's face fell, she looked aghast. It was plain to Ferdy that she was finding it all hard to believe. As he'd asked, she said nothing, but continued cutting vegetables.

'*Aagh*. Damn, I've cut my finger.'

'Can I get a plaster?'

'No, I'll manage. Damn, there's blood everywhere.'

'What can I do? Let me help.'

'I said *no*, I'll handle it.'

A sinking feeling crept into Ferdy's gut. This wasn't going well. But then, what did he expect after confessing to being an accessory to multiple murder?

He retreated to the far side of the kitchen and watched Phoebe strap her finger and mop up the drops of blood without a single glance in his direction.

At last she finished. 'I can't believe this, I really can't believe it. From the first moment I met you, I thought what a nice man you were: well mannered, polite and thoughtful. I got to know you a little better when you came here, and all the time my opinion of you rose. I thought we were kindred spirits. I really looked forward to you coming back and maybe staying longer. I even put off future bookings in the hope you would stay.

'And now this. You're not nice at all, you're despicable. How can I trust anyone ever again? If you're like this, is there a dark side to all my other friends as well?' Tears welled in her eyes.

Ferdy was staring at his long feet without seeing them. He raised his head to look at her. 'I'm sorry. I didn't mean to upset you. I thought it best to be honest.'

'You didn't mean to upset me? What the hell do you think your admission was going to do – get my sympathy?' She sniffed and gave him a hard, uncompromising look. 'I think it's best if you leave. I shan't repeat what you've told me to anyone, but you should go. You can stay in the house for tonight, but leave the village in the morning. I'll refund you for the lost days.'

'Please hear me out. I haven't finished.'

'Yes you have. Please go, Ferdy.'

'No. I insist you hear the rest, which is not about me, but about what happens next.'

Phoebe's mouth was set in a grim line. She didn't answer, but stared at him, waiting.

'Sally is observant. She detected a vibe between us and jumped to conclusions. She's certain that I have feelings for you, and you are therefore a tool for her to get to me. I'm so sorry, there was nothing deliberate in anything I did while I was here, but you are now in great danger. And that's why I'm here, to do my best to protect you.'

Who am I kidding? Ferdy thought. I couldn't begin to protect Phoebe if Sally came in now – I've no weapon, no clue what to do, and, most important, have no will to kill another, not even my own assassin.

His eye caught the TV. The news was on. The presenter was mumbling something, and the picture was of the front of a hospital. He leapt across the kitchen, past Phoebe, to turn up the volume. She jumped out of his way, thrusting her knife forward at him.

'Oh God. She's at it again. Already.' Ferdy gave Phoebe a look of desperation, ignoring the blade. 'Christ, we're in trouble.'

'*Keep away from me* … What do you mean?'

'Didn't you hear that? Attempted murder of a patient in hospital. That's Sally on Millie. She didn't waste any time, in spite of her injured arm.'

Phoebe let her knife-hand fall. 'Wh—? He didn't say all that. What are you talking about?'

'That's the hospital where I took Millie. Someone sneaked in and tried to kill her – cut her throat, most likely. Given who these women are, both killers, I think it's highly likely that

Sally – as Ratel – did this. What are the chances that two other people are involved at the same location?'

'*God*. So, what now? I don't want to be involved in all this. You must go – now, not tomorrow: tonight. Leave the village and disappear. I don't want to be dragged into your sordid, murderous world. Leave me alone.'

Ferdy spoke more softly. 'I wish it were that simple, Phoebe. But if I go, she'll drag you into the mess to lure me to her, no matter what you or I say. It's me she wants. So it's you who should go and hide. Once she has me, she'll ignore you. Please, you must go, and now. She believes I'm here, so she'll be here soon – tonight even.'

'I *refuse* to be a part of this. Go away and leave me alone. If you've gone and I don't know where you are, there's nothing this fantasy woman can do, is there?'

'She's not a fantasy, unfortunately. There's plenty of options when it comes to how to find me, but the easiest and surest is for her to threaten you and to let me know what she intends to do with you. If you're out of her reach, she'll have to find another way to find me, and you'll be safe. Please, Phoebe, please leave; now.'

'*No*. I'm not leaving, but you are.'

He shook his head, trying to think of another way to persuade her. 'I'll be down the road for tonight. If she comes, phone me and I'll be here.'

'If she's as vicious as you say, just what are *you* going to do about it? You're no match for this monster; how will you fight her?'

Ferdy looked down at his feet, turned and went out.

3

The burns from the back of Millie's thighs, over her buttocks and up onto her shoulders were excruciating. Every movement of the van, every slowing, every acceleration, every turn created friction between her skin and the seat. And whatever they had given her for pain had worn off. Where her skin was subject to first-degree burns there was an unrelenting sting. Where second-degree burns had occurred, blisters had formed and broken, leaving open wounds which were more painful, causing her to shift position to ease the pressure. In turn, this set her mildly scorched skin on fire. She could lean forward and ease the pressure on her back, but could do nothing about the areas she was sitting on.

She had broken her ankle and her forearm once when she peeled off a rock face in North Wales. That had been pretty painful, but she was tough and took it as a necessary experience in her climbing journey. That level of discomfort did not compare to the burns, though. And she hadn't had to endure that pain for the five hours it took her to drive to Upper Windon today.

To divert her mind, she reminisced on her path to the satisfaction she was now getting in her life. Everything she'd achieved had been through forcing her will upon others. She had dominated her class at school, bullying those who'd competed against her. She'd pushed and shoved her way up through the ranks in what was now her company, ultimately having her partner killed to gain control. Now, she was competing against an infamous serial killer to become the most famous murderer in Britain's history. Even in her recreational life – rock climbing – she had never been sporting with competitors. She had pushed, bullied and demeaned those less gifted, even putting some at risk so she could reach the pinnacle of her sport.

Millie had no doubt that her new opponent was just as forceful as she was. Although she didn't know Ratel, she instinctively realised that the woman was the greatest challenge she was ever likely to meet.

How to deal with her? There were no Marquess of Queensberry Rules in this fight, no Geneva Convention on humanitarian treatment – in fact, no human rights at all. It's winner-take-all, Millie, my girl, and if you have to shoot her in the back, so be it.

What about Ferdy? Shrug. What about him? Until August, Millie had carried on with her life of dominance without ever analysing her behaviour, even though she realised she was not like other people. It wasn't worthy of thought. The way she acted was the way she lived – why define it? Get over it. What she hadn't realised was that her lack of regard for others, her complete lack of empathy, was one characteristic of a psychopath.

But in August, Ferdy had organised that she kill a stranger. She had thoroughly enjoyed the excitement it brought her, without the slightest concern for her victim, nor the fat slob framed for the murder.

She owed Ferdy something. He had put her on this career path – if one could call it that – and he'd taken a huge risk in siding with her in her fight with Sally. It helped, of course, that there was no competition from him. So, was her mission to Upper Windon to help Ferdy or to further her own interests?

Was it even necessary to ask that?

CHAPTER THIRTY-THREE

Tuesday 1st November

AT HIS rental on Monday night, Ferdy couldn't sleep. He was too stressed over the inevitable arrival of the woman who was determined to kill him and his argument with the one person with whom he hoped to forge a relationship. It looked like that prospect was closed forever, even if he survived. But would Phoebe be all right? What could he do to keep her safe when she was adamant about being left alone? What could he do about anything?

His scale of confidence had descended into a joke. Taking score, the positive points were: his attempt to kill Simone (or get Ivan to do it); general lying to the twins (and getting away with it), in particular denying Millie's existence to Ratel; helping Millie to kill Ali, and now trying to organise how to eliminate Sally; rescuing Millie from the fire; and controlling the killers he employed. Points against were: weak will in the face of death; allowing himself to be ordered around by Ratel; and upsetting Phoebe, the one person who could be his support.

Verdict? There were more positives, but the negatives were more powerful.

He was pathetic, useless, incapable of decision, of action – he was just too weak a character. How to do better? He had to accept that he was quite likely to die, possibly in an unpleasant way. Therefore, he had nothing to lose by being bold. His spurts of confidence had to be made continuous. He had to plan. He had to outwit Ratel somehow.

His stomach felt empty. Well, it was, but the thought of eating was distasteful.

He sank a beer in a couple of minutes and went to the fridge for another.

No, you have to remain alert. But alert to do what, exactly?

But why not enjoy the last hours of your life?

And so it went. He opened the fridge and closed it three times before giving in and taking the half-litre can and not the small bottle. Back in the lounge, he allowed the huge armchair to envelop him, and curled up into the foetal position. Why couldn't he stop shivering?

The twins, Sally and Ali – Ratel – the state in which they'd left their victims: Cecil's body slumped to the ground and his severed head pinned to the tree with a crossbow bolt; Ivan, his face obliterated, his genitalia removed; another man, a pale corpse in an office chair with his entire blood volume taking up three quarters of the bucket beside him. What had he done?

A quarter to seven. *God*, he'd slept in the chair all night. It should be light soon.

A knock on the door sent a high-voltage bolt through Ferdy. He shot upright, heart pounding. His knees struggled. He groped for support. *Christ*, this is it. This is where I die. *Please* let it be quick.

Get a grip. Remember your resolve and calm down, it could be Phoebe.

He edged the bay window curtains aside to get a view of the front door. Phoebe. Thank God. Has she come to warn me that Sally is here? Or is she here to make peace? Does she need protection? He rushed to the door.

Low cloud hung over the lane, so low that its base reflected the house lights. Phoebe, her expression stern. No hint of reconciliation lay there – but something else was wrong.

'I want to set things straight, Ferdy. Too many things said in anger.' Phoebe's head was still, but her eyes kept flicking to her right.

'I know, I'm sorry.' What was wrong with her? Realisation struck and a shiver ran through him. Where was Ratel?

The answer came from the lane. 'Ferdy, step back inside and leave the door open.'

Sally emerged from the dark, at first a ghostly figure but, as she closed on Phoebe, her haggardness was plain. Her once gorgeous hair was lank and untidy, her sparkling green eyes were red-rimmed with shadowed crescents beneath, and her lips had somehow thinned into a grim line. She gripped a large knife in her right hand. Her left hand clutched her belt. Was it weak?

Ferdy took all this in, wondering how useful that left arm was, because she seemed to be protecting it. He did as he had been instructed and retreated into the lounge. In the old fireplace stood a modern log burner, the old fire tools to one side for decoration. A weapon, he had to have a weapon. A brass candlestick – too obvious; the iron handle for the fire door – too short; brass tongs – no weight in them; the poker, – yes, ideal, but how to use it? If he bent to pick it up, she would notice. It was too big to hide on his person. *Shit*, what to do?

Phoebe and Sally were at the front door. It slammed shut. Ferdy put the poker on the mantelpiece, the heavy brass handle projecting from the end, and stood with his back to the fireplace. What was he thinking? What was he going to do? Clear thought was essential, yet he had none.

Phoebe shuffled in. Shuffled because her head was bent right back to face the ceiling with Sally's left hand pulling on her ponytail. Sally's knife pricked into Phoebe's kidney area, urging her forward. With ashen skin and eyes clamped shut, Phoebe's expression was frozen in place, but she was unable to stifle the trickle of tears on her cheek.

Sally kicked the door closed. 'Right, Ferdy, this is what's going to happen. I want you to know so that you can prepare yourself. Over the next half hour, I want you to think on your betrayal. My beautiful twin has been killed. You instigated that. I'm wounded, a visit to hospital is impossible, and my life is in ruins.' She turned to Phoebe, a humourless grin on her face. 'Did you know that Ferdy was a virgin when I met him six weeks ago? With a little help from us, he turned into quite a good lover. Don't you agree?'

Phoebe didn't respond. Not a grunt of denial, nor a shake of her head.

'So, having initiated his member into some fantastic sex with gorgeous twins as a present, I believe I now have the right to remove his tool of the trade. Don't you agree, Phoebes? Isn't it my right?'

At first Phoebe didn't move. Then her eyes opened and she looked directly at Ferdy for a few seconds. He couldn't read her expression, but fear swamped whatever that glance meant. The urge to pee almost overcame him. He fought it with a desperate contraction of his pelvic muscles.

The knife was up at Phoebe's throat. Ferdy didn't know much about knives, but this one was ugly. Well, it was a beautiful shape, but it had an ugly purpose – a bit like its owner. The blade's cutting edge and back were straight and parallel until the one took a short curve up towards the tip. The back dipped in a short concave curve to the vicious point. The weapon spelt blood, sliced skin and sinew, severed arteries, mutilation and death. All that, in a nine inch piece of steel in the hands of a psychopath.

His breath was coming in short, rapid gasps. He was out of air and out of ideas.

'This is what is going to happen.' Sally didn't sound as if she was enjoying this; it was all being delivered in such a matter-of-fact tone. 'I'm going to tie your Phoebe to this chair. I shall then come to you. You will take off your clothes – every scrap of them. I shall proceed to cut off your penis. This knife is not as sharp as it should be. I might have to saw a bit. You will then sit down and watch, *if* I mercifully cut Phoebe's throat. I have no need to be cruel to her, she hasn't done anything to me, but she knows who I am. On the other hand, I may take the risk and let her live. The police will have a hard job finding me anyway.

'After that I shall carry out further cuts to your body. I'm still thinking of what. I'll get there. Eventually you'll prob-ably die of blood loss. If you try to resist, either now or later, I shall dispose of Phoebe immediately.'

'D-don't kill her. Don't, please.' Ferdy's mind scrambled to find an excuse when it was almost paralysed by fear. 'She's completely innocent and actually doesn't know who you are. I'm not sure I do. You're nothing like the woman whose computer I fixed. Phoebe only knows your face – like the rest of the population, it was on the news.'

Sally didn't answer, but held the point of the knife to Phoebe's throat and looked her in the eyes. 'Take off your belt.'

Phoebe did so with just a slight quiver of her hands. Sally took it, slid the knife under her own belt and forced Phoebe down onto the upright chair. 'Arms behind the chair back.'

Ferdy watched Phoebe comply without hesitation. At first, he was surprised she didn't resist, but then realised there was no point in her refusing when the outcome would be instant death. More time alive means more time to hope, and humans need hope.

Sally started to remove her own belt, a thin woven one. Her actions weren't smooth. She was favouring her left arm and, in struggling to thread her belt through the loops turned her back on Ferdy. Desperation stimulates courage. He slid the poker off the mantelpiece. He had it by the heavy brass handle. No time to reverse it to use the weight. One step forward.

Sally turned, the knife suddenly in her hand. She leapt forward at him. In a panic, he swiped. and hit her wrist. She screamed in pain and frustration, just two fingers still holding her weapon and scrabbling with one hand to get a better grip.

Ferdy had confidence now. He reversed the poker and aimed at her head. He couldn't strike too hard, he couldn't kill the woman. He winced as the poker handle met her skull with a crunch. The blow was weak, but Sally was down. He snatched the knife out of her hand. One slice and he was through the belt round Phoebe's wrists. Sally groaned and stirred.

Phoebe stood. She grabbed the chair for support as her legs trembled for a second, but her words were firm. 'Come on, let's get out of here before she comes to.'

'Where to?' he said. And, like a fumbling fool, he dropped the knife.

2

Phoebe raced out of the front door without waiting for Ferdy. Shock slowed his pace. He, little mild Ferdy, had actually hit a woman over the head with a poker. It had been a restrained blow; he'd been scared to hit her too hard in case he killed her. Never mind how evil Sally was, it would be murder. But had that left them with a problem?

Deep in thought, he hesitated his way down the front steps.

The sky to the south-east should have had the beginnings of a glow, but the cloud base was below the top of the ridge on the other side of the valley, so daylight was delayed. The first tiny drops of rain were cold on his head. A cock crowed in the farm somewhere. Another in the village tried to shout it down.

'Come on, Ferdy.'

'Sorry.' He sprinted after Phoebe. 'Where are we going?'

'The farm, to hide.'

'I don't know—'

Phoebe, brusque and angry: 'Of course you don't. That's why you listen to me.'

Along the lane, through the gates at the end, past the signs, 'No Entry' and 'Windon Farm' with its red 'Only' for emphasis, on past the great hulk of the combine harvester to reach the open entrance of a barn. They turned to go in.

Behind them, somewhere near the house, a car door slammed shut.

'Quick, Ferdy. Get inside.'

'Do you think she saw us?'

'Probably not in the dark. The combine covers the front of the barn – but we can't be sure. Hide.'

Although there was precious little light outside thanks to the clouds, it wasn't completely dark. It was pitch black in the barn, though, too dark to determine anything except bright colours. In front, barely distinguishable, was a massive four-wheel-drive tractor. Ferdy looked up, trying to assess its size. He had no idea tractors were this huge. Above his head was a yellow stripe labelled John Deere. He could only just see over the top of the front wheels, wide yellow things each clogged with more mud than he could hope to lift. Smells of oil, diesel, earth and hay.

Holding his hands up to protect his face from invisible spikes, Ferdy felt his way further into the barn to the rear of the tractor. Phoebe grabbed his arm and pulled him in behind it. He knocked his shin on some implement. '*Aah.*'

'*Shhh.*'

Ferdy peered round the back wheel. He started at a fleeting glimpse of a silhouette darting across the brightening entrance. She was here already. They had heard a car door shut. Why had she gone to her car if not to get something from it? She had a knife already. He should have taken it off her. Why was he so stupid? Did she now have a different weapon, a weapon with range: a gun? Or the crossbow she'd used before, perhaps? The twins had told him they didn't like guns: too noisy, and they left too much forensic evidence.

'Is there a back way out of here?' he whispered.

'Yes, but the door's rusty. It'll make too much noise.'

'What are we going to do?' He sensed Phoebe moving away. Where to? Should he follow? Since they were trapped in the barn, what was the point?

Sally called from the front of the tractor. 'Come out, Ferdy. If you come to me without a fuss, I promise I won't be cruel. You will die a quick and easy death. But if you choose to be difficult, then your end will be excruciating. I told you how. Be sensible, don't make me come in after you.'

He didn't know what to say. To volunteer to be killed would be to relinquish the will to live. He would be giving up hope. But if he prolonged what seemed to be inevitable, there was always the hope that something might intervene.

It was getting lighter in the barn. Little by little, the outlines of some tractor mounted implements became clearer. He recognised a spear fork-lifter for hay bales – he'd seen that in action as he drove north; a disc harrow – that was what he'd knocked his shin on – and one of those rotary mower things on a long arm that they cut hedges with. The only solid thing he could see to hide behind was the tractor itself.

Soon, as it got lighter, Sally would see him, if she hadn't already. Where was Phoebe? Had she found a safe place? If he gave himself up, would Phoebe escape?

It wasn't possible to see into the shadows against the light from the outside. Where the hell was Sally? He picked out an especially dark area. A good place to hide? He looked around and tiptoed towards it. What was going to happen when it got lighter? They had been stupid in trapping themselves in this barn when the only way out was past a fanatical killer.

'*Jees,*' he muttered under his breath as he knocked his shin on another piece of unforgiving steel. Where was that woman? Was he moving towards her, or to her side? Where was Phoebe now? Turning his head, he bumped it on something. '*Ssss.*' That was nearly his eye.

A clang of steel hitting concrete. Deep in the darkness, sounds of a scuffle and grunts. Ferdy froze. Where was that?

'*Let me go.* I've nothing to do with your problem.'

'Wrong. Stop struggling, or I'll cut you *now.*'

Silence.

'Furry Ferdy. I have your Phoebe here. I have a knife to her throat again, and this time I won't turn my back on you. Make your way to the entrance. I will meet you there with Phoebe.'

'Please let her go, Sally. She's no threat to you,' he called out. Then he added words he could not believe he was uttering. They shouldn't be coming from the man he knew himself to be: a little wimp, physically weak and only secure in his own environment. This situation certainly wasn't something he would create. He was a facilitator, not a doer. 'I will do as you say. Whatever you're going to do, I will give myself up, but first let her go, please.'

'Come outside, Furry.'

He weaved his way through the steel maze, looking up at every step to see his route and check for the two women who were only in this situation thanks to him.

'I'm coming Sally, but if you don't release Phoebe first, I'll run. You won't catch me and you won't find me.' He cleared his throat and swallowed before adding, 'You're wasting your time using Phoebe as a bargaining chip. We barely know each other, and to me, my life is worth more than hers. I'll take the risk that you'll kill her when you don't need to.'

3

Millie carreered down the lane towards Upper Windon. The day was still in the early stages of sunrise, so there was little chance of meeting another vehicle. She owned the road, banking on being able to avoid an early riser by seeing his lights before they collided. Hedges brushed the van on both sides. A wheel slammed into the odd pothole. Harsh braking in tractor-strewn mud caused a mini skid. Things had come loose in her tiny mobile kitchen and the rattle and crash of pots and cutlery was constant. Worse, her burns screamed at her on this rodeo ride.

She reached the field where she'd parked before killing Ali and turned in, once again hiding her van next to the hedge. In her backpack was an assortment of weaponry that she'd put together after careful thought of how she would handle different situations. From wild imaginings of life-threatening scenarios with armed police and vengeful rivals (as she herself was), she had built her armoury, supplemented by a few useful tools, cable ties, duct tape and a length of cord. Options for inclusion were her Korean Gakgung bow, a tonfa baton and a length of piano wire with handles for garrotting. She rejected a gun – unknowingly, for the same reasons Ratel had.

She'd assembled this collection over the period since taking care of Simone back in September – her first professional hit. In the intervening weeks, after it had dawned on her that she enjoyed murder so much that she wanted to make a career of it, she had stepped up her martial arts training and practised using selected weapons. Three murders boosted her convictions as she experimented with different methods each time.

But her ultimate test lay ahead – Ratel, a seasoned killer, intent on eliminating anyone threatening her superior position on the assassin's ladder. Millie was under no illusions that Ratel might have lost some of her effectiveness due to her sister's death; like her namesake, or any wild predator, she was all the more dangerous having been wounded. Ratel's (Sally's) strongest motive was to be rid of the upstart, her rival, Millie herself. After that she would focus on the simple target of Ferdy.

Millie didn't care about Ferdy as much as she'd let him believe. She didn't care about anyone actually. That was why it was so easy to dispose of people. But, she admitted, Ferdy had started her on this alternative career, and he had supported her in attacking Sally and had helped her to hospital and told her that this village was where she would find Ratel. So she supposed she owed him something. And he could still be useful. But he was expendable if it came to it.

Her belly ached, her back and thighs were burning – a mere discomfort compared to her life, so ignore it, she told herself. She half trotted, half strode down the lane towards the farm. Where were they? They were here somewhere. Did Sally have Ferdy at her mercy in the house? If not, where?

Ignoring the occasional raindrop, Millie circled the house, peeking in at the ground-floor windows. Nothing, and no sound from inside. Even with the cloud cover, it was getting light. In half an hour she would be visible from a distance. She tried the front door. It wasn't locked. In the hall she stopped and listened. Up the carpeted stairs without a squeak from the steps. Onto the landing. Pause: not a sound. She opened every door, half expecting to find a body. Nothing.

Outside again, voices came from the farm, but they were too indistinct to tell who it was.

CHAPTER THIRTY-FOUR

Tuesday 1st November

FERDY STEPPED away from the cover of the tractor and left the dark of the barn. Thirty metres away, in the middle of open ground, was a broad silhouette of indeterminate shape. The individual heads identified it as two bodies close together.

It could only be Phoebe with Sally behind her. As he got closer, more detail became apparent. Sally's right arm was around Phoebe's neck, holding her head back, baring her throat. Her wounded left arm held a knife, but not up to Phoebe's neck. Instead, it hung down at waist level.

So Sally was favouring that arm. It must have been giving her a lot of pain. It may even have become infected already and she was feeling feverish with weak muscles, sore joints and a distracting headache. She was right-handed, Ferdy knew, so she was using her strongest arm to restrain her captive while only minimum force would be needed to use the knife.

Was she too affected by her injury to fight well? Ferdy admitted he was no warrior, but he would try. He wouldn't just lie down and take it, he would fight for his life. He might even win with her in that state. But where was he getting this imaginary strength from? All he wanted to do was collapse and cry. He was talking brave while quaking inside.

He shivered, suddenly aware of the cold. His steps became hesitant as the gap to Sally and her knife closed. He stopped with ten metres to go.

'Come on, Ferdy, we haven't got all day.'

'Let Phoebe go and I'll come.'

'You have no choice, Ferdy. You either do as I say or I'll slit her throat.' She raised the knife. 'I'll give you ten seconds to obey me.'

'All right, all right. I'll do as you say.'

'Take off all your clothes.'

'But—'

'*Do it.*'

'All right, all right, I'll do it.' He held up his hand in a peace gesture, pulled it back and loosened his belt.

A movement behind Sally, at the side of the combine harvester caught his eye – Millie.

He pulled his shirt up and over his shoulders. With his head buried out of sight in its folds, he let his reactions loose for three seconds in a silent scream. Raindrops, more plentiful now, icy, pattered onto his bare back.

'Hurry up, Ferdy, this isn't a striptease for Phoebe. Shoes, jeans, underpants, get them off. Leave your socks. I think men look their most pathetic when they leave their socks on.'

Millie, for Christ's sake do something, and quickly.

His shoes and jeans were off. He was bent forward with his underpants round his knees, trying to maintain a final semblance of modesty. *Oh God* – his right sock had a hole at the big toe.

The late October morning air had its way with his skin, chest hair notwithstanding. With his hands covering his privates, undignified and stooped, he stood, and shivered. Sally was deliberately humiliating him in front of Phoebe. As a person without empathy, she would have no feelings about Ferdy's appearance. She would only be interested in how embarrassed he felt. As for Phoebe, in her situation she was unlikely to care whether Ferdy looked pathetic or not.

To hell with you, Sally. He knew he should march forward, chin up, chest out and swinging his arms. He should have marched to his death with pride, but he couldn't. He did manage to walk upright, though, but he couldn't tear his hands away from his genitals.

'Get out of here. Get off my land.' The double-barrelled shotgun looked like a pistol in the large calloused hands that held it. It was aimed first at Sally, then a fractional shift to Phoebe, before threatening Ferdy likewise. The owner had a weathered, ruddy face, and his eyes were narrowed in anger.

'*Get off my farm.* Bloody tourists. What do you think you're doing?'

Sally jerked round at the shock, relaxing her arm round Phoebe's neck. Her left hand dropped an inch, the knife with it. Phoebe swung her right leg round behind Sally's to trip her, gripped her right forearm and twisted her backwards.

Ferdy watched, open-mouthed. Floored and spitting with fury, Sally slashed through the air in front of her. Phoebe, astride the killer now, swayed back and blocked the swipe, then got a grip on the woman's weak knife hand. Sally punched her in the ribs with her right fist. Once, twice. Phoebe winced but bent that deadly hand over until the knife dropped to the floor.

No time to dress; Phoebe was struggling to hold Sally down. What if she wasn't able to for long? With only his socks on, Ferdy ran forward to help, his underpants dangling from a finger. He dropped to his knees and grabbed Sally's flailing arm, putting all his weight on it. His white bum was fully exposed. Phoebe glanced up as he appeared beside her, but quickly switched her attention back to her prisoner.

'What the hell's going on?' The farmer prodded Ferdy's bare bottom with the muzzle of his gun.

'It's all right, Joe. It's me, Phoebe.'

'*Phoebe*? Hello, luv. I didn't see you there. What's going on? Who's this spittin' cat you're sittin' on? She looks dangerous to me.'

'She's very dangerous. We need to get the police here as soon as possible. Will you phone?'

'Aye, I'll do that, but what's this silly bugger doin' with no clothes on first thing in the mornin'? Better not let my missus see 'im, she'd be after 'im down the lane with a horse whip.'

'Joe, we need something to tie her up with. Some rope or baler twine, maybe. There's no mobile signal here, so you'll have to phone the police, please. It's urgent. Tell them we've got Ratel, the serial killer.'

'Ratel? Is she Ratel? Saw her picture on the telly. Quite a looker, but now she's a prisoner and not nice at all. She looks ill to me.'

'Joe, please. It's urgent.'

'Urgent. Right. On me way.' The farmer ambled off, and then, as if suddenly realising what 'urgent' meant, quickened his pace.

Millie appeared, a big grin on her face. Ferdy could see the victory in her eyes, and that it tasted sweet. Ratel was out of the game, and now she held the blood-soaked crown.

She burst out laughing and put a foot on Ferdy's backside. 'Little man, you've such big feet. You're living proof it's not a fable. You know: the size of a man's feet are directly related to the size of … Put your pants on, you clown.'

Ferdy flushed. 'You hold her down then.'

'No need. She won't move. Will you, Ratel?' Millie had a pistol crossbow – the type used to hunt rats and squirrels – in her hand, and it was cocked and aimed at Sally's left eye. Range: six inches.

Millie stared down at her prize. She winced at the pain from her burns, then grinned. 'If looks could kill … Well mine will, won't they? Phoebe, you can leave her now. Mister, go and get some clothes on. You're making me feel cold and embarrassing your lady-friend.'

Ferdy stood and immediately turned his back to the women. Why was it so hard to get his big feet, especially damp feet, into a pair of underpants in a hurry? Why did they stick to the cotton every time? Not quite so exposed anymore, he ran to his other clothes, trod on a stone, yelped, and limped on. He struggled into his trousers, wriggled his feet into his shoes and, clutching his shirt and jacket, hurried back to the group.

Phoebe stayed where she was. Millie said, 'I don't suppose you two want to see what happens next? Of course, if you do, then be my guests. Otherwise, I suggest you go home immediately. Mister, I'll be in touch.'

'No Millie. I'm finished with all this. My business has stopped operating. I have no clients and I'm not accepting any more. Don't worry, I won't identify you and I won't talk. If I did, it would expose what I did, and that's no longer a part of my life.'

Millie never took her eyes off her prisoner. 'I understand that, Mister Facilitator, but what about your friend here? What's she going to do? She can identify me.'

'I have no idea who you are, and I'm not going to wait around to see what you do,' Phoebe said.

Sally's voice: bitter, vengeful. 'Kill her. Kill them both. You know they'll hand you in.'

Ferdy flourished his belt. 'We can use this to hold her hands while we wait for the farmer.'

'Sit up, Ratel. Hands behind your back.'

Sally kept her eyes on Millie's as she slowly raised her torso in time with the crossbow's withdrawal.

The thing about a crossbow is that, once fired, it takes a few valuable seconds to fit another bolt and draw the weapon.

Sally gave a violent swing of her head. So fast, so hard, that when Millie fired, the bolt embedded itself in the ground behind her. Sally was on her feet in an instant, the knife back in her hand. She lunged at Millie, who backed off, scrabbling for another bolt. The knife slashed the air in front of Ferdy, and Sally darted away. In seconds she was out of range of the mini crossbow and racing downhill through the field.

2

Almost at the bottom of the field, Sally stopped running. Ahead of her lay another pasture and a stream. The full height of the hill on the other side could not be seen as it lay enveloped in cloud, the flat base of which was like a ceiling above another farm. Some low tendrils even brushed the roofs as they drifted with the breeze. The house itself was hidden behind two large barns. There were no visible signs of life, but the throb of a heavy diesel engine came from some-where in the complex.

She was beside a dry stone wall between fields. A curve in the wall prevented anyone behind from seeing where she was, provided she kept her head down. Ten yards ahead was a gap where a gate had broken and lay twisted and hanging by its lower hinge. The passage was mud, mushed to a paste by a thousand hooves and rank with the stench of sheep droppings.

Sally ducked through the gap and glanced back up the hill. The copy-cat was far behind, but she was running.

The muscles in Sally's shoulders and down her back ached. She arched and bowed her spine to try and ease the pain, which worked for all of three seconds. In spite of the run, she was cold and therefore unwilling to get wet crossing the rivulet. A short distance to her left some rocks served as stepping stones. Soon she was on the other bank and climbing the slope, keeping close to the wall for cover. The throbbing of the diesel drew closer.

Fifty yards away, a man came round the side of the barn and stopped. Sally dropped to the ground between some cold, wet stones. Facing the valley, legs apart, the man began to urinate. Sally waited, motionless as a cautious squirrel while she watched his stream, willing it to stop. A month ago she would have been amused, even curious, but her current situation robbed her of any interest. She didn't need this delay; she was desperate to find shelter from the chilling rain, to find warmth and to think.

The man walked off zipping up his fly as he did so. Sally ran for the barn, her breathing shallow and rapid, her legs weakening after the first few steps. By the time she reached the building, she was gulping in air and trembling from the effort. Why? It should have been easy for her. But she knew why.

She looked back. The copy-cat had just crossed the stream. Damn that man having his leak and wasting her time. She peered round the end of the barn. Still no signs of life, but the wicket door set in the main door was ajar. Nothing could be heard from the inside of the building. The only noise was the diesel, but it wasn't in there. A strong smell of hay filled the air. Sure enough, behind a few tractor implements was a stack of bales.

If she could just climb on top and burrow down between them she'd be hidden and relatively warm – if she could: every physical movement was becoming more and more difficult. Gingerly, she touched her left upper arm. It was tender and, she couldn't deny it, swollen. It was inevitable that that was going to happen, but she hadn't expected to be on the run when it did.

Sally wiped her brow. It was damp. Sweat and cold, chills and shivers and aches. Her arm was badly infected, and her body wasn't going to heal itself.

That other idiot farmer must have already told the police that Ratel was in the area. The scramble to set up a manhunt for her must already be underway – it had to be. Officers would be visiting local farms and other possible hiding places. A blessing was the low cloud. It meant they might not be able to use a helicopter equipped with an infra-red camera that could detect her body heat. Helicopter or not, the main problem was going to be dogs. Once the animals picked up her scent, they'd be pulling their handlers off their feet to get to her. And sooner or later, they would find her.

She also needed proper medical care; if she delayed too long she might develop sepsis and probably not survive. But a hospital would mean questions and discovery.

It was so confusing. She had been taking her own antibiotics, but couldn't remember for how long. When did she start? Was it four days ago? Was the course nearly finished and hadn't helped at all? Or was it only two days and they hadn't had a chance to work yet?

Surely the farm would have a comprehensive medical kit? Antibiotics required a prescription, but maybe they had some. Would they be strong enough? Even the most powerful ones wouldn't kill her infection in less than a week. If someone found her looking for medication, the police would know exactly where she was. No, it was better to go to hospital where she might be able to fool them for a while.

But not before she had settled matters here in the hamlet of Upper Windon.

3

Millie bounded down the hill, eyes flicking from the rough surface at her feet to further ahead, where Sally should be. Was the bitch hiding behind the wall in the next field? Was she already up at the farm?

She slowed as a man came round the end of the barn and opened his fly. If he gave no sign of seeing an intruder, then Sally must not be close to him or had taken a different route. Millie waited until the man left then climbed onto the wall to get a better view. Nothing. No … wait. Yes, there she was, climbing up to the barn.

All this action had finally driven the drugs from Millie's system. She felt more alert, but her burned skin was tauter and drier and more sensitive.

She crossed the stream and started up the hill. Then she stopped, cursing her own stupidity. Ages ago, she should have woken up to the fact that a manhunt for Ratel was about to begin and that she, out in the open, was even more likely to be found than her quarry. Time would be wasted, Sally would escape and Millie would be in the police's field of vision.

Safer to stop now and walk away. But … there was something positive she could do. She fished in her pack and brought out her phone. No signal.

She climbed higher. Maybe that was all that was needed.

One bar – better than nothing.

'Fire, police or ambulance?'

'Police.'

'Police. How can I help?'

'You have a team hunting the killer known as Ratel. Tell them she's in the barn at the farm on the opposite side of the stream to Upper Windon.'

'What's your name Ma'm?'

'An-*oh*-ny Mouse. Byee.'

4

Phoebe strode away from the farm. Ferdy followed. She turned into his driveway and went up to the front door, which was still ajar. Marching in, she left the door open. Her tone was curt. 'Coffee. You still have some here?'

'Yes. Give me a moment. I need to wash my hands.' Ferdy climbed the stairs to his room, each step more difficult than the last. Why were his knees so wobbly? Reaching for the tap, he pulled his right hand back in horror. It was quivering, and he seemed powerless to stop it. No matter what he tried or willed, his hand shook. He gripped the basin's edge. His hand stilled, but the shake moved further up his arm to the elbow.

He got the tap on, but the soap slipped out of his grasp and thudded to the floor. He knelt, but his knees felt on the point of collapse, and he couldn't grip the bar without it slithering from his weak attempts to catch it.

From the foot of the stairs, Ferdy noticed Phoebe was at the front door, sitting on the top step and staring out at the lane. He was about to go to her, then thought better of it and went into the kitchen. He attempted to switch on the coffee machine, a simple push of a button, but his hand would not stay still enough to locate it. He tried to hold his right hand with his left, but that didn't work either. Frustrated, he put his fingers on the top of the machine and pressed the button with his thumb. What the hell was wrong? Shock, it had to be shock, and that would pass, eventually. But would he be able to hide it from Phoebe? He took a deep breath, and another, and a third.

Phoebe came in, grim-faced and pale. She sat at the table, put her elbows on it and sank her head in her hands.

Ferdy was hesitant, worried about her opinion of him and needing her friendship. 'Are you all right?'

She raised her head and stared at him. Ferdy tried to read her. Her cheeks seemed more hollowed than normal and her mouth was pinched. Tension radiated from her: anger, certainly; shock, naturally; but behind it all lay a cold determination. She said nothing.

'Are you okay?' he repeated.

'Of course I'm not bloody okay. Christ, Ferdy. Within a few days, a woman is murdered outside my house. She turns out to be a serial killer, run down by another psychopath. Then her psychopathic sister turns up and marches me around with a knife to my throat. She cut me, I'm bleeding. I'm held at knife point, millimetres from having my throat slit for an age while you try to bargain with her, even telling her I mean nothing to you – which means you were lying when we talked before. Then I had to fight this lunatic with her knife to get free, while this other murdering friend of yours stands and watches before taking over. And I have no idea whether this Millie will kill me or not. How do you think I feel? How the hell do you think I might be okay?' Phoebe took a deep breath.

Ferdy swallowed. His mouth dry. He opened it to speak.

But Phoebe hadn't finished. Her tone was calmer now, though. 'When I thought I'd found a friend, it turns out he was the one who brought these nightmarish people together. I don't like your friends, Ferdy. They should be in asylums. How could you let them loose in public?'

'They were not my friends, Phoebe. They were part of a business that went badly wrong.'

'*Not your friends? You were fucking two of them, for Christ's sake.*'

'I thought it was just the one.'

'*What fucking difference does that make?*' Phoebe shrieked and shook her head in bewilderment.

Minutes passed. Neither of them said anything.

Ferdy was staring at the floor. He looked up and met her eyes. Her anger had diminished – turned to sadness, he thought. 'I'm so sorry. I'm sorry you got dragged into this. I didn't mean it to happen. And I denied that you meant something to me because I wanted to strengthen my bargaining position. I was lying. Surely you can see that?'

Phoebe nodded.

'As for my relationship with them, I was a stupid, inexperienced idiot who was taken in by their charms. I believed she, whichever one "she" was, was in love with me. My life hung on a thread a few times too.'

Silence followed, then Phoebe asked, 'Is that Millie going to kill me?'

'I don't think so. She owes me, and she knows I won't betray her. If I give her the assurance that you won't either, I don't think she'll touch you.'

Phoebe sighed. 'There's no food in this house. I'm hungry. If you want breakfast, you'd better follow me.'

She still sounded gruff, although Ferdy wondered if the tension was easing between them. He wanted to prolong being in her presence for as long as possible, hoping things would eventually get back to normal. Breakfast, he didn't care about. 'Yes please.'

She stood and walked to the front door, he following behind her.

Millie was on the lower step, her backpack of tricks slung over one shoulder. 'Hello,' she said with a cheerful grin, which she quickly switched off.

Phoebe stepped back and trod on Ferdy's toe. He winced and shuffled out of the way.

'Hello, Millie,' he said, coming to Phoebe's side and forcing a smile. 'Er … all sorted?'

'No. She's gone into a barn on the opposite side of the valley.' Millie then told them why she hadn't followed Sally. 'They'll find her soon. With dogs it won't take long.'

'Once in custody, she'll be out of your reach.'

'Maybe. But remember, she's been shot through the arm. That wound can't have been treated properly, there's been no time, and she wouldn't go to hospital because of the questions they'll ask. I thought she looked ill, feverish. If she's caught, hospital might be the first place they'll take her. A lot hangs on this. If she talks, there'll be leads to me, and she'll definitely involve you, Mister, out of sheer spite. I have to get to her first, wherever she is.'

'I don't know that you should kill her. Let her serve a life sentence,' Ferdy said.

'Tut.' Phoebe's patience was clearly wearing thin. 'That's naïve, she'll be out in half the time and come for all of us.'

'She'll get a whole life sentence for every murder. She'll die in prison. And we won't be complicit in her death.'

'Nonsense,' Phoebe snapped at him. 'I'm not for killing anyone, but if we don't stop her now, she'll take us all down with her, even me. She's got to go – and before she talks. Millie?'

'Correct. It's not going to be easy, but I'll get on it.'

'Um … What about us? What are you planning to do with us?'

'Some people think I'm an unscrupulous bitch, Mister. It's a pretty accurate description of me, actually. I can be hard and cruel – but I've never gone back on my word. I told you already I won't kill you, so I won't.'

'That's fine, Millie. Thank you, but what about Phoebe? Won't you give her your word as well? Please.'

'I'd have to be sure she won't betray me before I make such a critical commitment.'

'If I betrayed you,' Phoebe said in a quiet, clear tone, 'I would fear for my life until you were put away forever. And if you were let out of prison, my fear would return. My whole life would be spent looking over my shoulder, double checking everything, to the left, to the right and in front of me, before I did anything at all: go to the shops, take a holiday, even go to sleep every night. That's no way to live. So, the stakes are too high for me to go to the police. I won't. I respect your word; you should respect mine.'

From the step below, Millie stared up at the woman who was a head taller than her, even on level ground. Ferdy thought she was eyeing Phoebe as she would an employee she was about to fire. After a tense wait, her expression softened, and she smiled. 'All right, Phoebe, since you're a friend of Mister Facilitator here, I choose to believe you. I will not kill you – but if I ever even think you've been to the police, I *will* come after you.'

'Your word and my word,' said Phoebe. 'The police will come here. Joe, the farmer, made the call to them so they'll start with him. He'll tell them who was involved, and that will include you. He doesn't know who you are, and we won't know who you are either. To us, you were a visitor who happened to come here at the start of a walk. We must protect you so that you can act. The police already know of Ferdy's relationship with Sally. But she's shown herself to be mentally disturbed. Why did she want Ferdy stripped, for heaven's sake? Is she a misandrist, or schizophrenic?' She held out her hand. Millie took it and put on a smile again.

'Ferdy,' she said. 'So that's your name, Mister.' She gave a quick wave and ran off up the lane.

Phoebe took a deep breath as they watched Millie's bobbing figure disappear behind the hedge. 'Food,' she said.

Ferdy, five foot eight in his shoes, and Phoebe, six foot in hers, walked to her house as the village began to stir. The aroma of bacon hung in the air. A man was putting rubbish in his wheelie-bin. Someone ahead of them was being pulled along by their straining, panting Labrador.

And the rain began to fall again.

5

Phoebe banged a pan onto the hob. A tea-towel hung from the rail in front of the cooker hood and obscured her view of the pan. She gave it an angry sweep. In an offhand manner, she said, 'I'm making myself egg and bacon, you want?'

'Perfect, thanks.' Actually, Ferdy didn't feel like a high-protein breakfast, but he was eager to bridge the gap between them, without a clue how best to do it. 'It's over. Do you feel happier, now?'

She rummaged and clattered through a drawer. 'Why can I never find anything in here?' Head down, she said, 'Can I trust her?' and came up with a spatula.

'I think so. She smiled at you. I thought it was genuine—'

'The smile of a cobra.'

'—Can you believe anything a killer says? I don't know, but I would relax and stick to your word. I know it's going to be difficult. The police are going to ask us questions eventually.'

The toaster popped. Ferdy put the slices on plates and eyed the egg he didn't want. It came anyway. 'Thanks. Phoebe, can we—?'

'I swore at you. It was rude. I don't usually swear like that, but I was a bit uptight just then.'

'You had every right. It's me who should apologise for everything, the way it's turned out, putting your life in danger. I'm so sorry. I don't know what I can do to make it up to you.' Then, in a stupid attempt to be normal, he added, 'Nice bacon, by the way.'

Phoebe ignored it. 'I was angry, shocked by what you'd told me. I still can't believe the incredible situation you created for yourself and others. How could you not see how wrong it was?'

'I don't know. It sort of slipped past me as I wasn't directly involved in the action. I merely facilitated what was going to happen, anyway – put together people who wanted others dead. My customers were going to have their targets killed whether I helped or not. I gave each of them an alibi and charged them less than a contract killer would. I kept myself apart from the violence, so I suppose I didn't recognise how bad it was. Only when Ratel became involved did the gravity of it all hit me. Then it became horrendous. There was nothing I could do but comply with her wishes.

'What I did was unforgivable, and I know I'm guilty of accessory to murder, or something like that, but I was blind to it at the time.'

'It was wrong, Ferdy, very wrong.' Phoebe said nothing else until she had finished cutting the last of her toast. 'I should be able to handle this, I was in the security service for years and exposed to all sorts of unsavoury things you don't want to know about. But actually having a knife to one's throat produces a different reaction to participating in an operation from behind a desk. This has upset me in a way I'm not proud of, because I'm angry at you for being a benign, essentially nice man who's a criminal on the quiet. But that shouldn't surprise me. I had colleagues in the Service who I'm sure were involved in some dark activities, perhaps even killed people. But they were nice guys, almost all of them, women too. A couple were good friends.

'The trouble is, for a person like you, who is part of my extended family, to be involved in murders shocked me. I suppose I shouldn't be shocked: we're all human, and I contributed to ops where people were sacrificed for the greater good – our greater good, anyway – maybe even killed. Rather like your activities, in a way, but the key difference between my actions and yours is that mine were officially sanctioned and done for the good of our country, whereas yours were purely to satisfy the needs of one or two selfish people.' She stared at him, shaking her head.

'I don't see you as an evil person, Ferdy. You're misguided, and have been incredibly stupid. If you want to come out of this with your head high, you need to prove to the world that you're the good man you have always pretended to be. You need to take demonstrable action.'

Ferdy stood and went to the window. The view was marred by drizzle on the pane. An old man, encased in his mac and wearing a deerstalker with the ear flaps down, was not deterred. Bent over his walking stick, he plodded steadily up the lane, then stopped to talk to someone out of sight. Some ducks squeezed under the gate on the other side of the road and began to feed on the grass verge. In spite of the murder and mayhem of the last few days, village life went on.

Ferdy wanted to ask Phoebe if she was willing to help him prove himself, make a suggestion on how, perhaps, but he was scared that her answer would be negative. Instead, he turned away from the window. 'The police will be here later today, probably. I doubt they'll get anything out of Sally very easily. On the other hand, if she thinks it's all over, she might tell them all about me – us – by way of revenge.'

'We'd better hope Millie gets to her first, then. Although I don't see that happening very easily. If you want more coffee, go ahead. The machine is the same as the one in your house.'

'Yes, thank you. I wanted to say that was an amazing move felling Sally like that. Did that come from your time in the Service?'

'Oh no, I didn't do anything like that then; I was desk-bound most of the time. I've practised judo since I was at school, and I've kept it up ever since. I'm a black belt, fifth dan, and I hold a class once a week in a village hall over the hill. It's a lovely sport.'

He almost joked that he would have to watch out, but Phoebe was hardly in the mood for that kind of humour. He would be seen as assuming too much, that one day they would have a relationship. He would have crossed a boundary – and he was suddenly conscious that he had no idea where her limits lay.

Phoebe began to stack the dishwasher. Ferdy watched for a moment. 'Thanks for breakfast. Let me help clear up.'

'No.'

'I'll go back and wait for the police, then.'

She didn't turn round. 'Okay.'

CHAPTER THIRTY-FIVE

Tuesday 1st November

SALLY EYED the end-on-end stack of cylindrical hay bales. Three-high on one side of the barn, and four-high on the other, where they almost reached the roof. So, room for another layer. She didn't know what they weighed – half a ton each, maybe – but she knew she'd never be able to move one.

Fighting back the pain and fever symptoms, she barely managed the simple climb to the top of the third level, something which she should have accomplished without taking a breath. Panting helplessly, she lay for a moment to recover and look around. Why was everything slightly blurred? She blinked again and again, but her eyes wouldn't clear. Precise focus seemed to have deserted her.

Because the bales were round, there was a narrow gap where four of them met. It was tight, but one bale had not been pushed deep into the stack, leaving a hole just big enough for her to squeeze into.

She inched down into it and found a foothold somewhere below. Her head protruded, but she could not be seen from the floor. At last she could relax and could let her breathing settle. Hay sounds cosy and soft, but the bales were compressed and hard and tightly wrapped in a mesh, with many prickly straw ends. That was a minor problem easily endured. Most important was that, degree by degree, her body warmth was building. All she needed was another two bales and she would be hidden from below, while the roof protected her from an airborne infra-red camera should the weather ever allow a helicopter to fly. Infection aside, she could stay here forever, hidden and safe.

By imagining suitable methods of revenge, Sally eased the torment in her mind. First, that usurper, Millie. The copy-cat who killed Ali. How was she to be dealt with? Dislocation of every joint in her body perhaps – fingers, toes, ankles, knees, shoulders, elbows. But not the spine. No, she had to be alive to feel the pain. And Ferdy? That little rat had betrayed the Ratel twins. What was a suitable punishment for him? Flay him alive, hear him scream, watch him pass out and then return to consciousness to feel the pull on the next patch of skin.

Sally almost dozed off, but was shaken by the sudden revving of the diesel. It moved – it must be a tractor outside. With a screech and a rattle, the main doors opened and more light flooded the barn. The diesel thundered inside the closed space. Sally kept her head down as the driver sat much higher than a standing man and might see her.

Across the top of the straw at her level she could see another bale rising from below, a great round half-ton thing clamped in a tractor-mounted grabber. Once at her height, it crept forward, pushing the bale in against the one behind her. Sally cringed; the slightest swing sideways and the grabber would knock her head off her shoulders. Coarse dry grass scraped her cheek. The grabber jaws relaxed and withdrew, brushing past her ear. The tractor left, but was soon back with another load. This one was going to box her in. If it wasn't too close, she would be hidden unharmed. If it was a tight fit, she would be squeezed into her crevice and not be able to move.

To her relief, it wasn't too tight. She relaxed, closed her eyes and felt the tension ooze out of her while she listened to the stacking of more bales further down the line. When the tractor left and she heard the screech of the closing doors, she tried to see how she could get out when the inevitable search had moved on.

But found she couldn't. Not without chewing at the netting holding the bale together and picking at the straws one by one. And she was so tired and so sore, and she needed to pee.

2

The urge to urinate was almost unbearable. Sally clenched her pelvic floor over and over, the effort exhausting. Meanwhile, she was unable to move, squeezed in to the tiny gap between the bales. She was going to be stuck here for a long time – until any search party had been and gone, and until she found the energy to fight her way out. There was no point in prolonging the agony.

The warm stream soaked her knickers and ran down her jeans. It was disgusting, but the relief was enormous. It was one less annoyance, and the loss of every little niggle was a blessing.

Her breathing had become more rapid, and her heart rate, normally in the low fifties, had accelerated to something over a hundred. She was not in a good place, but it didn't mean the end – she would beat this condition. She just needed time and a warm place to sleep...

The first sound of further trouble that she heard, muffled by the surrounding bales, was the distant barking of dogs. Then it was the voices of men nearby. Men and women, in fact, some authoritative, some taking orders. A car arrived, and the engine was switched off. The dogs were closer.

Dogs – if she were to be found, it would be thanks to the dogs.

The barn door screeched again, and with that the human sounds grew louder.

From her position, she could see through the narrow gap between the bales to the entrance and the far part of the barn floor. It was almost certain they could not see her. Uniformed police and three people in civilian clothes stood there. Judging by his work attire, another man was the farmer.

One of the dogs, a black German Shepherd, excited and barking, was pulling on his handler's lead. The pair came forward and disappeared below Sally's view.

The dog knows, the bloody dog knows.

'What work have you done in here today?' The voice was clear and sharp, the kind that travels far.

The farmer was pointing at the stack, waving his hand left and right, his words unclear.

'Right. Sorry about this, but I want you to take down all the bales you put up there today. That dog doesn't lie. Our quarry is up there, or has been. We need to find her, she's dangerous. Be careful, though. We don't want her injured.' The man turned to a firearms officer, pointed to the top of the stack, and said something indistinct.

The tractor rumbled into life. It entered the barn and started on the left of the row of bales in front of Sally. One by one, the jaws of the grabber lifted each bale and put it on the barn floor. There was only space for six.

Sally couldn't see, she could only feel and sense where the grabber was. The stack shook as each bale was raised. It was getting closer. She couldn't move. All she could do was shrink into her hole as far as possible. Her pulse was in overdrive. Her mind was scrambled, alternating between sickness, pain and exhaustion and a need to rebel against this monstrous grabber, a thing that could lift a ton with ease or rip her head off without knowing.

The urge to shout and tell them to stop this insane one-sided assault was strong, but that would be giving in, and

Sally did not give in. Ali had never given in, either. For Ali's sake, she'd hold fast. If they wanted to find her, they were going to have to work for it.

The tractor was back. The grabber was coming forward to the next bale, one away from her. One half of the jaws slide in around the bale in front of her, high and well clear of her head. It was black, made of tubular steel and shaped into a curve for this purpose. The jaws clamped tight around the bale, the diesel revved as it took the load, raised it and backed away.

Another sound above and behind her – what? The panting of a dog. She looked up. Angry dark eyes challenged hers. Drool hung from a black snout with bared yellow teeth. An unseen hand pulled the dog back.

'*Armed Police. Raise your hands.*'

Above her. Two of them. Automatic weapons aimed at her head. Shouted commands, designed to dominate and scare. Through her delirium, she stared, more with amazement than fear. Her eyes wanted to close, to shut out the image, to sleep, but the cry of '*Get your hands out, now*' kept her awake.

'*Drop your weapons. Get your hands out.*'

She struggled to lift her right arm out of the crevice. She had lost all feeling except pain in the left arm and couldn't move it. Her head sagged with exhaustion and defeat.

'*Get that left arm out. No weapons. Get it out.*'

She hadn't spoken out loud for hours. Her mouth was dry, her voice weak and hoarse. 'I can't. Wounded.'

'Get out of that hole. No mucking about, no weapons. Any tricks and you're dead, there are two rifles aimed at you.'

Sally tried to push up with her right arm and use her feet to climb, but the space was so narrow she couldn't get a purchase. The two officers watched her along the top of their rifle barrels and made no effort to help. Her strength was ebbing rapidly. She had always been a leader. She didn't recognise second place. Tears of frustration began to flow. Her head sagged; her right arm flopped across the bale.

'Are you ill?'

She didn't answer, merely nodded.

'*Sir.* I think she's wedged in there. She's weak and may be injured. We need to move this bale out a little so there's more space.'

What followed was a confusion of actions, commands, barking, and the noise of that bloody tractor. Vague recollections came to her later of the stack shaking, the gap she was in widening, hands under her armpits, lifting, general all-over muscle pain and the agony in her arm; then a stretcher, needles, outside the barn, light rain on her face, an ambulance, and a bumpy ride with fluid bags swinging from the roof; strange faces bending over her, police, paramedics, nurses; a hospital trolley speeding along polished corridors, ceiling lights flashing past; and finally a bed – a warm comfortable bed – and oblivion.

CHAPTER THIRTY-SIX

Wednesday 2nd November

MILLIE DROVE slowly through the hospital neighbourhood in her van, looking for a place to park. It had to be close and the route to it from the hospital doors short and, preferably, hidden. That would be ideal – in fact, too ideal to be true. To use the car park would be suicidal. There would be no quick getaway with number-plate recognition cameras and barriers. She found nothing suitable, so she changed her plan.

There were three council car parks in the town. Millie tried the one furthest from the hospital, but it had a height restriction bar lower than her van, so she moved to the next closest. That worked, and so, with the vehicle secure, she released her bike from the rear, feeling the stretch of the taut, burned skin on her shoulders. The bike hadn't suffered from its short spell underwater. There was a bit of additional mud which Ferdy hadn't hosed off, but the chain and pedals had been well oiled so it felt the same to ride as always.

The rain had stopped overnight, but the roads were still wet with puddles everywhere. She cycled at an unobtrusive and comfortable pace to the hospital – not too fast and not too slow. She didn't take her backpack: she didn't need any equipment for this mission, not for a bed-bound target.

Near a staff entrance was a small block without windows but with vents in its sides – a standby generator house, maybe? Alongside that was a shipping container. A narrow gap lay between the two. She could either chain her bike to a post or hide it in the gap. Chaining her bike would slow her escape, but if she didn't, and the thing was stolen, she'd have no means of getaway. Was it likely to be stolen outside the staff entrance? Would anyone even notice it in the narrow gap? No. She pushed the bike into the channel and strode towards the door.

Warm air welcomed her as she went in. She opened a door and found herself in a public corridor with her way blocked by an elderly lady shuffling along with the aid of a walker, an equally ancient man in support. The door was marked 'Staff Only' on the public side, and a fire extinguisher was mounted on the wall next to it. It was vital that Millie knew exactly where her escape route lay, so she memorised every detail and counted the doors as she passed.

The corridor linked the two main buildings and was also a tunnel, given that part of it was underground. Along its route lay the main kitchen, several numbered stores and many restricted rooms. A steady stream of visitors and staff moved in both directions. Millie controlled her impatience and moved along the corridor at the same leisurely pace as everyone else, except for the odd doctor or nurse rushing somewhere.

She emerged at the main entrance. A mass of people were queuing for four elevators, or milling about, waiting; still others studied the information boards. Too many for comfort, too many to block her escape. On the other hand, they could be camouflage – a crowd to hide amongst.

A box of surgical masks stood next to a hand-sanitiser dispenser. Millie took one, put it on, and approached reception.

'A woman was brought in yesterday with a police escort. Can you tell me where she is now, please.'

'Do you have a name?'

'Sorry, no.'

The receptionist tightened her lips and gave an audible sigh. Scanning her computer, she said, 'Intensive Care.'

Down one floor using the stairs-cum-fire exit, Millie followed the signs. The dense crowds were behind her. Only a few people were going her way; one, a staff member pushing a trolley of medical equipment, was in the passage to X-Ray, the theatres and the ICU, whose set of double doors was on the left. A cheap plastic chair stood to one side, and a large uniformed policeman was pacing back and forth across the entrance in an attempt to keep moving in the limited space, like a big cat in a zoo. What a job, Millie thought as she walked past. Reaching the waiting room for X-Ray, she turned round and strolled back to the ICU.

The officer was young, fresh-faced, and stood a foot taller than her. If she hadn't been wearing a mask, she'd have grinned at him. Instead, she said, 'You look bored.'

Other than a brief flick in her direction, his eyes never met hers. Instead they scanned the background. 'Yeah. Not much to do. Got to keep a watch, though.'

'You protecting someone, or have you got a prisoner in there?'

'Sorry, I can't discuss my job, particularly with reporters.'

He was undoubtedly junior and probably still determined to be diligent. 'Oh, I'm not with the press. I was just curious, with you pacing up and down as you were. We don't often see policemen on duty in the hospital.'

He gave a meaningless grunt. She wasn't going to get past him with ease. 'Oh well, I must be going. I hope your shift stays boring … Oh, that sounds terrible. It was meant in the nicest way.'

The officer flashed a weak grin. 'Bye.'

Millie walked on, but turned and looked back after a few seconds. The policeman was watching her and talking into his chest-mounted radio.

They know, she realised. That damn farmer must have told them of the woman who had Ratel a prisoner. But how did they know to look out for me here, a few steps from the killer's bedside?

She increased her pace, but a doctor overtook her, head down to his phone. His pager beeped. He grabbed it, read it, spun round, dodged Millie, and ran back towards the ICU.

2

Ferdy did not sleep well. He hadn't been shopping and there was no proper food left in the house. He had munched his way through a packet of biscuits for Saturday night's supper. That had left his mouth as arid as the Empty Quarter in Saudi Arabia. There was water, of course, but that wasn't what he wanted, and there was only one beer left. Drench his tonsils to relieve the drought today, or save it (or a flat half of it) for Thursday night had been his dilemma. Not exactly vital, this, but he was depressed, and muddled in his thinking. Little things were assuming too much importance for their real worth.

On Monday morning he gazed out of his bedroom window without seeing, his mind a dollop of scrambled egg. The police would be there shortly. What were they going to make of the second drama in ten days in a sleepy little hamlet in Yorkshire? What questions were they going to ask a mild little man who was present on both occasions? Were they going to deduce that this wee chap was a serious criminal who knew both these beautiful women? What on earth were they going to make of the fact that he was stark naked (except for his holed socks) on a cold October morning with a murderess dictating his actions? And what were they going to make of

Phoebe's presence at both incidents? And her connections to him? Phoebe was angry and disappointed in him – would she tell the police he was involved? Surely not, he'd begged for her life after all. But it was possible.

He couldn't deny that he knew Sally; the police at home knew perfectly well they'd been lovers, and his nosey neighbour had seen her coming or going from his house on numerous occasions. Up here, there were villagers who had seen her at Phoebe's B&B. And of course, Phoebe had met her too.

All he could do was to stick close to the truth, namely: he'd had a girlfriend named Sally, but she had been killed nine days ago. This other woman who attacked him (actually Sally) he did not know, and he had no idea why she had been intending to kill him. As for the random hiker, Millie, he had no idea who she was either, but he was beyond grateful that she had intervened.

And that was how his interview with a female inspector and a male constable progressed. They had already been to see Joe, the farmer, and were on their way down the lane to talk to Phoebe. They thanked him, leaving him in limbo, not knowing whether he'd passed a test or if there was more to come.

If there was more to come, he could be in trouble.

The greatest danger to him was what Sally might tell them. But Millie had thought Sally was seriously ill, and Ferdy agreed. If it were true, then maybe the police had not yet been able to interview her.

At the moment he was free to leave. The police had his address and could contact him again if they wanted to. They had given no sign that they were suspicious of him.

And Phoebe? If he was arrested, it would be all over for his hopes of being with her. Maybe it was time to swallow his disappointment over her and leave. He made himself another cup of coffee and went back upstairs to continue staring out of the window and ripping himself apart.

His desire for Phoebe to be a friend (being her lover didn't enter his troubled head) was intense. Was he in fact falling in love with her? Or was this simply a need for an ally in a time of crisis? He couldn't stand that this lovely woman was angry with him, even more so because she was right. What he had done with his life was indefensible.

Phoebe was coming down the road, and Ferdy's pulse quickened. She looked so 'country': her long stride, leather boots and heavy green shooting jacket. Was she on her way to see him, to invite him for breakfast again? No, she marched past the house without a glance and carried on through the farm gates. It was a perfectly natural thing for her to do. Why shouldn't she go and visit a neighbour? It was her business and nothing to do with him. He barely knew her, for heaven's sake. A wrench passed through his stomach, nonetheless.

A short while later, she came out of the farm gates. Would she come to see him now? He ran downstairs and struggled into his shoes – always difficult when in a hurry. He had the front door open as she raised her hand to knock.

'How did your interview go?' he blurted.

'Good morning to you too, Ferdy. I came to ask you the same question. I've just seen Joe. He told the police he didn't see much or what started the whole scene, but what we know he witnessed, he told them. I don't think there's anything damaging in what he said. What about you?'

'I stuck to our agreement. I have no idea who those women were. This crazy one comes and catches you and makes me strip, and then this hiker rescues us before disappearing.'

'When it's summarised like that, they're never going to believe it. I wonder what they got out of Sally?' Phoebe glanced through the kitchen cupboards and the fridge. 'There's nothing here except some milk and half a beer. What did you eat last night?'

'The second half of a packet of biscuits washed down with the first half of that beer.'

She turned away from him, but did a slight smirk cross her face? 'What are your plans? How long are you going to stay?'

'I'll feel very uncomfortable being far away before we know the outcome, what the police think or are going to do. I want to be here to confront it.'

'Well, you had better do some shopping, hadn't you? I can't continue to feed you for an indefinite period.'

'*No.* No, of course not. I'll go today. And … and if there's anything you want, I'll get it for you. You'll have to give me directions, though.'

'I will, but you had better come and eat something first.'

Why did she keep offering to feed him when she said she wanted him to go?

3

His shopping trip had taken an hour and a half, mainly because he got lost navigating the country lanes. But eventually Ferdy returned to the rented house and lugged his bags in with zero enthusiasm. Shopping was always a downer and, on top of Phoebe's scathing criticism, it had left him dispirited and depressed. His mood was not improved by the grey overcast, which had an air of permanence about it.

The radio was playing the last song before the news. He went back out to the car and tucked a box of beers under each arm, returning to hear of a major traffic incident on the M1 – boring. But the next item wasn't:

A woman who was allegedly under arrest for murder passed away in hospital this morning. She was under police guard at the time of her death, the cause of which has not yet been confirmed. Speculation that the woman was the infamous Ratel serial killer has been played down by police, who say that the arrest and the circumstances of her death are subject to investigation.

Ferdy didn't know what to feel. He sat at the table and stared out into the garden. He should be elated, but he felt a sense of loss in spite of the appalling characters she and her sister had been, and in spite of the ghastly non-future they had planned for him. Those two had given him his first experience of true love (on his side, anyway), and they had rid him of his virginity. Thanks to them, he was no longer the oldest virgin male in the world. Neither of those two epic milestones could be forgotten.

On the other hand, his life and Phoebe's life were no longer in danger from Ratel. Millie had given him her word that she wouldn't kill him, and he believed her. He believed she wouldn't kill Phoebe either – not without cause, anyway.

So, did he feel elated? Could he live free again?

He rose to his feet and began to stack his shopping into the cupboards and fridge. He kept it neat: baked beans in one row and tinned fish in another, pasta sauce, spaghetti and bread on the next shelf. Phoebe's goods he kept out: fresh veg, fruit and frozen fish.

The twins had given him a few serious life lessons, but they had also succeeded in teaching him something his dad had failed to do over an entire childhood – it's best to be tidy.

With everything put away, he had a weird feeling that he was growing in stature with such a massive weight suddenly lifted off his shoulders.

He was on the winning side, and most of the reason for that was through his own, sometimes ridiculous, efforts. Was it time to give himself more positive points for his work? If he summarised them, would the positives outweigh the negatives now? He'd played a significant part in bringing Ratel's activities to an end. That counted for a lot, but was it enough?

A more important question was: had he become a better human being? Only Phoebe's reaction could tell him that. If she accepted him as a friend, at least, then that would be good enough. He would have succeeded.

But if he couldn't be friends with Phoebe, then this saga was just another awful experience that would end without a satisfactory conclusion.

The news about Sally had to be shared with Phoebe, if she hadn't already heard. Maybe she would take a softer approach to him with the pressure off. He gathered her two bags and set off along the lane. The butterflies started to dance around his stomach again at the uncertain result of his visit.

CHAPTER THIRTY-SEVEN

Monday 31st October

PHOEBE'S FRONT door was ajar. Odd, as this was November and most people were conserving the heat in their homes. Something felt wrong, and Ferdy's neck crawled. With excessive care, he pushed the door. It swung open without a sound. Ahead of him was a short passage to the kitchen, to the right was the dining room, and to the left was an open arch to the foot of the stairs and another door to the lounge. A voice sounded to his left. He froze.

Millie.

What was she doing here? Whatever it was, it couldn't be good. There was no answer to whatever she'd said. Ferdy crept closer and snatched a look. Millie was facing away from him, looking up at Phoebe, who was standing on a chair, her back to the stairs. Her hands were out of sight behind her –

bound, no doubt. Round her neck was a rope which was tied to the handrail on the landing above the stairs.

Millie gave the chair a light kick. It edged an inch across the wooden floor. 'You broke our agreement, Phoebe. You told the police about me, gave them a description, didn't you?'

'I told you: no, I did not.'

'You must have done. That copper was on the alert for me. He called on his radio while he was looking straight at me. Our eyes met. I wore a mask, but I'm on TV now. They have CCTV of me in the hospital. They knew to look out for me. It had to be you, no one else knows anything.' Millie gave the chair another kick sending it a couple of inches further across the floor.

The chair could probably move another six inches before it left Phoebe's feet dangling in space. Ferdy dithered – what could he do? He ducked back out of sight but saw the recognition in Phoebe's eyes as he moved. What did he see in them? Hope, defiance, the desire to fight? At the front door was Henry's precious collection of walking sticks. A heavy blackthorn one with a bronze copy of an antler for its head stood out. His pick gave him confidence; his anger was building.

This is crap. I've had enough of these bloody killer women ruining my life and threatening my friends. I'm not having it anymore. It stops here and now, whatever the consequences. No more being the little man who organises but doesn't do anything. I don't care if she wins, I'll go down fighting. She won't expect me to fight. Tough, she's got another think coming.

He reversed the stick and felt the satisfying weight of its head so far from his hand. Which part to use, the long point of the antler or the blunt, roundish bit that fits under the heel of your hand? The antler tip looked vicious, it would go deep into her skull. Maybe too vicious.

'Why don't you admit you sold me out, Phoebe? If you do, I might stop kicking the chair. There must be just two more kicks before it falls out from under you.

'Did you know that a legal hanging is just a way to break you neck so you die instantly? That's because you drop a few feet before that hard knot jerks your head back while the noose tightens. Do you know what it's like being hanged without a drop to break your neck? It's slow strangulation. Painful, with the rope biting into your throat, made worse because you won't be able to stop kicking and struggling for air. And every movement, every jerk of your legs makes it worse still. I watched a documentary on public hangings once, so I know what it looks like. It's tortuous – not pretty.'

As Ferdy appeared in the doorway again, Millie gave the chair another kick. Phoebe said nothing, but her feet were only two inches from the edge. One more blow and it would topple.

The antler took on a mind of its own. It swung up in his hand and came down harder than he would have dared, thudding into Millie's skull. Ferdy swore he heard the wooden shaft creak as it struck.

Millie was down. She swung round to the left. Her foot caught the chair – sent it skidding across the wooden floor.

Phoebe was swinging. Ferdy leapt forward, grabbed her legs from the front, and lifted. She was coughing and gasping, but at least she could breathe. Ferdy couldn't hold that position for long, though. 'Try to put your feet on my shoulders. I'll hold one leg, keep it straight, get the other out.'

She coughed and rasped.

A desperate glance at the chair. That would save them, if he could get it. He could just reach it with an outstretched foot. But only if he took all her weight on his one leg. He wasn't strong enough.

It was out of reach.

'Are you with me, Phoebe?'

Whatever hell she was going through, her thoughts were obviously clear. Holding all her weight by clinging to her left leg with one tight arm, Ferdy loosened his grip on her right, allowing her to edge it out of his hug. She got that foot on his shoulder and followed with the left. Ferdy could stand with her balanced there for a while at least. But he was only small and not a powerhouse by any means. The time would come when he would collapse and Phoebe would hang.

'Can you rub away at whatever's tying your wrists?'

'No, there's nothing here. We need help.'

'And *now*.'

Phoebe screamed, '*Help, help!*'

Ferdy followed suit. They alternated, shouting for an age, but the village was silent.

The pressure on Ferdy's knees, on his feet, on all the vertebrae from his neck to his pelvis, was almost intolerable. The muscles in his legs were quivering. *Please*, somebody respond.

'Ullo?'

'*Help*!' Phoebe shouted.

Ferdy couldn't manage more than a squeak.

Joe stuck his head round the corner. 'What's up, lass? … *Ooh*. Bluddy 'ell.'

'Take her weight off me – please.'

The farmer, in a series of ponderous moves in his wellington boots and with great ham-like hands, went behind Phoebe and took her legs off Ferdy's shoulders. 'Right. Got her. Got you, Phoebe, lass. Nuthin' to worry about now. You better get up there and untie her, son. Sharpish, like.'

Ferdy could hardly move. He'd been compressed and was gradually expanding. He wasn't going to fight with knots. He walked, trying to hurry, but wobbling, to the kitchen and found a knife, got to the stairs and crawled up on all fours.

Phoebe kept her knives sharp, and it only took him a few strokes to sever the rope. Joe lowered her to the floor, keeping one of his massive paws on her shoulder. 'You all right now, Phoebe, lass?'

'Yes. Thank you, Joe. Thank you, Ferdy. That was close and bloody uncomfortable. Is that woman alive?'

Ferdy had almost forgotten Millie during his recovery from straining so much. Had he killed her? He turned her onto her back. It felt as if he was moving a bag of compost, and a sudden fear gripped him. Was this murder? He looked up at the others with a silent plea for support.

'Can you feel a pulse, Ferdy? In her neck?'

'Is she breathing? Hey, isn't this that woman from yesterday mornin'? What's goin' on here, Phoebe? What's all this murder and police and strangers and stuff these last few days?'

'I'll tell you, Joe, but right now we have to sort this woman out. Ferdy, for heaven's sake, is she breathing? Is there a pulse?'

'I … I don't think so.'

Phoebe dropped to her knees and pushed him out of the way to make a quick examination. 'She's dead. Joe, call the police.'

Joe ambled off to find the phone.

To the background tones of Joe telling the operator that there was an attempted murder and a dead killer in the village, Ferdy slumped back against the stairs. For months he'd been facilitating people getting killed – dealing in death. He'd even forced Ivan to do it (never mind that the little creep had failed). Now, the irony was that having left his life of murder behind him, he'd actually killed someone. Okay, it was to save Phoebe's life, but did he have to hit Millie so hard? Why did he do that? Why had he put so much force into the blow? Finally, after avoiding the law for so long, he was going to prison for defending an innocent person.

'Relax, Ferdy. You won't be arrested for murder, nor will you be convicted of manslaughter. If the police arrest you now, they'll release you after their investigation is over,' Phoebe said.

Ferdy realised he'd been mumbling his guilty predicament out loud.

'Between Joe and me, our statements will prove you acted within the bounds of self-defence. I'm going to put the kettle on.'

'Are you okay?' he asked.

'Not really. I'm a bit shaken, but I'm buggered if I'm going to let anyone notice.' She went out. Clattering noises and a kettle heating up could be heard in the kitchen.

Phoebe came back with three mugs of tea. Joe told them the police were on their way. 'But I can't wait for 'em, I've a farm to run. I'll just down this.' He raised his mug. 'They know where to find me.'

With the aid of a stair spindle, Ferdy worked his way up on to his feet. Weakness and lethargy had overcome him. He climbed three steps and sat down, his knees shaking. Regarding the body on the floor, he wondered if he should give himself another positive point to increase his confidence score. No, it was too late for that silly test now. Phoebe had to be his judge. Only her reaction should count.

'We can go to the lounge,' Phoebe said.

'I'm okay. I can sit and look at her body from here. Do you realise that, if I'd used the pointed end, she would have had a deep hole in her skull.'

'True. As it is, she's got a hole anyway, and it's bleeding out onto my floor. The sharp end would have been deeper, but either way, she's dead. Shift up.' She climbed the three steps and sat next to him. Ferdy put his head between his knees and closed his eyes.

2

Millie was inert. Phoebe stared down at the body, her mind racing over the events that led to this. Then her eyes narrowed for a moment. She glanced at Ferdy; his head was still down. She sat upright and put a hand on his shoulder. 'I think we deserve another mug of tea while we wait for the police. Your turn to make it, Ferdy. Everything is still on the counter in the kitchen. Just one sugar for me, please.'

She watched Ferdy get to his feet. He took a wide step over Millie's legs and disappeared down the passage. The roar of the kettle began. Phoebe descended to the floor, pulling her sleeve down to cover her hand. She lifted the walking stick and lined herself up with Millie's head; this had to be precise. 'You moved, Millie. I thought you were dead. Far better for all of us if you stay that way.'

The bronze antler head whacked into exactly the same spot as Ferdy's original blow. The kettle's roar peaked and died. Phoebe laid the stick down where she'd found it and once again checked Millie for a pulse.

3

Back on the stairs, Ferdy handed Phoebe her mug.

'Thanks,' she said. 'Cheer up and take that glum look off your face. One half of the threat to us has been eliminated. We only have to worry about what Sally tells the police.'

'She's also dead. Died of causes yet to be determined, this morning. It was on the news.'

Phoebe smacked his knee. 'That's fantastic, Ferdy. You're off the hook. No one knows your history now.'

Ferdy didn't answer. He continued to stare at Millie's body for several minutes. 'I can't believe what's happened. I've actually killed a person. I'm a murderer. *I'm a murderer, Phoebe.*'

She put her hand to his chin and turned it so he could face her. 'You saved my life by taking hers. You are not morally wrong, Ferdy. She chose violence. In doing so she had to expect violence in return. We may not like it, but much of the way the world is run, both seen and unseen by the public, is a matter of neutralising your enemy before they do it to you. Killing may sound extreme, but you've done nothing wrong. It was what happened in a fight that was started by her – that's it.'

'I suppose so. But how can you be so calm? You were literally inches from death a few minutes ago. Your life was hanging by a thread. Oh, that was stupid – sorry.'

Phoebe giggled. 'More a coarse rope, actually. Still punny, though.'

They fell silent for a few minutes, each digesting what had happened. Then Phoebe took a deep breath. 'I have a confession to make, Ferdy. I'm sorry I flew off the handle when you told me what you do for a living. It was hypocritical of me to judge you.

'I told you I spent my time in the Service behind a desk. That's not entirely true. Whilst I wasn't in charge, I did take a prominent role in an operation which ultimately resulted in the deaths of two people – and I knew beforehand what the result would be. When I was asked if I was willing to participate, I said yes, because I thought it would look good on my record. Afterwards, though, I became very uncomfortable with my role and tried hard to put it behind me, which I thought I had done. Then you confessed, and the memory, the guilt, came back and hit me like a slap in the face.'

Ferdy stared at her, scarcely able to believe what he was hearing from this woman who, his instincts told him, was the kind of person who was above the murky world he had been inhabiting. 'You have skeletons too?'

'Although I didn't have direct involvement; I did dupe the pair into believing that we were protecting them. I looked them in the eye and spoke with conviction. They trusted me. I even saw them onto the plane and waved goodbye. Deep down, though, I knew full well what was going to happen. After I learned of their fate, my shame and disgust at my contribution gave me the impetus to resign.

'The reason I was so angry with you was not just because of your awful business, but because you brought my own actions back to me when I thought I'd got over them. I thought that taking our relationship further would be a constant reminder of what I'd done, and that I'd never be rid of the guilt.'

'Then we have more in common than I thought.'

Phoebe's right sleeve still hung below her wrist from pulling it over her hand so she wouldn't leave fingerprints on the walking stick. She pulled it up. 'More than you realise, Ferdy. What separates us is that I was part of an official team and we all worked together. It wasn't seen as a crime. But I knew it wasn't right, and I went ahead anyway.'

Ferdy nodded. He pointed at the corpse. 'How did she overcome you – get you into that position?'

'She knocked me out. Crept up behind me, I suppose. I didn't hear her.' Phoebe ran her hand over the back of her head and winced. 'When I woke up, my hands were tied behind my back and the noose was round my neck. She'd already looped the rope over the banister upstairs, so when she pulled, it forced me to climb up onto the chair. She kept the tension on while she went upstairs and secured the rope. I couldn't move without being throttled. You saw the rest.'

Ferdy turned to look directly at her. 'Did you tell the police about her?'

A smile flickered across Phoebe's mouth. 'Mmmh. It might have slipped out in passing.'

'You promised not to.'

'Does that offend you, Ferdy? Would you rather let a serial killer roam free, or break a promise?'

'Sorry. You're right, but it seems wrong.' Ferdy stared at his feet without seeing them. 'Is it over? Is this the end of it, is there nothing more to dread?'

'Nothing. With Sally, you put your life on the line for me, Ferdy. I will never forget that.'

'Not really. She gave me the option of a clean death or a tortured one. That she might have let you go was just a bonus.'

'No. You could have run away, as you said, but you gave yourself up in the hope she'd let me go.' Phoebe suddenly started laughing.

'What's so funny?'

'That scene. You. Stark naked but for your socks, bending over that woman with your bare white bum in the air. That was very funny in retrospect. Weren't you cold?'

'Let me tell you, *I* wasn't amused. Yes, I was bloody cold, but what could I do? I had to hold her down. I was freezing.'

Phoebe giggled again. 'And then Joe prodded your bum with his shotgun. I know a cartoonist, I'm going to commission him to draw that scene.'

'Oh God.' Ferdy put his head in his hands and took a deep breath, the sort that precedes a meaningful utterance. 'Phoebe, my name isn't Ferdy. My real name is Felix, and I'm going to use that from now on to signify my return to a normal life.'

Phoebe smiled. 'Aah. That's been niggling me. I thought you weren't introduced to me as Ferdy, but I couldn't remember. One other thing I don't understand: why did Sally call you Furry? You're no hairier than many other men.'

'You haven't seen my feet, I had socks on. They're not so bad, she was just being her cruel self.'

'Oh … Having hair on your feet is hardly something to worry about.'

'You haven't seen mine.'

…

Silence.

…

'Phoebe … '

'Yes?'

'Can we start again?'

'I'd like that, Felix.'

*****

Before You Go

Thank you for reading *The Facilitator*. Hopefully you enjoyed it. If you did and have a moment to spare, writing a short review on your favourite site will be greatly appreciated. Authors depend on reader opinions in order to produce enjoyable works. Reviews help authors to further their careers.

To find out more about the author and his works please visit: https://www.helifish.co.uk where you have the option to subscribe to his mailing list.

You can also find him on Facebook: http://www.facebook.com/casole74

Also by C.A. Sole

Thirty-Four – The first Andrew Duncan story. Andrew is a unique specimen, and the secret in his DNA could change humanity. Big Pharma sees massive profits from learning his closely guarded secret.

Andrew is framed for a gruesome murder. There are two suspects in his eyes: the giant pharmaceutical corporation and a gang of child traffickers. Is there a connection between these two? He must find out to prove his innocence and employs barrister Kirsten Pearman to defend him. But her determination to destroy the gang goes beyond the professional – why?

As Andrew tries to dodge the tentacles of Big Pharma and avoid the police, he finds two abused children. He's torn between rescuing them or leaving them to their fate in order to bring down the entire gang of traffickers. All the while, with the help of his dog, he has to find a traditional, trained assassin before the man finds him.

#

Running Forever, the second Andrew Duncan book, follows on from *Thirty Four*. Andrew is still hiding from Big Pharma, so he takes a distant job hunting wild life poachers in Kenya.

His escape from the pharmaceutical giant's relentless pursuit finds him in the eastern Congo, a battleground of warring factions and a hub of wildlife trafficking, of which Jacques Mertens is the kingpin.

This cruel trade is so abhorrent that Andrew is compelled to fight it. Mertens will kill to protect his business – he's used to it.

When Andrew was ten, he witnessed the murder of his friend. All his life he has been looking out for this killer and, by sheer coincidence, in the Congo, the man appears before him. He too must be dealt with before Andrew can lead a peaceful life.

#

In *Scott's Choice,* Cuthbert Jonathan Scott is a young man with a dominant adventurous spirit. He grew up being indoctrinated by his father into an approach to life that was completely at odds with his nature: take no risks, caution in everything, settle down while young, save your money, on and on. A random event results in a decisive moment. He is torn between two options: following his father's teaching or being himself.

Two personae emerge. One, Jonathan, begins a life following his natural instincts. His spirit of adventure predominates. His choice has consequences which bring several life-threatening events but also great rewards.

Jonathan's alter ego, Cuff, is the brainwashed youth who tries to adopt the more cautious approach. But his nature conflicts with this and leads him on a dangerous path to escape the mundane existence which was the consequence of his choice. It seems he cannot avoid risk. Indeed, danger appears to seek him out.

Two independent stories develop in *Scott's Choice*.

The tales are linked only by his friends and enemies, who continue to influence and react to events in Cuff's life in one way, and in Jonathan's life in another. However, certain events are common to both and fixed in the calendar.

Nature's Justice is the first sequel to *Scott's Choice*. It traces Jonathan's life as he and Gudrun experience a horrific event in Southern Africa. Witnesses to the killing of a rhino and the sighting of the person responsible for the trade in horns, they are chased and hounded over a thousand kilometres from the Kruger Park through South Africa and Botswana to the Victoria Falls.

The Pilot is the second sequel to *Scott's Choice*. Cuff Scott tries to follow a career to become an airline pilot, but his attempts to lead a stable and prosperous life are ruined by events.

At the flying school where he instructs, he becomes aware of someone smuggling illegal immigrants into the country by night. That's not his only problem. One of his students is being stalked by an increasingly dangerous man, and she thinks it's him.

It seems that trouble seeks him out and brings his inherent instinct for adventure to the fore. He is forced to question whether he's really the persona he's trying to be.

#

A Fitting Revenge is a thriller about extraordinary events that happen to ordinary people.

Your friends are in deep trouble. What if you take a step too far in avenging them?

In rural southern England, Alastair is helping his close friend to avoid a punishing divorce from Sandra. But Sandra is ruthless, and determined to win.

As Alastair is drawn into a situation which he battles to control, the love binding him and Juliet is ripped apart. With the common goal of rescuing their friend, they strive to work together, but the tension between them only widens the rift as Alastair faces the ruination of his life.

Fighting his way out of the turmoil, Alastair stretches reason to exact a terrible revenge for the extortion and assault that has affected his friends. In doing so, he discovers a side to himself which he never knew existed.

Revenge must be taken, but is Alastair's 'eye for an eye' concept too extreme? Will Juliet remain a love lost?

#